P9-AGE-435

BLIND ALLEY

BOOKS BY IRIS JOHANSEN

Blind Alley
Firestorm
Fatal Tide
Dead Aim
No One to Trust
Body of Lies
Final Target
The Search
The Killing Game
The Face of Deception
And Then You Die
Long After Midnight
The Ugly Duckling
Lion's Bride
Dark Rider
Midnight Warrior
The Beloved Scoundrel
The Magnificent Rogue
The Tiger Prince
Last Bridge Home
The Golden Barbarian
Reap the Wind
Storm Winds
The Wind Dancer

IRIS
JOHANSEN

BLIND
ALLEY

DOUBLEDAY LARGE PRINT HOME LIBRARY EDITION

Bantam Books

This Large Print Edition, prepared especially for Doubleday Large Print Home Library, contains the complete, unabridged text of the original Publisher's Edition.

BLIND ALLEY
A Bantam Book / September 2004

Published by Bantam Dell
A Division of Random House, Inc.
New York, New York

This is a work of fiction. Names, characters, places, and incidents either are the product of the author's imagination or are used fictitiously. Any resemblance to actual persons, living or dead, events, or locales is entirely coincidental.

ISBN 0-7394-4654-1

Manufactured in the United States of America
Published simultaneously in Canada

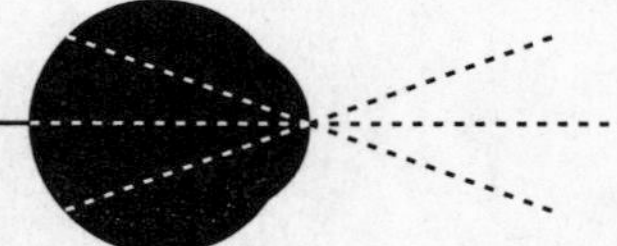

This Large Print Book carries the Seal of Approval of N.A.V.H.

BLIND ALLEY

ONE

Calhoun, Georgia

Joe watched the body wrapped in a dark green tarp being carefully lifted from the grave by the forensic team.

"Thanks for coming, Quinn." Detective Christy Lollack was walking toward him. "I know it's not your case but I needed you. This is a weird one."

"What's weird about it?"

"Look at her." She moved toward the stretcher where the corpse had been placed. "The kids who found her nearly threw up."

He followed her and watched as she drew back the tarp.

There was no face. Only a skull remained. Yet from the neck down the cadaver was only slightly decayed and intact.

"It appears someone didn't want her identified." He looked down at her hands. "He bungled it. He should have taken the hands. We'll be able to get a fingerprint match right away. DNA will take longer, but that will—"

"Look closer. Her fingertips are burned," Christy interrupted. "No prints. Trevor warned me there might not be any."

"Who?"

"Some Scotland Yard inspector. Mark Trevor. He sent an e-mail to the department after he read about the Dorothy Millbruk case in Birmingham and the captain dumped it in my lap. He stated he sent the same e-mail to most of the cities in the Southeast warning them that the perpetrator might be heading into their jurisdictions."

Millbruk . . . It had been a sensational homicide of a prostitute that had taken place four months ago. Joe mentally went over the details he remembered. "The Millbruk case was no connection. It didn't have the same MO. The woman was burned to death and left in a trash disposal."

"But she didn't have a face by the time the fire got through with her."

"No attempt was made to keep the Birmingham police from finding out who she was. They were still able to check prints." He shook his head. "Not the same killer, Christy."

"I'm glad you're so sure," she said sarcastically. "Because I'm not. I don't like this. What if he didn't want us to make a connection? What if he peeled her face off to slow us down so that we wouldn't know he'd moved into the area?"

"Possible." His gaze narrowed on her face. "What do you want from me, Christy? It's not like you to ask for help."

"As soon as forensics gets through with her, I want you to take the skull to Eve to find out what that woman looked like. I don't want to wait until I find out who she is."

It was the answer he'd expected. It wasn't the first time he'd been asked to be an intermediary between the department and Eve. She was probably the best forensic sculptor in the world and the captain wasn't about to ignore a valuable asset. He shook his head. "No way. She's backlogged and working her ass off right now. I'm not loading anything else on her."

"We need to know, Joe."

"And I don't want her wearing herself out."

"For God's sake, do you think I'd ask you to do this if I didn't think it was urgent? I like Eve. I've known her and Jane for almost as long as I've known you. I'm scared. It's necessary, dammit."

"Because of some nebulous tip from Scotland Yard? What the hell do they have to do with this?"

"Two cases in London. One in Liverpool. One in Brighton. They never caught the killer and they believe he moved from the U.K. to the U.S. three years ago."

"Then they can wait for ID or Eve to get out from under."

Christy shook her head. "Come back to my car and I'll pull up Trevor's e-mail."

"It's not going to change my mind."

"It might." She headed for her car.

He hesitated and then followed her. She opened her laptop and accessed the e-mail.

"There it is. Read it and do what you like." She turned away. "I've got work to finish up here."

He scanned the letter and report and then flipped to the victim's page.

He stiffened with shock. "Holy shit!"

Lake Cottage
Atlanta, Georgia

She couldn't breathe.

No!

She would not die, she thought fiercely. She hadn't come this far to lie forever in darkness. She was too young. She had too many things to do and see and be.

Another turn and still no light at the end of the tunnel.

Maybe there was no end.

Maybe this was the end.

It was so hot and there was no air.

She could feel a scream of panic rising in her throat.

Don't give in. Panic was for cowards and she'd never been a coward.

But dear God, it was hot. She couldn't bear—

"Jane." She was being shaken. "For

God's sake, wake up, baby. It's only a dream."

Not a dream.

"Dammit, wake up. You're scaring me."

Eve. Mustn't scare Eve. Maybe it was a dream if she said so. She forced her lids open and looked up into Eve's worried face.

The worried frown was replaced by relief. "Whew, that must have been a doozy of a nightmare." Eve's hand stroked Jane's hair back from her face. "Your bedroom door was closed and I still heard you moaning. Okay now?"

"Fine." She moistened her lips. "Sorry I bothered you." Her heartbeat was steadying and the darkness was gone. Maybe it wouldn't come back. Even if it did, she had to make sure it didn't disturb Eve. "Go back to bed."

"I wasn't in bed. I was working." She turned on the bedside lamp and then grimaced as she looked down at her hands. "And I didn't wipe the clay from my hands before I came in here. You probably have bits of it in your hair."

"That's okay. I have to wash it in the

morning anyway. I want to look good for my driver's license photo."

"That's tomorrow?"

She sighed resignedly. "I told you yesterday that I'd need you or Joe to take me."

"I forgot." She smiled. "Maybe I'm in denial. Getting your first driver's license is sort of a rite of passage. It could be I don't want you to be that independent."

"Yes, you do." She met her gaze. "Ever since we've been together you've made sure that I could take care of myself in every way. You've done everything from giving me karate lessons to having Sarah train Toby as a guard dog. So don't tell me that you don't want me to be independent."

"Well, not independent enough to walk away from Joe and me."

"I'll never do that." She sat up in bed and gave her a quick, awkward kiss. Even after all these years, loving gestures were difficult for her. "You'll have to kick me out. I know when I've got it good. So which one of you is going to take me to the Driver's License Bureau?"

"Probably Joe. I have to finish this skull right away."

"What's the urgency?"

She shrugged. “Search me. Joe brought the skull home from the precinct and asked me to make it top priority. He said it had to do with linking a group of homicides.”

Jane was silent a moment. “A kid?”

Eve shook her head. “A woman.” Her eyes narrowed on Jane’s face. “You thought it might be Bonnie?”

Jane always thought it might be Bonnie, Eve’s daughter who had been murdered when she was seven and whose body had never been found. The tragedy had been the impetus that had made Eve study to become a forensic sculptor to identify murder victims and bring closure to other grieving parents. The search for Bonnie and her passion for her career still dominated her life. She shook her head. “If you suspected it was Bonnie’s skull you were working on, you wouldn’t have even heard my stupid caterwauling.” She held up her hand as Eve opened her lips. “I know. I know. You don’t love me less than you did Bonnie. It’s just different. I’ve known that all along. From the beginning. She was your child and we’re more . . . friends. And that’s okay with me.” She settled back in bed. “Now, you go back to work and I’ll go back to sleep. Thanks for coming in and waking me. Good night, Eve."

Eve didn't answer for a moment. "What was your nightmare about?"

Heat. Panic. Darkness. A night without air or hope. No, there had been hope. . . .

"I don't remember. Has Toby come back yet?"

"Not yet. I'm not sure it's a good idea to let him out at night. He's half wolf."

"That's why I let him roam. Now that he's grown, he has to have more freedom. He has too much golden retriever to be really dangerous to anything but squirrels. Probably not even them. He caught one once and all he wanted to do was play with it." She yawned. "Sarah said it was okay, but I'll stop him if you say the word."

"No, I guess not. Sarah should know." Sarah Logan was Eve's good friend as well as the canine search-and-rescue specialist who had given Toby to Jane. "Just keep an eye on him."

"I will. I'm responsible for him. You know I won't let you down."

"You never have." She stood up. "And we'll have a little celebration when you come home from getting your license."

Jane smiled slyly. “You going to bake a cake?”

“Don’t be ugly. I’m not that bad a cook. It would serve you right if I did.” She grinned as she headed for the door. “I’ll have Joe stop at Dairy Queen and pick up an ice cream cake on the way home.”

“Much more sensible.”

Eve glanced at her over her shoulder and her expression became troubled. “Maybe too sensible. I wonder if we’ve made you a little too responsible, Jane.”

“Don’t be silly.” She closed her eyes. “Some people are born responsible. Some people are born to be butterflies. You had nothing to do with it. For Pete’s sake, you’re not even my mother. Good night, Eve.”

“Well, I guess I’ve been told,” Eve murmured. Her gaze was caught by a sketch lying on the window seat. It was a picture of Toby sleeping on his bed by the fireplace. “That’s very good. You’re getting better all the time.”

“Yes, I am. I’m not going to be a Rembrandt but genius isn’t what it’s cracked up to be. I’ve always thought being driven by art was for the birds. I want to be in control of any career I choose." She smiled. "Like you, Eve."

"I'm not always in control." She looked from the sketch to Jane. "And I thought you wanted to be a search-and-rescue worker like Sarah."

"Maybe. Maybe not. I guess I'm waiting for a career to choose me."

"Well, you have plenty of time to make up your mind. Although your attitude is a little surprising. You usually know exactly what you're going to do."

"Not always." She smiled impishly. "Maybe it's my adolescent hormones getting in the way."

Eve chuckled. "I doubt it. I can't see you letting anything stand in your way." She opened the door. "Good night, Jane."

"And don't work much longer. You've been pulling too many late nights in the last couple weeks."

"Tell that to Joe. He really wants this reconstruction."

"That's weird. He's always the one who tries to make you get more rest." Her lips tightened. "Don't worry, I'll tell him. Someone's got to look out for you."

Eve smiled as she opened the door. "I'm not worrying. Not with you in my corner."

"Joe's in your corner, too. But he's a guy and they're different. Sometimes things get in the way of their thinking."

"Very profound observation. You must repeat it to Joe."

"I will. He can take it and he likes me to be up-front with him."

"Well, you're certainly that," Eve murmured as she left the room.

Eve's smile faded as she closed the bedroom door behind her. Jane's remarks had been typical of her; fierce, protective, and far beyond her years. Eve had gone into the room to comfort and Jane had given her comfort instead.

"Something wrong?" Joe was standing in the doorway of their bedroom. "Is Jane okay?"

"A nightmare." Eve moved down the hall toward her studio. "But she's not talking about it. She probably thinks nightmares are a sign of weakness and heaven forbid she show any weakness."

"Like someone else I know." Joe followed her. "Want some coffee? I could use a cup right now."

She nodded. "Sounds good." She went back to stand before her pedestal. "Can you go to the Driver's License Bureau with her tomorrow?"

"Sure. I'd planned on it."

"I forgot." She grimaced. "You're a better parent than I am, Joe."

"You've been working your ass off." He measured coffee into the coffeemaker. "And that's my fault. Besides, Jane never wanted parents when she came to us. She wasn't Orphan Annie. Hell, she may have been only ten, but she was as street-smart as a woman of thirty. We've done the best we could to give her a good home."

"But I wanted her to—" She stared blindly at the skull. "She's seventeen, Joe. Do you know I've never heard her talk about going out on a date or to the prom or even a football game? She studies, she plays with Toby, and she sketches. It's not enough."

"She has friends. She stayed the night at Patty's last week."

"And how often does that happen?"

"I think she's very well balanced considering her background. You're worrying too much."

"Maybe I should have been worrying before this. It's just that she's always acted so mature that I forget she's just a kid."

"No, you didn't forget. You just recognize that the two of you are as alike as two peas in a pod. How many proms did you go to when you were a teenager?"

"That's different."

"Yeah, you had a drug addict for a mother instead of growing up in a dozen foster homes."

She made a face. "Okay, so we both had it tough when we were kids, but I wanted something better for Jane."

"But Jane has to want it too. She probably thinks proms are pretty silly. Can you see her in a frilly dress, getting into one of those stretch limos the kids hire these days?"

"She'd be beautiful."

"She *is* beautiful," Joe said. "And she's strong and smart and I'd want her behind me if I was ever in a tight corner. But she's not frilly, Eve." He poured her a cup of coffee and brought it to her. "So stop trying to force her into the role."

"As if I could. No one forces Jane to do anything she doesn't want to do." She sipped the coffee and then grimaced. "You made it strong enough. You really want to keep me awake to finish this skull, don't you?"

"Yes."

"Why? You're acting out of character. Even Jane noticed it."

"It's important to the case. Have you named her yet?"

"Of course. She's Ruth. You know I always name them before I work on them. It's more respectful."

"Just asking." He moved toward the front door. "I think I hear Toby."

"And you changed the subject."

"Yes." He smiled over his shoulder. "After all these years I need to maintain a little mystery. If I become too predictable, you might get bored with me."

"No chance." She looked away from him. "I might have thought I could tell what you'd do next at one time but not anymore."

"Son of a *bitch*."

She looked up to see Joe glaring at her. "Sorry. I shouldn't have said that."

"No, you damn well shouldn't," he said roughly. "Even though I know you're thinking it. When are you going to trust me, for God's sake?"

"I trust you."

"Within limits."

"Don't yell at me. You set those limits."

"I lied. I deceived you. But you damn well know I only did it to stop you from hurting."

"You let me think I buried the bones of my Bonnie instead of another little girl. You did it on purpose." She met his gaze. "I told you it would take time for me to forgive that. I try. I try every day. But sometimes it comes back to me and I say—I love you, Joe, but I can't pretend all the time. If that's not good enough, it's your call."

"And you know what that call will be." He drew a deep, ragged breath. "I'll take what I can get. I won't let you go." He opened the screen door. "Every month, every year we're together is a bonus. We'll get past this. Where's that damn dog?" He went out on the porch and she heard him whistle. "Toby!"

He was angry and hurt. If she hadn't been so tired, she wouldn't have let those words tumble out. She was usually more careful. When she had decided to stay with Joe, it had been with the intention of making the relationship work. She had known it would be hard, but most worthwhile things weren't easy. Most of the time life was good, they were good together.

"I've got him." Toby bounded into the room ahead of Joe, panting and full of joy. "He's been on the hunt. That wolf blood is becoming more predominant. I'm not sure Sarah is right about letting him roam."

"That's what I told Jane." Joe was clearly ignoring the tension of the past few minutes and she eagerly followed his lead. "She said she'd stop him if we liked."

He reached down and stroked Toby's head. "We'll keep an eye on him. Maybe a touch of wolf in any creature isn't all that bad. I always feel safer when he's with Jane." He looked up at Eve. "That's probably why Sarah gave him to Jane. She thought you'd feel easier if Jane had protection."

"Because Bonnie didn't." Eve nodded. "God help me, I didn't dream she'd need it. I couldn't imagine anyone hurting my Bonnie. She was so . . . wonderful that—" She stopped and was silent a moment. Even after all these years the pain and anger were ever present. “But you know all about the monsters who kill the innocent. You’re a cop. You deal with them every day.” She began to measure the tissue depths again. “Is it another monster who killed this woman, Joe?”

“I think so. There’s a chance he may have been killing for a long time. Only not in this area.”

“When are you going to tell me about her?” She looked at him over her shoulder. “And don’t tell me it’s confidential. I’m not buying it. You know damn well you can trust me.”

“We’ll talk about it when you finish.” He gestured to Toby. “Come on, boy, I’ll let you in Jane’s room before you start howling to get in. That’s enough to give anyone nightmares.” He started down the hall and then stopped. “You know, I think she had a nightmare last week. I was up doing paperwork and I heard her . . . panting.” He frowned. “Maybe crying? I don’t know. When I peeked in, she was sleeping quietly.”

“If she’s having frequent nightmares,

maybe she's not as well balanced as you think."

"Two isn't frequent."

"And how many could she be having that we know nothing about?"

"All you can do is be there for her if she wants to talk about them. You have nightmares of your own. God knows you don't want to talk about them."

Yes, she'd had her share of nightmares and dreams of Bonnie. The nightmares were gone, but the healing dreams remained, thank God. "I asked her about her nightmare and she said she didn't remember. I think she did. Maybe she'll talk to you tomorrow."

"I'm not giving her the third degree. If the subject comes up . . ." He shrugged. "But I don't think it will. She's too absorbed in this driving test."

She smiled. "She wants to make sure and get a good photo. That's the first sign of vanity I've seen. I was encouraged."

"Good. But you'd better be contented with a hint of vanity." He winked. "Because you'll never get frilly."

* * *

"I got it!" Jane parked the SUV and jumped out of the car and ran up the steps to the porch where Eve was waiting. "It was a pretty easy test, Eve. They should make it harder. I don't like the idea of being on the road with kids who could pass that level of— Get down, Toby." She hugged his neck and then pushed him down. "But I got it and the photo isn't too bad, is it, Joe?" She handed the license to Eve. "At least, it's better than my learner's license. I hated looking as idiotic as one of the Three Stooges. It wasn't dignified."

"Is that why you were so upset? Why didn't you tell us? We could have waited until you had another one taken."

"You were in a hurry. It didn't matter."

Eve frowned. "And you could have gotten this license last year on your sixteenth birthday. You never mentioned wanting to do it."

"You were snowed under all last year. And Joe was in and out of Macon for months on that homicide case. I decided I'd do it on my seventeenth and then we could all enjoy it. Like I said, it didn't matter." She turned to Joe. "Thanks for taking me. I'll pay you back by fixing dinner for you and Eve."

"No, you won't." Joe got out of the passenger seat and got a sack of groceries out of the back. "This is a celebration and you're the guest of honor. I'll grill some steaks." He climbed the steps. "And she came out with a perfect score on that 'easy' test, Eve. Cool as a cucumber."

"I didn't expect anything else." Eve glanced down at the driver's license. The photo was very good. Jane's brown eyes were shining from that triangular face that was more fascinating than pretty. Eve had always thought she looked a little like Audrey Hepburn with those winged brows and high cheekbones but Joe couldn't see it. He said Jane was an original and if she looked like anyone it was Eve. The same red-brown hair color, the same well-shaped mouth, the strong chin. "It's a great photo, Jane."

"Yeah, I look like I might have a modicum of intelligence. You finished with Ruth yet?"

"Getting close."

"That's good." She looked away from Eve as she bent down and patted Toby. "Then don't worry about stopping to have dinner. I'll bring you a sandwich. We'll celebrate some other time."

Another delay after Jane had waited a year because it hadn't been "convenient" for Eve and Joe? "No, we won't." She handed the license back to Jane. "This is an important occasion. Ruth can wait."

"Really?" Jane glanced up and a brilliant smile illuminated her face. "You sure? It's not as if—it was a pretty easy test."

"I'm sure. I wouldn't miss it. I'm very proud of you." Eve turned away. "But I'll have to work until supper is ready. Okay?"

"Okay." She turned away. "But if you change your mind, I'll understand." She ran down the steps. "Come on, Toby. Let's go for a run by the lake." She glanced over her shoulder. "Call me if you need help, Joe."

"I think I can manage." Joe opened the screen door. "You and Toby need to get rid of some of that energy. You may not have been nervous, but you're charged. Don't come back until you're more mellow."

Jane laughed but didn't answer as she streaked down the lake path with Toby at her heels.

"She's happy." Eve was smiling as she

followed Joe into the cottage. "It's good to see her like that."

"That's not new. It's not as if she stumbles around with a gloomy puss all the time. She's usually pretty happy. She lives every minute to the hilt."

"I know. But this is different. Do you think we should buy her a car?"

"No, she wouldn't take it. She's already talking about getting a part-time job so that she could earn the money to buy one herself."

"It will take forever. Can we give her one for her birthday?"

Joe gave her a glance. "What do you think?"

Eve sighed. "That she'd see right through it."

"Right." He started unloading the groceries onto the kitchen counter. "So the best we can do is try to find her the best-paying part-time job in the area and find ways to get her transport." He unwrapped the steaks. "Now you'd better get back to work. How close are you?"

"I might be able to finish up tonight. I'll start the final phase as soon as Jane goes to her room."

"Good idea." He picked up the bag of charcoal and carried it out the front door.

No protests about her overworking. No suggestion that she put off the completion of the job until the next day.

A tiny frown creased her forehead as she moved across the living room to her studio area. Ruth's features were blank, waiting for the final smoothing and forming to bring them to life.

Life.

She glanced out the window at Joe lighting the charcoal in the stone barbecue pit at the side of the cottage. So many small acts made up life. So many hours, so many experiences. Jane had gone through one of those experiences today. . . .

But Ruth had been cut off before she'd had a chance to experience more than the beginnings of womanhood. Early twenties, Joe had told her the forensic report was guessing. So young.

"I'm getting close," she whispered. "Just a little more measuring and we'll go for it. I'll bring you home, Ruth."

* * *

The woman was damn heavy.

His chest was laboring as he carried the tarp-wrapped body up the hill.

She was too heavy. Too voluptuous. He had known it wasn't Cira, but she was similar enough that she had to be eliminated.

He couldn't take any chances.

Not with Cira. Never with Cira.

He grunted as he reached the top of the hill. He dropped the body on the ground and looked down at the sloping bank that dropped into Lake Lanier. The water was deep here and he'd weighted the tarp. She might not be discovered for weeks.

And if she was found earlier, then it was too bad. It changed nothing but the difficulty.

He drew a deep breath and then gave a shove that sent the body rolling down the bank. He watched the tarp disappear beneath the water.

Gone.

He lifted his head and felt the breeze caress his face. A tingling excitement was coursing through his veins and he felt more alive than he had since that first moment when he had realized what he had to do.

He was close to her. He could *feel* it.

* * *

"Okay," Eve murmured as she turned the pedestal to the light. "Here we go, Ruth. Measurements only take us so far. Help me out. I can't do this alone."

Smooth.

Start on the cheeks.

Work fast.

Don't think.

Or think about Ruth.

Think about bringing her home.

Do the upper lip.

Smooth.

A little less?

No, leave it alone.

Smooth.

Her hands moved swiftly, mindlessly.

Who are you, Ruth?

Tell me. Help me.

The middle area between nose and lip. Shorter?

Yes.

Smooth.

Smooth.

Smooth.

It was three hours later when her hands fell away from the skull and she closed her eyes. "It's the best I can do," she whispered. "I hope it's enough, Ruth. Sometimes it is." She opened her eyes and stepped back from the pedestal. "We'll just have to—*My God!*"

"You haven't finished her," Joe said from the doorway. He came over to her workbench and took out her eye case. "You know which ones to give her."

"Damn you, Joe."

He took out two glass eyes and handed them to her. "Give her eyes."

She jammed them into the sockets and whirled on him. "What the hell are you doing?" Her voice was shaking. "For Christ's sake, why didn't you tell me?"

"The same reason you never let anyone give you photos of your subjects. It might have influenced you."

"Of course it would have influenced me. What the devil is happening?" Her gaze flew back to the skull. The likeness was remarkable. The face was fuller, more mature, the eyes a little closer together, but the features were very similar. Shockingly, frighteningly similar. "It's *Jane*, damn you."

TWO

"I agree she looks like Jane might in ten years or so." Joe studied the reconstruction. "I was hoping to hell she wouldn't."

"Because this woman looks like Jane and she was murdered." She folded her arms across her chest to ward off the chill. "And you knew what I'd find when I finished this reconstruction. You knew that it would be Jane."

"For God's sake, it's not as if I was trying to keep it from you any longer than I had to," he said roughly. "I did what I had to do." He took the drop cloth on the worktable and threw it over the skull. "Now it's done and we know."

"We don't know anything. At least, I

don't." She whirled and went over to the sink and started to wash the clay from her hands. They were shaking. Don't panic. It couldn't happen again. Not twice. Not after Bonnie. "But I'm going to know, Joe. I'm going to know everything. You tell me what's happening."

"I'll tell you what I know now. We'll find out the rest. I promise, Eve." He went across the room to the coffee table and opened his laptop. "The woman was found in a shallow grave outside Calhoun. Her fingers were burned and her face was just a skull. The rest of the body was intact. Christy said that she'd been warned by Scotland Yard that the perpetrator might be moving into this area after allegedly killing a woman in Birmingham."

"Allegedly?"

"It's not exactly the same MO. The woman was burned to death. And no real attempt was made to hide her identity. Except her face was destroyed." He pulled up the case history. "She was a prostitute and an illegal alien and they didn't find a snapshot until a few weeks later when the story was on page five. I had to dig to find it." He swiveled the laptop around toward Eve.

"Not as close, but the resemblance is there."

Another Jane.

Thinner, lips not as firm, skin not glowing with youth but similar features.

"What is this?" Eve whispered.

He didn't answer, but brought up another screen. "Inspector Mark Trevor's e-mail. Four victims from the U.K."

She knew what she'd see but it still came as a shock. "They all look like Jane."

"Not entirely. They're not identical, but close enough to be sisters."

And they were all dead. She moistened her lips. "Same serial killer?"

He nodded. "In every case he destroyed the face. By fire, by peeling it off, once it was done by some undetermined chemical."

"To hide their identity?"

"That didn't seem the purpose except in the last case."

She drew a shaky breath. "Then he did it because he hated the way they looked. And that's why he's targeting them."

"It seems the logical conclusion."

"Logical? I don't feel logical. I'm scared to death." Her voice was uneven. "Calhoun is just down the highway and if he peeled off her fingerprints he was trying to make it look like the work of a different killer, with a different MO. He didn't want anyone to know he was in this area. Why?"

"Maybe he didn't want the women in this city to be on the alert."

"But not all of them have Jane's face." Her hands clenched into fists. "And that's what that crazy is looking for. He's trying to destroy everyone who looks like Jane."

"He doesn't know about Jane."

"Then someone who looks like an old girlfriend or his mother. Someone with Jane's face."

"It would follow the serial killer profile."

"Oh, yes, I know all about those profiles," she said jerkily. "I did a lot of studying after Bonnie was murdered, until I almost drowned in them. Well, he's not going to substitute Jane in any of his sicko fantasies. That's not going to happen again."

"No, it's not," Joe said quietly. "I won't let it. Do you think you're the only one who cares about Jane?"

No, of course he loved Jane. But he hadn't lost a daughter. He didn't know the constant terror of it happening again.

"I know." Joe was studying her expression. "You should realize I know how you're feeling. Who knows you better?"

No one. And she wasn't being fair. Fear was clouding her judgment. "I'm sorry. You're as worried as I am. Now what do we do?"

"Contact Trevor and find out all we can about what they know about this creep. His e-mail was scanty at best. I called his cell phone at three this afternoon and got his voice mail. I told him to call me back." He glanced at his watch. "It's after midnight. We may not hear from him for a few hours. It's only five A.M. there."

"Call him again. I don't care if we wake him up."

He nodded. "And we do need to know how they knew the killer moved across the Atlantic if they couldn't put a name to him. The Yard has to have some theories if they've been working on this case for the last three years. We have to know reasons before we can anticipate his movements."

"They only have to look at those photos to know why he's doing this." But she didn't want to look at those photos any longer.

They frightened her too much. She turned away. "I'm going to check on Jane."

"She's okay, Eve. We're right here in the next room."

"That's probably what those parents of that little girl in California said before that murderer came into their home and took her."

"Jane's not a little girl. She's a tough, smart kid and anyone who messes with her had better look out."

"No one's going to mess with her. No one's going to hurt her," she said fiercely. "I'm not going to let that happen. Not again. You just call that Trevor and pump him dry. We're going to find that bastard before he finds Jane."

Jane was sleeping peacefully.

No dreams tonight, Eve thought as she looked at her. Or, if there were dreams, they were good. Or were they? She couldn't remember Jane ever telling her about her dreams. Perhaps she should have asked before this. Jane had fit so effortlessly into their lives that it had been easy to take her for granted. It was odd since Jane's personality was as strong as her own. But Jane had never wanted to challenge her. She'd given them both affection, worked hard for her place in their family, and never asked for anything.

What a wonder of a person she was.

And no one was going to destroy that wonder.

She turned and left the room. The next moment she was passing Joe, who was on the phone, presumably with Trevor, and went out onto the porch. She sat down on the top step and leaned her head against the post. The air was clear and cold and the lake was still tonight. It was all beautiful and familiar and home.

But home could become a place of desolation and terror. Who could know better than she that no one was really safe?

"No one, Mama. But you shouldn't worry until there's something definite to worry about. Life's too short."

She turned her head and saw Bonnie sitting in the porch swing. Her legs crossed, dressed in jeans and the usual Bugs Bunny T-shirt. "That's what Joe says. I'm not listening to either one of you. He's too damn logical and you're a dream. I think I have a hell of a lot to worry about."

Bonnie sighed. "I'm not a dream, I'm a ghost. Deep down you know that's true."

"I don't know any such thing. I probably invented you when I was so depressed that I had to have a way to cope or kill myself."

"Yeah, that's why I first came to you." A smile illuminated her face. "And because I missed you."

Eve felt her throat tighten. "I miss you, too, baby."

"You'd miss me less if you let Joe come closer. I thought for a while that you were going to be okay but you pushed him away."

"You know why I did that."

She sighed. "Me, again. It was a mistake but he did it because he loved you."

"I know all that. We're working on it." She looked back at the lake. "Why are you here? You haven't come to me for months."

"You need me. I'll always be here when you need me."

Why was she looking at the lake when she could look at Bonnie? It didn't matter if she was a ghost or a dream, she was Bon-

nie. She turned and gazed hungrily at her. "I do need you. Every minute of every day."

"I can't be here all the time. And you have other people who love you. Joe. Jane."

"Jane may be in trouble. I'm afraid for her."

Bonnie nodded soberly. "I'm afraid for her too. He's close."

"Who's close?"

"The bad one." She unfolded her legs and they dangled above the floor of the porch.

Such a little girl, Eve thought. So small and dear . . . "You don't know who he is?"

She shook her head. "Only that he's bad."

"Like the man who killed you?"

"I can't think of that time, Mama. It's gone. So I can't answer you. But I know that the man who killed Ruth is twisted and dark."

"I'm glad you can't remember that time, baby." She cleared her throat. "But it's damn convenient you can't tell me any concrete facts. What good is a ghost if she's not useful?"

Bonnie threw back her head and laughed. "I'm useful. I keep you from going around all gloomy and suicidal. Besides, I don't have to be useful. You'll love me anyway."

"Yes, I will."

"And you'll love Jane, no matter what."

"I'm not sure she believes that."

"She's afraid to believe it. She's been hurt too many times."

"That was a long time ago. Joe and I have tried to make up for all those years."

"She's not like me. The bad times are still with her."

"So what the hell can I do?"

Bonnie shook her head. "She has to work her way through it."

"If she has time. If some bastard doesn't kill her like he did you."

"You won't let that happen." She tilted her head, listening. "I think Joe's almost finished talking on the phone. I'd better leave you. Do you know when I'll know you don't need me any longer?"

"I'll always need you."

She shook her head. "You won't need me when you're so close to Joe that you'll share me with him. When you tell him I come to see you."

"And have him tell me I'm nuts?"

"See, you're not ready." She suddenly frowned. "Jane's dreaming again. She's scared. You'd better go to her."

Eve rose to her feet. "She was fine before I came out here."

"She's not now. Wake her. She can't do anything right now. She wants help, but there's nothing that— Wake her."

Eve headed for the front door. "If she's not dreaming, your credibility is going to be zilch."

Bonnie smiled. "Wake her. Good-bye, Mama. I'll see you soon."

"You'd better."

She opened the screen door and saw Joe still sitting on the couch talking on the phone. She glanced back at the porch swing and saw what she expected. Vacant. No Bonnie.

"I'll be right with you," Joe said when he saw her in the doorway. "Give me a few more minutes."

She nodded. "I'm going to check on Jane anyway." She moved down the hall toward Jane's room. "It shouldn't take me long."

* * *

Joe had hung up the phone and was pouring coffee from a freshly brewed pot when she came back in the room. “Okay?”

She frowned. “No, she was having another nightmare. I got her a glass of water and talked to her for a few minutes.”

“Did she tell you about it?”

She shook her head. “She said it was probably indigestion from too much of that ice cream cake after dinner.”

“Well, at least she didn’t blame my steaks.” Joe handed her the cup and poured one for himself. “Did she settle down?”

“Yes, or pretended she did.” She sat down on the couch and glanced down at his notepad. “I gather you got through to Trevor?”

“Actually, he called me back before I started placing the call. He said he was an early riser and thought since I sounded so urgent that he’d take a chance on reaching me.”

“What did he tell you?”

“Not much. He said that they’d virtually come up with nothing in all these years. That they had no idea of the identity of the killer.”

"Then how did they track him here?"

"By following a trail of murders with the same MOs. He said he knew that killings like these were a compulsion that wouldn't stop and there were no more reports in the U.K. . . . So he started monitoring the killings in Europe and on this side of the Atlantic."

"Then he has to know more than we do. Couldn't you get him to talk?"

"I did most of the talking. He zeroed in on Ruth and wouldn't let go. He was very interested in the fact that her fingerprints were obscured."

"You told him about Jane?"

"No, I told him I wanted a complete report on all the victims sent to me immediately."

"Good. When can we expect it?"

"One-thirty this afternoon. He's bringing it himself."

"What?"

"He's catching the first flight from London. He wants to be here on the scene. He offered his assistance."

"We don't need Scotland Yard."

"But we may need Trevor." He stared thoughtfully down into the coffee. "I caught something in his . . . I think this case may be an obsession with him. Sometimes it happens that way when you devote years to trying to find a killer."

" 'Years' is the key word. Why hasn't Trevor found him before this? Before he came to the U.S.? Before he became a danger to Jane, dammit?"

"I'm sure you'll ask him," Joe said. "As soon as he walks through that door." He took a final swallow of coffee and set his cup down on the coffee table. "But in the meantime I'm going to take that reconstruction back to the precinct and see if we can find out who Ruth is and set the wheels in motion to track down who she might have been with in the days before her death."

"It's nearly four in the morning, Joe."

"I couldn't sleep." He got to his feet. "I called and arranged for a police car to set up a stakeout to watch the cottage. They should be here soon."

"Jane will wonder why they're here when she gets up."

"Then you'll have to think of an explanation. Because they're staying here when I'm not around."

"I'm not arguing. I want all the protection I can get for her." She took her cup and Joe's to the sink. "It was just an observation. And I won't lie. She wouldn't forgive me for not being honest with her." Her lips twisted ruefully. "And she'll probably think I'm stupid for being so terrified. She's braver than I am."

"She only has different experiences." He kissed her lightly on the lips and headed for the door. "No one has more guts than you do."

"Yeah, sure."

He glanced over his shoulder and saw her weary expression. He muttered a curse, turned on his heel and came back to her. He gave her a kiss that was definitely not light. It was hard and passionate and completely dizzying. She found her arms sliding around him, pulling him closer.

He lifted his head. "No one has more guts or endurance or beauty and don't you ever forget it." He stepped back. "I'll try to get back in a few hours, but if I don't, I'll be here to lay this Scotland Yard whizbang at your feet this afternoon."

"Okay," she whispered. She didn't want him to go. She wanted to go to bed and forget Ruth and the danger to Jane and everything but the raw, wonderful sex that always bridged every abyss that threatened them.

"Me, too." As usual, Joe had read her thoughts. He touched her lips with his forefinger. "Double. Say the word and I'll call the squad car and say I'm staying here for a few more hours. I probably won't be able to find out much at this hour anyway. I can leave at six."

Her arms tightened around him. Joe . . . He was strength and life, and, Jesus, she needed him.

"Call them," she whispered. "Six is soon enough."

London

Trevor hung up the phone and leaned back in his chair. "That was Quinn. I think he was impressed to find we start work early over here. I leave for Atlanta at nine."

Bartlett smiled. "You said you'd get him. Do you want me to go with you?"

"Not now." He got up and headed for the

closet. "I'll call you if I need you. Dig out that file on Quinn and Eve Duncan for me while I pack. I've got to be prepared for them. I need to know them inside out."

Bartlett had already retrieved the file and was glancing through it. "You may have a problem. They're both pretty complicated. Eve Duncan grew up in the slums with a drug addict for a mother. She had an illegitimate daughter as a teenager and it turned her life around. She went to college and worked at straightening out her mother. Her daughter, Bonnie, was taken and presumably killed by a serial killer when she was seven. The body was never found. It was thought that Bonnie was recovered a few years ago, but it was discovered later that it was another child."

"And Quinn?"

"Born of privileged parents and was an FBI agent for a while before becoming a detective for the ATLPD. He owns a lake cottage and extensive acreage near Atlanta. That's where Quinn and Duncan live." He glanced up at Trevor. "He's tough and smart and tenacious as a bulldog."

"Weakness?"

"Eve Duncan. No doubt about it. He's

been with her from the time of her daughter's death and he may have stayed in Atlanta instead of continuing with the FBI to be near her."

"A button to push."

"Not unless you want to set off a chain explosion."

"Sometimes explosions are necessary." Trevor smiled recklessly. "I'll risk it."

"You always do." Bartlett's smile faded. "They're tough. Both of them. Be careful that explosion doesn't take you out."

Trevor snapped his suitcase shut. "Why, Bartlett, I believe you're worried about me."

"Nonsense. I'm just too lazy to look for a new contact. Are you taking this file with you?"

"Not if you've covered the high points." He set the suitcase on a chair. "I'll just glance at the MacGuire file while you go downstairs and hail me a taxi."

"Again? You should have it memorized by now. There's not much there. Jane MacGuire's only seventeen, grew up in foster homes, and she's been with Duncan and Quinn since she was ten. She's an honor student and never been in trouble.

But she's too young to have much experience or history."

"I disagree. Look at her face. She's young, but there's a world of experience in that face. And he'll see it. It will draw him like a magnet." He gazed down at the face of the girl staring boldly out of the photo. "The taxi, Bartlett."

"Right away."

Trevor barely heard the door close behind him. Excitement was soaring through him and he had to suppress it. He had to think coolly and clearly if he was to win this battle. And he *would* win it, dammit.

His finger delicately touched the cheek of the girl in the photo. She was close. Remarkably, marvelously, close.

"Close enough, Aldo?" he murmured. "Cira?"

THREE

"Ruth really looked like me?" Jane gazed in disappointment at the empty pedestal. "I wish I could have seen the reconstruction before Joe whisked it away. May I go down to the precinct and take a—"

"No, you may not," Eve said firmly. "You can see the photograph. You're sticking close to home for a while."

"Because of that creep?" She shook her head. "I'll stick around here today but I've got a trigonometry test scheduled for Monday and I'm not going to let him stop me from taking it." She went to the doorway and gazed at the patrol car parked down the road. "He'd be crazy to make a move when he can see Joe has me under surveillance."

"He *is* crazy," Eve said. "Nothing could be clearer. No one goes around killing women just because they remind him of someone else unless they're nuts. So your argument doesn't hold water. And that test isn't worth any risk."

Jane turned to look at her. "You're really scared."

"You're damn right I am. I'm not having anything happen to you even if I have to tie you to your bed."

Jane studied her expression. "You're remembering Bonnie. I'm not Bonnie, Eve. I'm not an innocent little girl who can be lured to her death. I intend to have a long, good life and I'll go for the jugular of anyone who tries to take that away from me."

"You may not get the chance. This man has killed at least six women that we know about. All of them older and more experienced than you."

"And they probably weren't suspecting anything. I'll be suspicious of everyone." She smiled. "You know I'm not the most trusting person in the world."

"Thank God." Eve drew a deep breath. "I'm scared, Jane. Don't make me more scared by defying this monster. Please."

Jane frowned. “I hate letting him keep me from doing what I need to do. Bastards like him shouldn’t be able to control us.”

“Please,” Eve repeated.

Jane sighed. “Okay. If you’re really going to worry.”

“I am going to worry. Count on it. Thank you.”

Jane’s eyes twinkled. “Come on, I didn’t have much choice. You threatened to tie me down.”

Eve smiled. “Only as a last resort.”

“How long do you think it’s going to take to catch him?”

Eve’s smile faded. “I don’t know. Soon, I hope.”

“I’m not going to hide forever, Eve.” She glanced back at the patrol car. “Do you believe in fate?”

“Sometimes. Most of the time I think we’re in control of our own destiny.”

“So do I. But this is a funny coincidence, isn’t it? First Bonnie and then me. What do you think the odds are that you’d be faced with this kind of situation again?”

“Astronomical. But I am.”

“Then maybe . . .” She paused, working

her way through it. “If there is some kind of fate, this might be a second chance.”

“What do you mean?”

“Maybe it’s like . . . a circle and comes around again and again if it goes wrong the first time.”

“You’re getting too deep for me. I don’t know what the devil you’re talking about.”

Jane shook her head as if to clear it. “Me, either. It just occurred to me that—” She started for the door. “All that thinking is giving me a headache. Let’s go for a walk.”

“I have to be back in time to meet with Trevor.” She glanced at her watch. “An hour.”

“I don’t think he’ll leave if you’re not on the doorstep. From what you said he wants to cooperate. Besides, he’s probably one of those proper, methodical, slow-moving types.”

“Just because he’s Scotland Yard? They’re very efficient, from what I hear.”

“They didn’t catch Jack the Ripper, did they? Joe would have caught him. He thinks out of the box.” She nudged Toby with her foot as she started down the steps. “Come on, lazy. Just because you like to run at night is no reason you get to sleep all day."

Toby yawned and then got to his feet.

"You know those policemen in the car will be trailing us," Eve said as she followed Jane down the steps.

"The exercise will do them good." Jane smiled at Eve over her shoulder. "And it will do you good, too. You've been stuck in the house working on Ruth for days. You need fresh air and a change of scene. The sun's shining and there's not a cloud in the sky."

She was wrong, Eve thought. There was a terrible, dark cloud hovering over them. But Jane's expression was radiant, bold and without fear. Eve felt her own spirits lift as she looked at her. "You're right. It's a great day for a walk." She caught up with her. "But just to the head of the lake. Trevor may not be that eager to see me, but, stiff and proper or not, I'm damn interested in meeting him."

"Ms. Duncan? I'm Mark Trevor." He rose to meet her as she came into the cottage. "I'm delighted to meet you." He gestured to Joe, who was standing at the kitchen bar, before moving across the room with hand extended. "Quinn was telling me what a magnificent reconstruction you did. I can't wait to see it."

"You'll have to go down to the precinct. Joe took it in this morning. I didn't even get a chance to take any photos." He had a firm, hard handshake and as he met her eyes, she felt a ripple of shock.

Trevor was obviously courteous but that was as far as Jane's description applied. He couldn't have been more than thirty, was dressed in jeans and olive sweatshirt, and was tall, broad shouldered, and muscular. Every ounce of his body appeared charged with energy. Short, curly dark hair framed an amazingly good-looking face dominated by dark eyes that shone with interest and intelligence. His smile exuded a charisma that warmed and flattered at the same time. Good God, he looked more like a male model or actor than a policeman.

"I've already asked him for permission to take a look." Trevor took the cup of coffee Joe handed him. "We have our own forensic sculptors that work with us at the Yard and I'm a great fan. They've done some amazing reconstructions."

"So I've heard." Joe handed Eve her cup. "Where's Jane?"

"Playing with Toby. She'll be along. She was right behind me." Her gaze went to the briefcase on the coffee table. "Case histories?"

Trevor nodded. "But I'm afraid you're going to be disappointed. As I told Quinn on the phone, we have nothing concrete." He unfastened the briefcase. "The killings appeared to be random and we didn't make the similar facial connection until he'd moved out of the U.K. . . ." He sat down on the couch. "But please help yourself. You can keep these records if you like. They're copies."

"You have to have found out something," Eve said. "In this age of DNA no crime scene is sterile."

"Oh, we have fiber and DNA, but we have to have a suspect for comparison."

"Witnesses?" Joe asked.

Trevor shook his head. "One night the victims were alive, the next day they were dead. No one saw them with anyone suspicious. Aldo obviously saw them, stalked them, and then moved in when it was safe for him."

Eve stiffened. “Aldo? You have his name?”

Trevor shook his head. “Sorry. I didn’t mean to raise your hopes. Aldo is only my name for him. I made it up because after all these years of tracking I couldn’t think of him on an impersonal level.”

“Why Aldo?”

He shrugged. “Why not?”

“I don’t care what you call the bastard,” Joe said. “I just want to nail him. The woman in Birmingham was burned to death and the medical examiner says that there are signs that Ruth was smothered. No similarity.” He gestured to the files. “What about these women?”

“Jean Gaskin was smothered. Ellen Carter was burned to death. He seems to be fond of those two means of killing his targets.” He took a sip of coffee. “However, he doesn’t limit himself. Julia Brandon died of a lethal poison gas she inhaled.”

“What?”

“Presumably forced to inhale. Unusual.”

“Horrible.”

“Yes.” He nodded. “And Peggy Knowles, the woman from Brighton, had water in her lungs. She was drowned.” He set his cup down on the coffee table. "Aldo's never in a hurry. He allows himself the time to make his kills in the way he's planned."

"Can't you identify who he's trying to punish by killing these women? Records? Databases?"

"It would be a needle in a haystack, Eve," Joe said.

Trevor nodded. "And unfortunately we don't have any technology that sophisticated. We have no central photographic database. However, we did make the attempt to check all our records and came up with nothing." He paused, his eyes sliding to the window before he brought his attention back to Eve. "However, I have a theory that even if the odds weren't so huge we might not have been able to find him in our records."

"Why not?"

"When I was digging for information after the last killing in Brighton, I found records of a killing in Italy and one in Spain before the first murder in London. Both women smothered, both with faces destroyed."

"Christ, we can't even narrow down his country of origin?" Joe asked in disgust. "What about Interpol?"

Trevor shook his head. “Do you think I haven’t scanned every bit of info during these last years? If he did kill other women, there’s no record I could find.”

“And he didn’t leave any calling cards as some serial killers do?”

Trevor was silent a moment. “Well, yes, he did.”

“What? Why the hell didn’t you tell us that to begin with?” Eve said.

“I thought you might already know.” He turned to Joe. “Haven’t you received your forensic report on your Jane Doe?”

“Not everything. It’s coming in bits and pieces.”

“Then they haven’t analyzed the ashes yet?”

“Ashes,” Eve echoed.

“They found ashes with Ruth’s body,” Joe said. “We thought it might be evidence she was killed in the woods and the campfire was—”

“Not wood ashes,” Trevor said. “And no cozy little campfire. The report will come back volcanic ash.”

“Shit.” Joe started to dial his phone. “You’re sure?”

“Quite sure. Particles of volcanic ash

were found with every body. Your Birmingham police were understandably negligent in having the ashes analyzed in a case where the victim burned to death. They'd naturally assume any ashes were produced by the fire itself."

"Then why didn't you notify them?"

"I'm notifying you now. It's your case." He rose to his feet and moved swiftly toward the window. "Hadn't you better check on her?"

Eve was suddenly aware of Trevor's tension. The easy composure was gone and he was alert, restless, totally focused. She stiffened as she remembered how his gaze had slid to the window moments before. "Jane?"

He nodded curtly. "You said she was right behind you."

She glanced at Joe.

He shook his head and hung up the phone. "I didn't discuss her with him."

Trevor stiffened, his gaze narrowing. "There she is." He turned to Eve. "You shouldn't have left her alone."

"If you'll look a few yards behind her, you'll see that she's not alone." Eve went to stand beside him at the window. Jane was coming up the path with Toby at her heels and the two policemen trying to keep up with her. "I'd never leave her without protection." Her voice was cold. "You can never tell who you can trust in this world. How did you know about Jane?"

He turned to look at her. "I'm sorry. Of course you'd protect her. I spoke impulsively."

"How did you know about Jane?" she repeated.

"Your suspicions are very healthy. I approve. But I'm the last person you should be concerned about. To make sure that she's safe is the reason I'm here." He reached into his wallet and pulled out a creased and faded newspaper clipping. "I've had my assistant scanning all the major city newspapers for some time and lo and behold he came up with this photo of Jane MacGuire."

Eve recognized the photo. It had been taken when Jane had entered Toby in a charity dog show for the Humane Society three months ago. It was a little blurred but Jane's face was clear. Terror iced through Eve.

"He may not have seen it." Trevor was

reading her expression. “I don’t know how he picks his victims. Some have to be random. The Millbruk woman in Birmingham. Peggy Knowles in Brighton. She was a prostitute, too. Neither of them had their photos in the newspaper.”

“And the others?”

“One had just won a gardening award a week before.”

“So he does look at the newspapers.”

“Possibly. But he can’t be sure of finding his victims by reading the newspapers and, if they were a source, he’d have to limit himself to certain areas because of the sheer magnitude of the task. I’d say he has some other way of targeting.”

“Another theory?” She was chilled. “You found her, dammit.”

“But the chances were against it. I was really having my colleague Bartlett doing routine checks to see what he could come up with.”

“And you came up with Jane.” Joe took the photo from Eve. “And it’s too damn clear. Why didn’t you notify me if you thought she was in danger?”

“The e-mail,” he reminded him.

"Damn the e-mail. You should have been specific."

"I didn't even know he was in your area until the Millbruk murder and that was two months after this photo was taken. And if he'd seen this photo, it wasn't likely that he'd waste time and effort on any other target. He'd have come straight to her."

"Why?"

"Look at her." Trevor's gaze went to the photo. "She's so vibrant she almost jumps out of the picture. When you compare her to the other victims, they're like counterfeits compared to the real thing."

"All the more reason why you should have let us know."

"There might have been no threat to her."

"You bastard, we should have been told."

"I assure you we've been keeping an eye on her. The moment I saw this photo, I sent Bartlett here to watch her. But I'm sure I would have felt the same way if I were in your shoes."

"You don't know how we would have felt," Eve said fiercely. "You cold son of a bitch. I don't care if you catch your killer. I want to keep Jane safe."

"So do I." He met her gaze. "There's nothing I want more. Believe me."

She did believe him. There could be no doubting either his sincerity or the intensity of his feeling. It didn't lessen her anger.

"And do you mean you've been spying on us without—"

"I think your policemen are afraid of Toby, Joe." Jane was laughing as she came into the room. "He growled when they came too close behind me and they stopped so short they almost got whiplash. You'd think they'd realize Toby is—" She stopped as her glance went from Eve to Trevor. She gave a low whistle. "Do I sense a rift in Anglo-American relations?"

Trevor smiled. "Not on my part. I'm solidly in your camp. You're Jane MacGuire, aren't you? I'm Mark Trevor."

Jane was silent, staring at him. "Hello. You're not what I expected."

"You're everything I expected." He crossed the room and took her hand. "And more."

Jane was gazing at him in fascination and Eve could understand why. She had felt the same response to that smile and charisma when she'd first seen him. But that was before she'd realized how cool and ruthless he could be. In the space of minutes he'd changed from an ally into an adversary. She had an impulse to run across the room and jerk Jane away from him. "Mr. Trevor was just leaving."

Trevor didn't look away from Jane. "Yes, I'm afraid I've put myself in their bad books. I blew it." He smiled ruefully. "I was skimming along famously and then I got worried they weren't taking proper care of you and I opened my mouth and let all my hard work go up in smoke."

"What hard work?"

"They'll explain."

"I want you to explain." She gazed directly into his eyes. "You've been trying to catch that murderer. What have you been doing and how does it affect me?"

He chuckled. "I should have known you'd be like this. You're a delight."

"And you're bullshitting me."

"I'm not, you know." His smile faded. "You want the truth? You're a target and I've known for some time that there was the possibility that you might be under the gun. I watched and waited. And Ms. Duncan and Quinn quite rightly are outraged that I didn't immediately surround you with all the protection you deserve."

"Yes, we are," Eve said. "Because I can think of only one reason why you'd wait. If you had her watched, then you may have wanted to set her up as bait."

"The possibility occurred to me." He looked back at Jane. "But I would never have let anything happen to you. No one's going to hurt you. I promise."

"Which means zilch," Jane said. "I'm responsible for what happens to me. Not you or Eve or Joe. I take care of myself. I don't care if you played some kind of game to trap that creep. As long as you didn't hurt anyone I care about." She took a step back. "But I think you'd better leave now. You've upset Eve."

His brows lifted. "And that's a sin, I take it."

"Yes, it is." She gestured to the door. "Good-bye, Mr. Trevor. If you can catch that creep, good luck to you. But don't come back unless you have a darned good reason."

"And don't upset Eve."

"You've got it." She turned to Joe. "It's suppertime. Do you want me to warm up those leftovers from the steaks you grilled last night?"

"I appear to be dismissed." Trevor smiled and headed for the door. "I'll be in touch, Quinn."

Joe nodded curtly. "Like she said, you better have a good reason."

"The very best. I won't darken your door until I do," Trevor said. "May I commandeer one of your policemen to take me to town?"

Joe nodded again. "He'll drop you at a hotel." He paused. "Or the airport."

Trevor gave a mock shiver. "The welcome mat has definitely been yanked. I can only hope that I can reinstate myself in your good graces."

"You were never in them," Eve said. "We don't know you and now we don't trust you."

He paused at the door. "You can trust me," he said quietly. "If you searched the world over, you wouldn't find anyone who wants to keep Jane safe more than I do." He reached in his pocket, pulled out a card, and placed it on the table by the door. "That's for you, Jane. My cell number. If you need anything, call me. I'll be there for you." The door closed behind him.

"Whew." Jane went to the window and watched him as he moved toward the police car. "He's definitely not stuffy or slow moving, is he?"

"No." Eve's gaze narrowed on her face. "What do you think of him?"

She glanced at Eve. "Why?"

"When you first met him, you couldn't take your eyes off him. He's very good-looking, isn't he?"

"Is he?" She frowned. "I suppose he is. I didn't really notice."

"That's hard to believe. It was pretty clear you were fascinated."

"He reminded me of someone."

"Who?"

"I don't remember. Someone . . ." She saw Eve's expression and she smiled. "You're worried. You think I developed a crush on him in the few minutes he was here? I don't have crushes, Eve. You know that."

Relief surged through her. She smiled. "There's always a first time. I'd be glad to see you have a crush or two. I keep hoping and waiting for a breakthrough." She shook her head. "But pick a rock star or a football player. Not him, Jane."

"Definitely not him." Joe headed for the door. "I think I'll escort him into town myself. Don't bother to heat up the steaks. I'll pick up Chinese on the way back."

Jane giggled as the door closed behind him. "He reminds me of the sheriff in a spaghetti western. Only he'd be running the outlaw out of town, not escorting him to the hotel." She moved over to the door and picked up Trevor's business card on the table. "He really upset both of you. You'd think he was attacking me instead of only doing his job."

"He should have notified us of any threat. That's what any policeman I know would have done."

"Maybe Scotland Yard is different."

"Are you defending him?"

"I suppose I am." She stuffed the card in the pocket of her jeans. "Do you remember when I was little and stole food to feed Mike when he was hiding out in that alley? I didn't want to do it. I knew it was wrong, but Mike was six years old and would have gone hungry if I hadn't found a way to feed him. Sometimes you have to do bad things to keep worse things from happening."

"It's not the same. You were only ten."

"If I couldn't find any other way, I'd do it today. Maybe that's why I understand Trevor."

"You can't understand him," Eve said curtly. "You don't know him."

"I just don't see what all the fuss is about. You told me that Joe thought he was obsessed with this case. I can see why anyone who felt that deeply would be willing to snoop around a bit and see if he could spot anyone suspicious before he let me be surrounded by cops that might scare him off."

"That's more than I can see." Eve's lips tightened grimly. "And why are you keeping his telephone number?"

"Because I believed him when he said he wanted to keep me alive." She met Eve's eyes. "Didn't you?"

Eve wanted to deny it, but it wouldn't have been honest and Jane would have known it. "Yes. But that doesn't mean I'd trust his ways and means."

Jane nodded. "I see what you mean. But sometimes you take what you can get. Trevor may be unconventional but I'd bet he's very good at what he does." She moved toward the bedroom. "Now I'm going to do my homework so that I can enjoy that Chinese food Joe is bringing home."

Eve watched the door shut behind her. Jesus, she wished Jane wasn't so damn smart. From the time she was a child she'd always known her own mind and trusted her judgments.

And her judgments were usually good, better than most adults'. That didn't mean that she was infallible. Trevor was smart and charismatic and both qualities would appeal to a teenager like Jane.

But there weren't any teenagers like Jane. She was an original and her reactions were distinctly her own.

She'd kept his telephone number, dammit.

She sighed. Who knew which way Jane would jump? She might be worrying for nothing.

After all, she'd kicked him out of the house just because he'd upset Eve.

"This is the Peachtree Plaza." Joe pulled up before the front entrance. "I made reservations for you for two days. I didn't think you'd be here any longer."

"And now you hope I won't be." Trevor got out of the car as the doorman opened the door. "My assistance is no longer required."

"I imagine I'll be able to find out all I need from those files you brought. We don't need you."

Trevor smiled. "But you've got me. And how do you know I put everything I know into those files?"

Joe's gaze narrowed on his face. "For instance."

"The volcano that produced those ashes. You'll notice the geologists couldn't come to any conclusion."

"But you know where they originated?"

"I have theories."

"Theories aren't proof."

"But they're a starting point."

"And do you have a theory about why he scatters those ashes?"

"Maybe." Trevor tipped the doorman as he grabbed his duffel. "What's certain is that we could be valuable to each other, Quinn. And you're coming in late on a case that I've lived and breathed for years."

"Do you think I don't know you're trying

to play me?" Joe said coolly. "You're dangling little morsels of information in hopes that I'll forgive all and let you edge back into the investigation. But you haven't given me anything. Zilch."

"Jane used that word too." Trevor smiled. "It's a warm and heartening thing the way families pick up words and traits from each other." He pretended to think. "You're right. I've told you nothing really. Theories are so difficult to substantiate. And you have all the time in the world to formulate your own and then investigate, don't you?" He didn't wait for a reply but turned and walked into the hotel.

Bastard.

Joe sat at the wheel, his gaze fixed on the door. Trevor would take a sly pleasure out of having him run after him. He'd be damned if he'd do it. Even if logic told him he should wring every bit of information Trevor possessed out of the mocking son of a bitch, he'd wait until he was certain that he couldn't get it any other way. Trevor was a force to be reckoned with and he didn't need a wild card spinning the investigation out of Joe's control.

He pressed the accelerator and glided back to the street.

Ashes from a volcano . . .

Weird. Maybe the scientists they had on this side of the Atlantic could come up with an answer. But if they did, they'd have to be damn quick. Trevor's last remark had hit the bull's-eye. They might be running out of time for Jane.

The thought sent a bolt of panic through him and tempted him to turn around and go back to Trevor. To hell with Anglo-American cooperation. There were other ways than persuasion to get information from the son of a bitch. Two could play that game. Trevor had violated his position by not informing him about the danger to—

His phone rang and he glanced at the ID. Eve.

"I've just dropped him off," he said. "I'll be home in forty-five minutes. Everything okay?"

"No, I don't think it is." Eve's words came hard and fast. "I was sitting here going over these files and something occurred to me. I think everything may be wrong as hell."

* * *

Trevor watched Quinn's car disappear around the corner before he turned and moved toward the registration desk.

He'd done all he could. A few tantalizing tidbits and a subtle threat to someone Quinn loved. Either one might do the trick. God, he hoped it would be enough. Today hadn't been his most shining hour. He'd come here prepared to be clever and conquer on all fronts and he'd made a gigantic mistake that was impossible to cover. Maybe if Eve Duncan and Quinn had been less smart, less perceptive, he might have been able to smooth it over, but they were as formidable as Bartlett had told him. He was lucky to have gotten out of there with—

He stopped short in the marble foyer as the realization sank home.

Perhaps not so lucky.

They were both smart and very, very perceptive. He had the experience to recognize those qualities and he'd seldom met anyone who'd filled him with more wariness.

And that experience was sending out vibrations that were triggering every instinct he possessed. He reached for his phone and dialed Bartlett. "I'm in Atlanta. Are you at the flat?"

"Yes."

"Get out of there. You may have company." He glanced around the lobby and then headed for the restaurant. There was almost always a street entrance to a hotel restaurant. "I blew it."

"I can't believe it." Bartlett chuckled. "All that slickness and you were knocked for six? I would have liked to have been there to see it."

"I'm sure you would," he said dryly. Yes, there was a street door at the back of the restaurant. He headed straight for it. "And I'd deserve to have you give me a hard time. Jesus, I was stupid. I behaved like a stinking amateur. I never expected to have that reaction."

Bartlett was silent a moment. "Jane MacGuire?"

"I'd been waiting too long. I got panicky even before she walked in the room."

"Panic? I've never seen you panic in any situation, you icy son of a bitch."

"Well, you would have seen it today. I was scared to death she'd be lost before I even got a chance at her. And then I saw her and I tried to mend my fences but it was too late."

"Is it her?"

"God, yes. She took my breath away. Even Aldo would be satisfied." He opened the street door and hailed a cab. "But you were right about Quinn and Eve Duncan. It's only a matter of time before they start asking the same questions I would." He settled in the cab. "I'll call you back later. Don't leave anything there. Clean as a whistle."

"You may have behaved like an ass, but I won't, and I value my efficiency. I'll do my job." He hung up.

As he should have done his, Trevor thought in disgust as the cab pulled away from the curb. But who the hell would have expected him to fall apart like that? "Hartsfield Airport," he told the driver.

He should have expected it. It had been too long and every day had seemed a century. He'd thought he was prepared but evidently you couldn't prepare yourself for something like this.

So pick up the pieces and start again.

No, not again. His clumsiness had only caused him to take a step back. Because

Jane MacGuire was here, only minutes away. He'd seen her, touched her. He was ahead of the game.

He was ahead of Aldo.

So far.

FOUR

"I'm sorry, Detective Quinn." The desk clerk glanced up from the computer. "Mr. Trevor hasn't checked in yet."

"Look again," Joe said impatiently. "I know he's here. I dropped him off fifteen minutes ago."

The clerk did another search and then shook her head. "I'm sorry," she said again. "Maybe he stopped off in the bar. Or perhaps he was hungry and went to the restaurant."

Or perhaps he'd flown the coop, Joe thought as he turned away and headed for the bar. He was going to find out in a hurry even if he had to question every employee in both places.

* * *

"He went through the restaurant and hopped into a taxi," Joe told Eve twenty minutes later. "I've called the taxi company and a cab dropped off a man of his description at the airport ten minutes ago. I'm on my way."

"Can't you call and have him picked up by airport security?"

"Not without risking a lawsuit against the department or an international incident. No proof, Eve. As Trevor would say, pure theory."

"I've heard enough of Trevor's theories," Eve said. "Have you called the precinct?"

"I've asked Christy to do the work since she's the one who connected me with Trevor. I'll call you back when I know something."

"Make it soon. I'll be waiting."

"You didn't get him," Eve said as she saw Joe's face when he walked into the cottage three hours later. "How did he get away?"

"Well, he didn't get on a plane. I checked with all the taxi dispatchers and he didn't take a taxi from the airport." Joe dropped down on the couch and wearily rubbed the back of his neck. "My bet is that he hopped on MARTA and took the subway back into the city. A nice slick exit, hard to track and easy to lose."

"Very smart."

"What did you expect? He is smart. And he has damn good instincts. I don't think he had any intention of going on the lam when I dropped him off. He was playing me for all I was worth."

"Did you get the report from Christy?"

"Thirty minutes ago. She called Scotland Yard directly and spoke to Inspector Falsworth. No Inspector Mark Trevor. But there's someone by that name who works in the evidence lab. Trevor wouldn't want to impersonate a real inspector. It could be an instant giveaway. But a title could possibly be confused and he'd want a bona fide name in case someone called the office instead of his cell number. They never sent that e-mail regarding our serial killer. They never suspected he was here in the States. They're still looking for him in the U.K." He glanced at her. "Why did you think Trevor might be a phony?"

"I didn't think. It was pure guesswork. I got to wondering after you left how unusual Trevor's behavior was for a policeman. Proper procedure is drummed into all of you and he violated one of the cardinal rules." Eve's lips tightened. "And then I started playing the what-if game. Could we be certain Trevor was who he said he was? What proof did we have? I'm sure he showed you his credentials, but they could be forged. And this e-mail could have been bogus too. It would have been difficult and nervy for him to infiltrate the Scotland Yard Web site and use it to send official e-mails, but not beyond the skills of an expert hacker. It was worth checking out."

"Yes, it was. I only wish I'd been able to collar him before he slipped out." His gaze went to the hall. "Did you tell Jane?"

"I told her we were checking on him. She didn't say much. She probably thinks I'm paranoid." She headed for the kitchen. "I heated up a leftover steak for Jane when I knew you wouldn't be picking up Chinese. Do you want one?"

"I'm not hungry. But I'll take a glass of milk." He got up and sat down at the bar. "Christy asked Scotland Yard to try to run a computer check on Trevor. She needs a good description."

"They'll need more than that. Trevor's probably not his real name. I saved the coffee cup he used, to dust for fingerprints." She set the glass of milk before him. "Jane might be able to help. She could give Christy a sketch of him." She grimaced. "If she'll do it."

"If she knows he's lied to us, she's not going to protect him."

"Maybe. She was talking about how she used to do bad things for good reasons when she was a little girl. I don't like the way she was identifying with him." She moistened her lips. "Do you think it's him? Do you think he's the one who killed Ruth?"

Joe didn't answer for a moment. "I was thinking about that all the way home. Pretending to be an investigator would be a smart way to get close to Jane." He glanced at the file on the coffee table. "And he paved his way with very tempting bait."

"Bastard."

He nodded slowly. "It's safer to assume he's a danger to Jane until we know different."

Her gaze narrowed on his face. "But you have your doubts."

"I think he wanted to be part of the investigation."

"It's not completely uncommon to have a serial killer trying to insinuate himself into the investigation. Look at Ted Bundy."

"I know that." He finished his milk. "I just think I would have spotted that kind of sick reaction. He pissed me off but not for one moment did I doubt that he wanted—" He shrugged. "Who the hell knows what he wanted? We'll find out when we find him. If he's still in the city."

"Oh, he's still in the city," Eve said jerkily. "Didn't you see his face when he was talking to Jane? There's no way he'd leave her." She rinsed out the glass. "Did you get a report on Ruth?"

"Give it some time. Her photo will be in tomorrow's paper. Maybe someone will identify her."

"I hope so. I wanted something good to come out of this." She paused and then whispered, "I'm scared, Joe. What if that murderer was in this cottage, shaking Jane's hand?"

"Jane's safe, Eve."

"Is she? God, I hope so." She drew a deep breath and squared her shoulders. "Of course, she's safe. And we'll keep her that way." She put the glass on the sink and came around the bar. "And now I'm going to see if Jane's still awake so I can talk to her about that sketch. Why don't you check and see if Christy has heard anything more?"

Aldo smiled as he studied the photo in the newspaper. It was an amazingly close likeness. The artist who had rendered the reconstruction was obviously very talented. Almost as talented as he'd been when he'd carefully removed those features with his surgical knife. He'd thought it would take much longer to put a face to the woman they were calling Ruth.

Her name wasn't Ruth. It was Caroline and someone would probably identify her soon. She wasn't a prostitute or vagrant this time. He'd seen her coming out of a downtown office building and he'd done his duty and removed the Cira possibility.

Jesus, he was getting weary of that duty.

There was always an explosion of pleasure when he performed the act but he was tired of the searching. There was no doubt that her likeness must be banished from the face of the earth but he had to find the true Cira. Every night before he closed his eyes he murmured a prayer that he be given that one gift.

And he had the feeling that his prayer was to be answered soon. The excitement was too intense, the anticipation escalating with each passing day.

He pushed the newspaper away and scooted his desk chair back to the computer. He couldn't count on finding Cira by random chance. He'd decided long ago he wouldn't deserve that final pleasure if he just cruised the streets looking for her.

So type in the stolen password.

The monitor screen lit up.

He was in!

Now avoid all the security walls they had put up to protect Cira.

He settled down and began to flip through the pages. There were thousands but he was very patient. Even though his eyes grew blurry and his back ached from hours of leaning over the computer, he wouldn't give up.

It was the road that led to Cira.

"Here it is." Jane dropped the sketch on the table in front of Joe the next morning at breakfast. "It's as good a likeness as I can do." She went to the refrigerator and got out the orange juice. "What are you going to do with it?"

"Send it to Scotland Yard and they'll probably send it to Interpol." He studied the sketch. "This is very good. You've caught him perfectly."

"He's easy. Very strong features." She poured orange juice into her glass. "Besides, as I told Eve, he reminded me of someone. He felt . . . I don't know . . . familiar." She sat down at the table. "Where's Eve?"

"Outside taking coffee to Mac and Brian, who are on the stakeout." He looked up from the sketch. "Eve thought that you might object to doing this for us."

"Why? I don't even know this Trevor. And my loyalty is to you and Eve." She smiled. "Always, Joe."

"That's good to know."

"That being said, I don't think Trevor wants to hurt me. And I can't see him skinning any woman's face off."

"Just because he has such a pretty face himself?"

"No, I told you I hardly noticed that he was good-looking. He's got a lot more going for him than what's on the surface."

"How can you judge? As you said, you don't even know him."

"You have to trust your instincts." She sipped her orange juice. "You've always told me that, Joe. I'm just following your lead."

"Now you blame it on me?"

"Sure, why not?"

"Because your character was already formed by the time you came into our lives. If anything, you're the one who nudges us along."

"Not true. I wouldn't presume. So when do you think you'll hear about Trevor?"

"Soon, I hope."

"Good. I'm curious about him." She finished her orange juice. "He's interesting. I'd have offered to do the sketch even if Eve hadn't asked me."

"Now, that surprises me."

"Why? He pushed into our lives and he deserves to have us push back a little."

"Maybe a lot," Joe said grimly.

"We'll see." She scooted back her chair. "Now I'm going to find Eve and ask her to take me to school to get my assignments." She smiled. "Of course, I could borrow your car and go by myself. I'm legal now."

"I think we'd prefer you to have company for the next few days."

"I thought you would." She headed for the door. "So much for my brand-new license."

"Ruth's name is Caroline Halliburton," Christy said when Joe walked into the precinct three hours later. "She worked at a brokerage office downtown and her parents live up north in Blairsville. She has an apartment in Buckhead and she didn't show up for work last Monday. On Wednesday she was reported missing by a friend who worked with her."

"Is that who identified the photo?" Joe asked.

"No, actually one of our clerks in the department remembered seeing the photo when they were processing the missing person report."

Joe swore in exasperation. "We did the usual missing person check before I released the photo to the newspaper. We came up with nothing."

"So what's new? Since the latest budget cuts we're a month behind in paperwork and at least four months behind at the DNA lab." Christy glanced at the sketch Joe had tossed down on her desk and then gave a low whistle. "This is damn good, Joe. Is it accurate?"

"Absolutely."

She grinned. "He's a real pretty boy. I'd let a con artist like him talk me into almost anything. It's no wonder Jane was impressed enough to remember him."

"She didn't notice he was particularly good-looking. She just drew what she saw."

"Yeah, sure. For God's sake, she's seventeen, Joe. Appearance is everything to teenagers. He's as sexy as a damn movie star." She held up her hand as Joe opened his mouth. "Okay, she's above all that. She's not like my daughter Emily, or ninety-nine percent of her age group." She made a rude sound of derision and stood up. "I'll get this scanned right away and sent to Scotland Yard."

"Thanks, Christy."

She grinned. "My pleasure. I'm not like Jane. I like looking at handsome devils like him."

"He may well be a devil," Joe said. "You call him a con man, but we don't know that he didn't do the killings himself."

"No, we don't." Christy's smile faded as she looked down at the sketch. "Pity."

Joe watched her as she moved away through the row of desks before he flipped open the Caroline Halliburton file in front of him. He'd been prepared for the photo but it still gave him a shock. The photo made from Eve's construction had been true to life, but this was the picture of the woman herself. She'd been twenty-four at the time of her death, but this photo had been taken a few years before and the resemblance to Jane was very strong.

It scared the hell out of him.

"Joe."

He looked up to see Christy standing before him. "That was fast. I wouldn't think you'd have time to—"

"We've got another one." She turned off the cell phone on which she'd been talking. "Lake Lanier. Some scuba divers found a body, marked the location, and notified the authorities."

Joe flipped the file shut and jumped to his feet. "You're sure?"

"As sure as I can be." She grabbed her purse and headed for the door. "She had no damn face."

It was her!

Aldo couldn't believe it. It was a miracle.

His heart was beating hard as he gazed at the photo.

She was staring out at the world with a boldness that dared all comers. Fresh, young, and impregnable.

No, not impregnable, Cira. Not from me.

He wrote down the name.

Jane MacGuire.

Not Jane.

Cira. Cira. Cira.

He quickly copied the address on the record.

He was shaking, he realized. Trembling with delight that the moment had come. The others had been close but she was exact, perfection. There could be no doubt that this was the face he'd seen all his life and in his nightmares. He was quivering with fear that something or someone would snatch her away from him.

No, that mustn't be allowed to happen. He'd traveled too long, devoted too much time to the search, purged too many Cira pretenders.

But Jane MacGuire wasn't a pretender. She was Cira.

And she deserved to die.

Darkness.

No air.

No time.

She wasn't going to make it.

The hell she wasn't. She wasn't going to die in this tunnel. Let those other cowards give up. She'd fight until she broke free.

She'd smashed all the chains that held her captive before and she wouldn't let death make her a final captive.

Was the ground shaking?

No air.

She fell to her knees.

No!

She struggled up and lunged forward. Which way? It was too dark to—

She turned right.

"No, that's a blind alley. This way."

He was standing in the tunnel behind her. Tall, shadowy but she knew who it was, damn him. "Get out of my way. Do you think I'd trust you?"

"There's no time to do anything else." He held out his hand. "Come with me. I'll show you the way."

She'd never take his hand again. Never trust him to—

She staggered down the tunnel.

"Come back!"

"The hell I will." Her voice was only a whisper from a throat that was painfully dry.

Run.

Hurry.

Live.

But how could she live when there was no air?

"Dammit, Jane, wake up!"

She was being shaken. Eve again, she realized sluggishly. Eve afraid. Eve trying to save her from the dream that was no dream. Didn't she know that she had to stay here? It was her duty to—

"Jane!"

The tone was demanding and Jane slowly opened her lids.

Eve's face was taut with alarm.

"Hi," Jane murmured. "Sorry . . ."

"That's not good enough." Eve's voice was as alarmed as her expression. "I've had my fill of this." She stood up and headed for the door. "Get on your robe and come out on the porch. We need to talk."

"It's only a nightmare, Eve. I'm okay."

"I know about nightmares and there's nothing okay about them. Not when they happen every night. Come out on the porch." She didn't wait for Jane to answer.

Jane slowly sat up and shook her head to clear it. She was still logy and half-dazed and the last thing she needed was to confront Eve with a fuzzy head. She went to the bathroom and splashed cold water in her face.

That was better. . . .

Except for her lungs that were still tight and burning from the night with no air.

That would go away soon and so would the lingering panic.

She drew a deep breath, grabbed her robe from the bed, and shrugged into it as she walked down the hall toward the porch.

Eve was sitting on the swing. "At least you look awake now." She handed her a cup of hot chocolate. "Drink it. It's chilly out here."

"We could go inside."

"I don't want to wake Joe. He'd think I'm exaggerating your problem. Hell, he might not even see it as a problem. He's all for patience and letting you work it out for yourself."

"Maybe he's right." She sipped her hot chocolate and then sat down on the top porch step. "I don't see it as a problem."

"Well, I do. And it's up to you to convince me I'm wrong." She lifted her cup to her lips. "By telling me what the devil you're dreaming about."

She made a face. "Chill, Eve. It's not as if I'm suffering some deep psychological trauma that's connected with you or Joe or even the way I grew up."

"How do I know that? How do you know that? Dreams aren't always clear and they can be interpreted in a number of different ways."

"Yeah, by some shrink who gets paid a couple hundred dollars an hour to make dumb guesses."

"I'm not that fond of psychoanalysis myself, but I want to know that I haven't failed you."

Jane smiled. "For heaven's sake, you haven't failed me, Eve. You've been everything that's kind and understanding, and that wasn't easy with a hard nut like me." She took another drink of hot chocolate. "But I should have known you'd blame yourself for something that has nothing to do with you."

"Then show me it has nothing to do with me. Tell me about that damn dream."

"How do you know it's the same one every time?"

"Isn't it?"

Jane was silent. "Yes."

"At last." Eve leaned back in the swing. "More."

"Well, it is and it isn't. It starts out the same way, but every dream seems to take a step forward." She looked out at the lake. "And sometimes . . . it doesn't . . . I don't know if it's really a dream." She moistened her lips. "I know it sounds crazy but I'm *there,* Eve."

"Where?"

"I'm in a tunnel or a cave. Something like that. And I'm trying to find the end, the opening, but I don't know where it is. And there's not much time. There's no air and it's getting hotter and hotter. I keep running but I'm not sure I'm going to find the way out."

"Hell?"

She shook her head. "That would fit the bill, wouldn't it? Hot and no air and an endless chase. But this is a real tunnel. And I'm not dead, I'm alive and fighting to stay that way."

"That's no surprise. You've been a fighter all your life."

"Yes, I have." She kept her gaze on the lake. "But in the dream when I remember fighting . . . it's different. They're not my memories, my battles, they're hers." She shook her head in confusion. "I mean mine, but they're not mine. Crazy . . ."

"You're not crazy. You just need help to understand all this."

"Yeah, and the shrink would tell me I'm

trying to escape reality by climbing into someone else's shoes. Bullshit. I like my reality."

"But you don't like those nightmares."

"They're not so bad. I can live with them."

"Well, I can't. Maybe if you took a sedative, you'd be too deeply asleep to have—"

Jane's head swung around. "No!"

"I don't like drugs either but it might—"

"I'm not afraid of taking a sedative. I just can't— I have to finish it."

"What?"

"I have to get to the end of the tunnel. She'll . . . I'll die if I don't get out of there."

"Do you know how irrational that sounds?"

"I don't *care*. I have to do it." She could see Eve was about to protest and hurried on. "Look, I don't know what's happening to me but I think . . . no, I *know* there's a reason for it. That's a hard thing for me to admit because I don't believe in much that I can't see or touch." She tried to smile. "I believe in you and Joe and what we have together. That's good and real. But what's happening in that tunnel is real too. And if I don't keep on trying to help her, she may be lost."

"You said 'she' again."

"Did I?" She hadn't realized it. "So what are you thinking, Eve?"

"I don't know what to think." She frowned. "If it's not you, tell me who you think this woman is. Do you believe it's some telepathic connection with someone in distress? I've heard of things like that."

"Not to people like me. I'm not psychic."

"Anything is possible."

Jane smiled. "I thought you'd try to find a way to believe in me, even if I sounded bonkers. That's why I told you."

"After I pried it out of you."

"I had to make you work a little." Her smile faded. "I don't have any answers, Eve. I have a lot of questions and every one of them scares me."

"When did you start having these nightmares?"

"Two months ago."

"About the time Aldo appeared in the Southeast."

"But I didn't know it. So he couldn't have triggered them." She smiled again. "Go ahead. Tell me everything is possible again.

I like that line." She finished her hot chocolate. "Since I don't have any answers, it's very comforting." She stood up. "Don't worry about this, Eve. Maybe it will just go away on its own." She crossed the porch and gave her a quick hug. "And if it's any comfort to you, no serial killer is chasing me down that tunnel. That's not why I'm running."

"Good. I'm glad you're alone. We're having enough trouble without that bastard following you into your dreams."

She hesitated. "Well, I'm not exactly alone. There's someone behind me. A man. But I'm angry, not afraid of him."

"Who is it?"

She shook her head. "Shadowy." She shrugged and smiled. "Well, now you know everything I know. And it's probably all bunk and the result of my deprived childhood. But I'm not going to let any shrink tell me that. So let's forget it and go to bed."

"I'm not going to forget it."

"I know you won't." Jane felt a surge of warmth as she looked at her. "All these years you've tried to bring home all those lost ones and you don't like the idea I might join the ranks even in a small way. I'm not lost, Eve. There's a way out of that tunnel. I just don't know where she—I'm going."

"Then tell me when you have another one and we'll figure it out. Two heads are always better. I'm not about to scoff at anything you say to me. I've found that sometimes dreams are the only salvation."

"I know you have."

Eve suddenly stiffened as she caught an odd note in Jane's tone. "Jane?"

Lord, she hadn't meant to say that, Jane thought. She should back down and lie to her. No, she'd never lied to Eve and she wouldn't start now. "I . . . heard you."

"What?"

"You were sitting out by the lake and you didn't know I was on the trail behind you."

"And?"

"Bonnie. You were talking to Bonnie."

Eve was silent for a long moment. "In my sleep?"

"I guess so. You were leaning against a tree. I don't know. I only know you were talking to someone who wasn't there." She could see the shock on Eve's face and added quickly, "That was over three years ago. I knew you wouldn't want to talk about it so I never— I should have kept my mouth shut. Stop looking like that. It's okay. You have a right to— It's okay."

"Three years." She looked at her in wonder. "And you never mentioned it. . . ."

"What was there to say? You were hurting. So you talked to your dead daughter. It was your business."

"And it never occurred to you that I might be a little . . . off center?"

"Not you." She fell to her knees in front of her and laid her head in Eve's lap. She whispered, "And if you were, I wanted to be just like you. Everyone in the world should be so crazy."

"Lord, I hope not." Eve gently stroked Jane's hair. "No questions?"

"I told you, it's your business. I'm sorry I mentioned it. I didn't mean— Don't let it make a difference between us. I couldn't stand that."

"It will make a difference."

Jane swiftly lifted her head. "You'll feel awkward around me? Please don't do—"

"Shh." Eve's fingers on her lips stopped the flow of words. "I don't feel awkward. If anything, I feel warmer and closer to you."

"Why?"

She chuckled. "Because you think I'm a

little bananas but you still love me. Because you didn't say a word to me for three years because you thought it might hurt me. I'd say that's pretty special, Jane."

"No, it isn't," Jane said unevenly. "You're special. You're good and you're kind and I'm lucky to be allowed in the same house with you. I've always known that." She stood up. "So it's okay? You're not upset with me?"

"I'm not upset." She grimaced. "When I get over the shock, I believe it will even be good to share Bonnie with someone."

"Joe doesn't know?"

Eve shook her head. "It's . . . difficult."

"I'll never tell anyone. Not even Joe."

"I know you won't."

She glanced away from her. "I do have one question. If you don't want to answer, that's okay."

"Ask it."

"Is Bonnie . . . is she a dream like the ones I'm having?"

"I like to think she's a dream. She tells me she's a bona fide ghost and that I'm in denial." She smiled. "Sometimes I believe her. So I obviously have no right to question what you're experiencing, Jane."

"You have the right to do anything you damn well please." She moved toward the screen door. "And I'll fight anyone who says anything different. Good night, Eve."

"Good night, Jane. Sleep well."

"I'll try." She smiled at her over her shoulder. "And if I don't, then I'll come running."

"I'll always be here for you."

Jane was still feeling the warmth engendered by those words when she reached her bedroom. Yes, Eve would always be there to comfort and support her. She had never had anyone to trust before Eve had come into her life, and after the confidences tonight, she felt closer to her than ever.

Now to go to bed and get to sleep and hope that she wouldn't be pulled back into that other place. Not yet. Each dream was becoming increasingly draining. It was like being on a treadmill whose speed kept escalating. She needed to recover strength before she faced it again.

"I'm coming," she murmured as she pulled the covers up. "Just give me a little rest. I'm not abandoning you, Cira. . . ."

FIVE

It was too damn dark and they hadn't turned on the porch light.

Aldo lowered the binoculars with profound disappointment. When the two women had come out on the porch, he'd thought he'd be able to see them clearly but they'd both only been a shadowy blur.

But he knew which one was Jane MacGuire. He could feel the exquisite life force, the singing strength, the poetry that was such a part of her. When she'd knelt before the other woman and laid her head on her lap, it had been so characteristic, so familiar. She could move the heart with a gesture, control those around her with a smile or a tear, he thought bitterly.

She was doing that now with the woman who must be Eve Duncan. The woman was still staring after her and Aldo could almost feel the love radiating between them. He had not been surprised when he'd discovered that Jane lived with the same forensic sculptor who had reconstructed Caroline Halliburton. It had just been another sign that the circle was tightening.

Even the police car parked down the road had not intimidated him. He could move in these woods as silently as a forest animal. And those policemen standing guard were only an indication that she knew he was near and was filled with fear.

As she should be.

Joe was lying still in the darkness when Eve slipped into bed but she could sense that he wasn't sleeping.

"Jane had another nightmare," she said as she pulled the blanket over her. "I had to talk to her."

"And?"

"Running down a tunnel, unable to breathe, someone in the tunnel with her but no threat." She cuddled closer and laid her head on his shoulder. “It sounds like typical stuff but nothing’s ever typical about Jane. We’ll have to keep an eye on her.”

“I don’t think there’s any question about that,” Joe said dryly. “Particularly under the circumstances. And if it was as typical as you’re saying, I don’t think you’d have been out there on the porch for so long.”

Eve was silent a moment. “She says sometimes she’s not sure it’s a dream.”

“Now, that’s not commonplace.”

“And a little scary?”

“No, it just has to be handled.” He gently stroked the hair at her temple. “You had your share of dreams about Bonnie and we fought our way through.”

Oh, yes, she remembered those first years after Bonnie’s kidnapping when he’d been her rock in a seething whirlpool of despair. But she hadn’t shared these last years of healing dreams of Bonnie with him. It was too bizarre. How would he handle those visions if she did?

“Eve?”

“What if she’s right, Joe? Sometimes I wonder. . . . How do we know what are dreams and what’s real?”

“I know.” His lips brushed her forehead.

"Don't get all philosophical on me. You want to know about reality? Ask a hardheaded cop like me. We live and breathe it."

"That's right, you do."

He must have sensed the slight mental withdrawal because his arm tightened around her. "Okay, I'm not the most sensitive guy in the world. But I'm here for you and Jane. So take what I can give you."

"You are sensitive, Joe."

He chuckled. "Yeah, sure. The only reason I'm sensitive to you is that I love you so damn much that you can't take a breath without me knowing about it. Otherwise, I'm a tough son of a bitch and that's the way I want to stay. Tough isn't bad. Not if it keeps you and Jane safe."

That was Joe, she thought. Loyal, smart, and denying any hint of softness. Jesus, she loved him. She turned her head and kissed him. "No, tough isn't bad," she whispered. But she knew she wasn't going to tell him tonight.

Not yet, Bonnie . . .

"I'm on my way," Bartlett said. "I'm changing planes at Kennedy now. I couldn't get on the direct flight but I should be at Atlanta in a couple hours. Unless the police pick me up."

"I think you're still safe," Trevor said. "They would have stopped you from entering the country if Quinn had been able to trace your connection with me."

"That's comforting. Where am I supposed to meet you?"

"The lobby of the Best Western Hotel at Lake Lanier. Don't check in. We'll be leaving right away."

"And where are we going?"

"Quinn's lake house. Well, not the house itself. I've been sleeping in the woods for the past two nights."

"Why? As I recall, I leased you a nice comfortable lodge north of the city. I was quite proud of how thoroughly I buried the paperwork."

"I have to keep close to her. Sooner or later Aldo will show up there." He paused. "He may be there now. But I haven't run across him yet. Quinn's got a lot of acreage and Aldo is woods savvy."

"So are you. But then I haven't come across anything you're not good at. It's very depressing. Of course, you're not as well versed in the outdoors as you are in a casino. I'd judge the odds aren't nearly as good. But what do I know? You've proved me wrong before. However, I'm here to state that I'm not looking forward to any damp, earthy sojourn in the forest primeval."

"You'll adjust."

"Promises. I'll see you at nine at the hotel if you don't get your ass caught flitting around there." Bartlett hung up.

Trevor pressed the disconnect and looked out over the lake. Jane was in that cottage. Even though it was the middle of the afternoon and she should have been in school, they were keeping her home, keeping her safe.

Or so they thought. There was no safety where Aldo was concerned. He was totally relentless and his patience was inexhaustible.

So that's how patient Trevor must be. Jesus, it was hard. He'd never been this close before. Well, he had to be patient. Jane MacGuire was a bright beacon that Aldo wouldn't be able to resist and he only had to watch until the bastard ventured too close to the flame.

Aldo would want to kill Jane with all due ceremony. No long-range rifle shot for him. And if he was right, the chances were good that Trevor would have time to get him before he could murder the girl.

"The odds aren't nearly as good."

Well, Bartlett was wrong. The odds were always as good as the effort you made to make them come up a winner. He just had to divorce himself from all emotion and use intellect and logic. He had to forget that moment when he'd looked at Jane and seen the spirit and the vitality that shone from her face. She mustn't matter to him as a person, only as a means to an end. He'd made one mistake. He couldn't afford another one.

Or Jane MacGuire would be dead within the next few days.

"It's definitely volcanic ash forensics found with Caroline Halliburton's body," Christy said when Joe picked up the phone. "We're trying to determine from which volcano. No luck yet."

"Scotland Yard can't help?"

"No conclusions about the ashes found with the other victims."

"That's what Trevor said. How the hell did he know if he's not connected with the Yard?"

"There's the obvious answer."

"Yeah." And he should accept the probability. To hell with instinct. His training should dictate what he thought in this case. "Any report on Trevor?"

"Not yet. No info on a Mark Trevor in their data banks and it takes a long time to get a photo match from a sketch. No report on the fingerprints either. They sent them out to Interpol. I'll let you know when I hear something."

"You'd better."

"How's Jane?"

"Restless, impatient. A hell of a lot better than Eve and me. She doesn't like being cooped up."

"That sounds like Jane." Christy chuckled. "But she's not dumb, Joe. She's not going to do anything foolish."

"What she considers foolish may not be what I consider foolish. She won't stay in the cottage. She says that having a police escort constantly on her heels is enough of a hassle without being made a total prisoner."

"A visible police guard is usually an effective deterrent, Joe."

"Usually." He went to the window and watched Jane as she strolled down the lake path. Mac and Brian were several yards behind her but in clear sight and Toby was gamboling beside her. "I don't like to count on it. Get back to me the minute you hear anything."

"Any news?" Eve asked as he hung up the phone.

"Volcanic ash. No location determined." He turned to face her. "Nothing on Trevor."

"Dammit." She joined him at the window. "What's the use of all this technology if they can't pull up information when you need it?"

"Trevor impressed me as being very smart. He may not have any criminal record."

"Yes, he's smart. But he tipped his hand with us. And if he made one mistake, then he could have made others." She frowned. "And no one is an island in this day and age. What about the fingerprints? Even if he doesn't have a criminal record, he must have gone to school, gotten a driver's license. Something . . ."

"We're checking." He slipped his arm around her waist, his gaze on Jane, who had just sat down on a log beside the lake. "It's only a matter of time."

He should be in hiding, Aldo thought. It was daylight and there might be more policemen than the two following the girl combing the woods. Screw it. He'd go to ground soon but he'd take this moment. It was the first time he'd been able to see her clearly.

He gazed hungrily at the girl sitting on the log across the lake. She appeared totally unafraid and was truly exquisite. So confident in her youth and power. The young always thought they were immortal, but she should know better. Had she no memory?

She must remember. She was just displaying her usual arrogance. She wouldn't admit to fear because she'd look upon it as a defeat.

But she'd admit it soon. She'd look into his eyes and he'd see the terror.

It was only a matter of time.

* * *

Was he out there?

Jane stared at the woods across the lake. She couldn't see anything, but she felt . . . something. It was weird to think of a man stalking you, wanting to kill you for no reason other than that he didn't like your face. It was crazy and she should be more afraid.

She felt more than just fear. She was filled with curiosity and excitement and anger. The idea of prey and hunter intrigued her. What would he do if she became the stalker? If she tried to turn the tables on that creep?

Not that she'd do anything like that, she thought regretfully. Eve and Joe would have a cow and there was no way she'd worry them. Eve was already too concerned about her after their talk last night. She'd understood Jane more than anyone else would have but in spite of her saying she had no right to judge, it had still troubled her. No, she wouldn't willingly cause Eve any more worry.

But the key word was *willingly*. It wouldn't be her fault if she was drawn into the whirlpool Aldo was stirring. And she couldn't be expected not to fight back, could she?

Jane picked up a rock and sent it skimming over the surface of the lake.

Did you see that? Are you watching, Aldo?

Yes, he was watching. She could *feel* it. He was close and getting closer. She would be forced to confront him soon.

It was only a matter of time.

"We've got a report on Mark Trevor," Christy said when she called that night. "Interpol came through."

Joe signaled Eve to pick up the extension. "Criminal record?"

"Not exactly."

"What do you mean 'not exactly'? He has a record or he doesn't."

"He was on their watch list because of casino activity in Monte Carlo. Among other talents, he's a superb card counter. He took several casinos on the Riviera to the cleaners before they caught on to what he was doing and banned him. Since card counting is a talent and not a criminal activity they couldn't charge him, but the local police wanted to keep their eye on him. There was every chance one of the casinos would take a contract out on him."

"No other charges?"

"Not so far as we can find out. But he must have forged identity documents as he moved from country to country. The name he used in Monte Carlo was Hugh Trent."

"A British citizen?"

"No, the Brits can't believe they wouldn't have been able to find some record in their computers. They're very frustrated because they regard it as an insult to their professionalism."

"He sounded British."

"The casino in Monte Carlo thought he was French. The one in Germany was sure he was German. He evidently speaks several languages fluently. Every report indicates that he appeared to be well educated, brilliant, and slick as glass."

"And he doesn't have any history of violence?"

"I didn't say that. When the Zurich casino was looking for Trevor to squeeze some of their money out of him, they ran across one of his contacts, Jack Cornell, who said he fought with him when he was a mercenary in Colombia. That was over ten years ago and Trevor wasn't much more than a kid, but he was one lethal son of a bitch."

"And still may be. The military can be a great training ground."

"You should know. You were in the SEALs, weren't you?"

"Yes." He paused. "And, kid or not, he could well have been seduced by the dark side."

"Dark side? Come on. You sound like something out of *Star Wars*."

"Do I? The phrase struck a note when I first heard it. Violence can be addictive if you don't pull yourself away fast."

"Maybe he did. Card counting is a mental exercise."

"But very dangerous if you do it on the scale Trevor was playing. Like walking a tightrope. Serial killers get off on taking chances too. Did they find out anything on a personal level from Cornell?"

"Not much. Cornell said that Trevor was quiet and never talked about himself. He was always reading or playing with those Rubik-type puzzles. He was a whiz at that kind of stuff. But once he did mention being in Johannesburg."

"At last, something concrete. And did Interpol follow up on it?"

"Negative. There wasn't any reason. No crime and Trevor had disappeared from their radar scope. They have enough to do without borrowing trouble."

"Well, he's back on the scope with a vengeance now."

"And they're sending out feelers, but we may not get lucky anytime soon. I'll send you a copy of the fax I received from Scotland Yard and I'll let you know if we get anything else." She hung up.

"It's not much." Eve replaced the receiver. "They don't even know his nationality."

"It's more than we knew before."

"We know he's brilliant and shady and was trained to kill. That's not very encouraging."

The bell on the machine signaled the incoming fax.

"Are we going to let Jane read about our Mr. Trevor's past?" Joe asked.

"Hell, yes. We tell her anything we can that will cause her to stop identifying with him. A mercenary isn't a role model." She went over to the fax machine and took out the two pages. "Besides, she'd resent it if we tried to keep anything from her. I don't blame her. So would I."

Joe nodded. "You're a lot alike." He smiled. "But I'm not sure that she's going to instantly condemn him for that."

"Why not?"

"Because I didn't." He opened the screen door. "And she's a lot like me, too."

The lights in the cottage went out.

Soon she'd be sleeping, Aldo thought. She'd be lying defenseless in her bed not realizing how close he was to her. He might be able to climb in her window and—

No, he might be able to kill her but he'd never be able to do it as it should be done. No quick, merciful death for her. He'd disposed of even her counterfeits with the usual ceremony and he wasn't about to cheat himself of the pleasure with the true Cira.

So, watch and wait?

No, he couldn't stand to do that. Not this time. Not with her.

Then find a way to bring her to him and put an end to waiting. Make her kneel as he had those other women. Submission was hateful to her and the perfect revenge.

Yes, that was what he had to do. Make her come to him.

"You have to come this way. Don't be foolish." His voice echoed behind her as she ran down the tunnel.

Whose voice? she wondered hazily. That's right, the man who had come out of the smoke and was standing at the fork of the tunnel. But she didn't know him. . . .

No, that wasn't true. Jane didn't know him but she did. Antonio. His name exploded out of nowhere and with it came all the memories, bitterness, and anger again. "I'd be foolish to believe you. I won't make that mistake again. I know what you want."

"Yes, I want it. But I also want you alive. This isn't the time for battles."

At least he was being honest.

Or clever. Antonio was always clever. It was the quality that had first drawn her to him. Clever and self-serving and ruthless.

But she had those same qualities and had no argument with them.

Until he had turned them against her.

"Why do you think I followed you?" There was anger in his voice. "I know the way. I could have left you to die."

"Or you could get me lost in this cave and then tell me you won't show me the way out until I give you what you want. Do you think I don't know that you always take advantage of every opportunity, Antonio?"

"Of course you do. Because we're alike. That's why you took me for your lover. You didn't trust me, but you knew me. You looked at me and it was like looking in a mirror. You could see every scar and feel the hate and the hunger that drives you."

"I wouldn't have betrayed you."

"I made a mistake. I'd been poor too long. I didn't realize that you were more important than—"

"Liar." Hot. It was getting hotter and her lungs felt tight and sore.

"Yes, I'm a liar and a cheat and I've been a thief. But I'm not lying now. Let me help you."

"Go away. I'll help myself. Just like I've always done."

"Then die, damn you." His tone was harsh. "But you'll die alone. I'm going to live and become rich as an emperor and make the earth shake at the wave of my hand. What do I care if you burn, Cira?"

"I didn't ask you to care if—"

He was no longer there. His shadow had disappeared from the tunnel opening.

Alone.

Shake off this despair. She'd always been alone. This was no different. She'd been right to depend only on herself. He had betrayed her once and it was clear he was as ambitious as ever. Even if he knew the way out, he might have turned her over to Julius at the end of the tunnel.

But he wanted to live and he hadn't followed her down this tunnel. He had taken the path on the left. If he did know the way out, then she would be stupid to be stubborn and continue on this course. She had no idea how to get out of here. She would follow him down the other path. He would not have to know she was behind him. Use him as he had used her.

She turned and started back toward the branch of the tunnel. The earth was becoming hot beneath her sandals and the rocks on her right were beginning to glow dimly in the darkness. Her pace quickened as she felt a surge of panic.

There wasn't much time. . . .

Jane was panting as she opened her eyes.

Hot. She couldn't breathe.

No, that was Cira.

Jane wasn't in the tunnel. She was lying in bed, in the cottage. She lay still and drew several long, deep breaths. In a few minutes her heartbeat steadied and she sat up. She should be used to this aftereffect but it was always new and terrifying. But this time it hadn't been as horrible as usual. The panic had been present but there had also been hope. Cira had thought she had found a way to bend fortune to suit herself as she usually did. She was always happier when she could take action.

And how was Jane so certain of that? Who the devil knew? Maybe she was echoing Antonio's words and Cira was Jane's mirror image. It felt strange to know Cira's name without understanding how she knew it. Or maybe Cira was some kind of manifestation of a split personality.

No, she wouldn't accept that explanation. She wasn't nuts and she didn't have any alter egos running around in her head. So she had weird dreams. They didn't do her any real harm and she found Cira fascinating. Every dream was like turning the pages of a novel and discovering something new with every sentence. If that story became a little too exciting at times and she woke scared to death, that went with the territory.

At least she evidently hadn't been screaming or whimpering this time or she would have had Eve or Joe running in here. She swung her feet out of bed and padded to the bathroom to get a glass of water. She glanced at the clock on the bedside table. It was almost three in the morning and in a few hours Eve would be getting up and starting to work. She didn't need to get up early and come in here to comfort Jane, she thought as she padded to the bathroom. She would get a glass of water and then go out in the living room and cuddle Toby on the couch until she was drowsy enough to go back to sleep.

She suddenly stiffened.

There was something wrong.

She turned to look at the Orvis dog bed on the floor beside her bed.

"Toby?"

SIX

Toby's red collar was lying on the top porch step.

Jane slowly knelt to pick it up and saw a piece of paper fastened to it.

She heard the howl as she straightened.

Panic soared through her. "Toby! Toby, come."

Another howl. Far away. Across the lake.

She started down the porch steps and then stopped.

Bait for a trap. It couldn't be clearer. She should call Joe and Eve.

She slowly unfolded the note on the collar.

Come alone and the dog will live.

The implication was clear. If she didn't

come alone, Toby would die. If she called the policemen in the squad car or Joe and Eve and set them to searching the woods, her Toby would not live through the night. Agony twisted through her at the thought.

"Is everything okay, Ms. MacGuire?"

She looked up to see Mac Gunther walking toward her from the squad car.

No, it wasn't okay, she wanted to scream at him. Toby . . .

Her hand holding the collar slipped behind her back. She forced a smile. "Fine, Mac. Just getting a breath of air. I couldn't sleep."

"Can't blame you." He smiled sympathetically. "But let us know when you decide to come out on the porch. You gave us a start."

"Sorry. I didn't think." She turned and started up the steps. "I'll just go back to bed. Good night."

"Good night."

She watched him turn and stroll back to the squad car as she opened the screen door. Give it a little time before she slipped away.

She heard Toby howl as it closed behind her.

"No," she whispered as she closed her eyes in pain. "You dirty bastard, stop it. I'm coming."

The howling pierced the night like a knife.

Bartlett jumped. "Jesus, what the hell was that? A wolf?"

Trevor began to curse. "Son of a bitch." He straightened away from the tree. "He's got her dog."

"What?"

"I'd bet on it. It's her dog, Toby. I've been here three nights and never heard that dog howl before."

"That doesn't mean— Where are you going?"

"I'm going to follow the sound," Trevor said curtly as he faded into the shrubbery. "Just like she's going to do."

"Should I go with you?"

"Hell, no. Go to the car and wait for me to call you. You make too much noise in the woods. If he hears you crashing through the brush, Aldo will kill the dog and then Jane MacGuire will kill both of us. She loves that dog."

The dog howled again.

"This could be a break," Bartlett called after him. "If you can get to the dog before the girl, you might be able to take down Aldo."

"I know that." And if he didn't get there in time, Jane MacGuire would be either butchered or taken prisoner. Some break. It wasn't the scenario he'd have planned if given a choice.

Well, choices had been few and far between since this macabre charade had begun. He'd have to take the hand that was dealt him. Don't think about the girl. Forget her. This was the closest he'd been to Aldo since Brighton. Think only about what he'd do to him when he got his hands on him.

Toby howled again.

She was closer.

Toby's last howl had sounded much nearer.

She stopped on the trail and closed her eyes, waiting for him to howl again.

If she could get a fix on his location, then she wouldn't be so vulnerable. She knew these woods. She and Toby had run and played over every inch of them for years.

The minute she figured out the location, she could picture it and find a way to get there without blundering into Aldo's trap.

"Come on, Toby," she whispered. "Tell me where you are."

He howled again.

To the south. At least a hundred yards from here. Concentrate. Don't think what Aldo is doing to make him howl. He's alive. Now keep him alive. A hundred yards south. There was nothing but a glade surrounded by pines.

Where better to stake out Toby than an open glade? To get to him she'd have to go through the pines where Aldo would be waiting. At the thought her hand unconsciously closed on the butcher knife she'd taken from the cutlery drawer in the kitchen. Would she use it? The thought of stabbing someone made her shudder.

But it didn't make that bastard flinch. He'd killed before and now he wanted to kill her.

And he was hurting Toby.

Hell, yes, she'd use the knife.

Okay, was there any other path she could take to elude Aldo?

Not unless she circled around and entered the lake in the one place where the pines were scraggly and sparse. She would be able to see any waiting attacker as she approached from that angle and, if she was careful, he wouldn't see her as she crawled up on the bank.

Was there any other way?

Toby howled again.

If there was another plan, she had no time to discover it. She had to get to Toby.

She moved quickly to the edge of the lake, took off her shoes, and waded into the cold water.

"Jane!"

Eve jerked upright in bed, her heart pounding.

Joe opened his eyes, totally alert as he always was when he woke. "What is it?"

"Jane."

"Is she having another dream? Did you hear something?"

"I didn't hear—or maybe I did." She threw the covers aside. "I'm going to go check on her."

Joe sat up on one elbow and watched as

she grabbed her robe and headed for the door. "I didn't hear her call—" He stopped, tilting his head, listening. "Go check on her." He swung his legs to the floor. "Now."

She was already flying down the hall.

Empty bed.

No Jane.

She ran to the bathroom. "Jane!"

Jane's nightgown lay in a pool on the floor.

"She's gone?" Joe was behind her. He'd pulled on his jeans and was shoving his arms into his wool sweater.

She nodded numbly. "He's got her. He just came in and got her."

"I don't think so. He would have to be pretty stupid to try to get by Mac and Brian." He pulled the sweater over his head. "Get your clothes on. I'll meet you outside."

Eve didn't argue. "Where are you going?"

"To the squad car. They might have seen her." He headed down the hall. "Or Toby."

"Toby?"

"I didn't hear Jane call out, but I thought I heard Toby howling."

Terror iced through her. "Oh, God."

"Maybe I was wrong." He opened the screen door. "Toby doesn't often—"

And then they heard the howl.

The dog was staked out at the edge of the glade. All four legs were tied and his left hind leg was bleeding in several places.

Trevor muttered a curse. Christ, he hated those bastards who preyed on the helpless. Children and animals should be exempt from the cruelty of the world.

Yeah, sure. No one was allowed a free pass. He should know that by now. Close out the anger. Where was Aldo?

He had to be somewhere close to Toby to make the poor animal howl.

Trevor adjusted his infrared glasses and then studied the nearby trees.

Nothing.

His gaze shifted to the left.

Noth—

Maybe.

Yes!

A blurred shadow but definitely a human shape.

Aldo.

He moved silently forward through the underbrush.

The cold wind struck Jane's soaked clothes and sent a shudder through her body. She scarcely noticed as she crept through the sparse trees toward the glade. Be careful. The full moon that enabled her to see would also allow her to be seen. So far her memory had served her well. The glade should be right ahead. . . .

And then she saw him.

Toby!

Tears ran down Jane's cheeks as she caught sight of Toby's bleeding leg.

Hurt. That son of a bitch had hurt him.

And was going to hurt him again.

Someone was coming across the glade. It was too dark to distinguish anything about his appearance except that he had a large, powerful body, medium height and shoulder-length hair that could be sandy.

But there was nothing blurred about the glitter of the knife in his hand.

He dropped to his knees beside Toby.

"No!"

She didn't even realize she was running toward him until she'd almost reached him.

"Don't you *touch* him!"

He swiveled on his knees. "You're here." His voice was exultant. "I knew you'd—" He screamed as the knife in her hand entered his shoulder. "Bitch!"

His own knife lunged upward.

A hand closed on her shoulder from behind, spinning her away from that deadly knife. "For God's sake, get out of here. Now!"

Trevor?

A crashing in the underbrush. Voices. A dozen flashlight beams pierced the darkness of the trees surrounding the glade.

Aldo cursed and leaped to his feet. "Whore. I told you not to bring anyone. Did you think I wouldn't kill him?" His knife plunged down toward Toby.

"No!" She leaped forward but Trevor was already there, knocking Aldo to the ground and then rolling sideways to protect Toby.

"Stop! Lay down your weapons." Joe's voice. Joe running out of the forest toward them.

Aldo was cursing as he struggled out from under Trevor. The next moment he was on his feet and running toward the cover of the trees.

"Okay, Jane?" Joe asked, and when she nodded, "Eve and Gunther will be here in a minute. You stay where you are, Trevor." He took off after Aldo with the four policemen on his heels, guns drawn.

Jane fell to her knees, her anxious gaze on Toby. Aldo's knife thrust had not gone home, she realized with relief. "It's okay, boy. Everything's going to be fine." She crawled the few steps toward him and started sawing through the ropes binding him. "No one's going to hurt you again."

"You shouldn't have run at Aldo," Trevor said in frustration as he got to his feet. "Why the hell didn't you give me a few minutes more? I'd have had him."

"He was going to hurt Toby." She didn't look at him. "No one hurts my dog." But someone *had* hurt him, she thought in agony as she looked at the wounds on his leg. They appeared shallow but one was still bleeding. "Give me something to wrap around his leg. Everything I have on is soaking wet."

"I don't have time for canine first aid. I have to get out of here before Quinn gets back. I've no desire to end up in jail while Aldo is running free."

"After you give me something to wrap around Toby's leg." She glared up at him. "Take off your sweater."

He gazed at her in disbelief and then started to laugh. "You look like you're freezing. You need it more than he does." He pulled his sweater over his head and tossed it to her. "Anything else?"

"No." She turned back to Toby. "If you go south over the hill, you'll find a drainage pipe that will take you to the highway. I'll tell them you went north. It may buy you enough time to get away." She wrapped the arm of the sweater tightly around the dog's leg. "Go."

"I'm going." He stopped as he turned to leave. "May I ask why you're helping me?"

"I don't want you in jail either." She stroked Toby's head. "I can't be sure Joe will catch Aldo. No one else has been able to do it all these years. If Aldo gets away, I want everyone in the world to be on the search. You may be everything Eve suspects you of being, but you want to catch him. I saw that tonight and you know things. . . ."

Toby turned his head and licked her hand and it nearly broke her heart. "Poor boy . . ."

She glanced up at Trevor and added fiercely, "I'm going to catch him, Trevor. He's not going to hurt any animal or woman again. Now get out of here so that you can help me do it."

He smiled and slowly nodded. "By all means." He ran south through the trees.

She could still hear Joe and the policemen crashing through the forest as she held the compress over Toby's wound. They might catch him. Lord, she hoped they did. Anyone who would torture a helpless animal was a total monster. On one level of her mind she had understood how evil Aldo must be but it had taken this cruelty to make it sink home.

"Let me look at it."

She turned her head to see Eve standing a few feet away. "The bastard didn't sever any arteries. I think he's going to be okay."

"I wasn't sure you were going to be okay." Eve turned to Gunther hurrying behind her. "It's okay, Mac. Go on after Joe and the others."

He nodded and took off at a run.

Eve dropped to her knees beside Jane and looked down at Toby's leg. "When I saw him lift that knife, I nearly had a heart attack. And then when he didn't kill you, I wanted to murder you myself." Her hands were shaking as she tightened the compress. "Why didn't you tell us, dammit? Don't you ever close us out like that again."

"He said he'd kill Toby. He's my dog. I was stupid. I should have kept him inside. It never occurred to me that he'd go after Toby. My fault. He's my responsibility."

"And you're our responsibility. How do you think we'd have felt if he'd killed you?"

"Terrible." She met Eve's gaze. "But you'd have done the same thing."

Eve's glance fell away first. "Maybe. It was Trevor who tackled Aldo? It was pretty dark, but I thought I recognized him."

She stiffened. "Did Joe?"

"Probably. And he must have realized he was helping you."

"He saved Toby."

"But then he ran away."

"He knew Joe would still have arrested him."

"As he should do."

"He saved Toby," she repeated. "And he'll do us more good out of jail."

"How do you figure that?"

"He wants Aldo." She stroked Toby's head. "And I don't care about forging documents and impersonating a police officer and all of that stuff. If he can find him, then that's all that matters."

"Maybe it will be a moot point if Joe catches Aldo tonight."

"I don't think he will."

"Why?"

She shrugged. "Just a feeling. I don't think it's his time."

"I hope you're wrong."

"Me, too."

"Where's Trevor?" Joe was striding toward them, his expression grim. "Which way did the bastard go?"

"Aldo?" Eve asked.

"We lost him for the moment. He had a motorboat parked beneath the trees. I sent an all-points bulletin out. We may still pick him up." He looked down at Toby. "How is he?"

"We'll have to get him to a vet right away but I think he'll be fine."

He turned back to Jane. “Which way did Trevor go?”

She hesitated. She hadn’t realized it would be this difficult to lie to Joe. “North.”

She felt Eve’s startled gaze on her face. That’s right, she must have seen Trevor take off toward the drainage pipe. She looked Eve in the eye. “North,” she repeated.

She waited.

Eve was silent a moment and then looked down at Toby. “I’ll need a couple men to lift Toby on a stretcher and get him to a vet.”

Jane felt relieved and guilty at the same time. It was bad enough to lie to someone she loved, but now she had pulled Eve into the deception.

“I’ll get Mac to arrange it.” Joe turned away. “I’m going to be busy.” He strode toward the policemen standing at the edge of the glade.

“Thank you,” Jane whispered.

“Don’t thank me.” Eve gave her a cool glance. “I did it because I agreed with you and I didn’t want to put Joe on the spot by asking him to go along with a lie.” She looked over her shoulder at Joe and then smiled. "And the point may not even be applicable. He's splitting up the force and sending some of them south. You should have known Joe was too sharp not to read you. We may be having to do some explaining."

Jane sighed resignedly, her gaze on Joe, who was gesturing with his usual dynamic forcefulness toward the south. "Well, I did my best. Trevor's on his own."

"I'm sure he doesn't expect protection from anyone."

"I didn't do it for him, I did it for me. I may need him."

"Don't talk like that. I know you're upset about Toby but you leave Aldo to Joe and the department. You're out of this, Jane."

"Tell that to Aldo. He doesn't think I'm out of it." She gently stroked Toby's head. "And I know I'm not. I just have to wait until the next time comes around."

"Next time?"

"He'll come back. He'll always come back. Until one of us is dead."

"How can you know that? This attempt may have discouraged him."

Why am I so positive? Jane wondered.

The words had come from her lips and mind with absolute certainty.

The circle. Inescapable, always there, always repeating.

But she couldn't say that to Eve. Why should she understand when Jane couldn't? "A hunch." That was as true as any other explanation. She changed the subject. "I saw his face. Not clearly, and just for an instant. But I'll be able to give Joe a sketch."

"Good. But he would rather have had Trevor." Eve raised her head. "Here comes Mac with the stretcher for Toby. I'll be glad to get both of you home."

He was bleeding.

Aldo could feel the blood running down his shoulder, but he couldn't stop to tend it. He had to reach the bank where he'd hidden his car and get out of here before Quinn chased him down. It didn't hurt anyway. He was too full of rage and frustration to feel pain.

The bitch. She had sunk her fangs in him and then lived to see him run like a fox from the hounds. He'd not even been able to punish her by killing the dog.

Trevor's fault.

Trevor barging in and interfering. Trevor stepping in front of Cira and keeping him from punishing the whore.

Whore. Yes, that's what she was. She'd managed to ply her wiles on Trevor and he was now as much her slave as all the others. Why else would Trevor have tried to save the dog when he could have taken his shot at Aldo?

Bitch. Whore. She was probably laughing at him.

Not for long, Cira. I almost had you. You're not such a difficult target.

Next time.

"Move!" Trevor said to Bartlett as he jumped into the car. "Get out of here."

"I take it we're being chased?" Bartlett stomped on the accelerator as he moved onto the freeway. "Aldo?"

"Quinn and the ATLPD." Trevor glanced at the side mirror. "No one yet," he murmured. "Maybe she did toss him a red herring."

"The girl?"

Trevor nodded. "I wasn't sure. She's not predictable. She could just as well have told me to go this way and then had a covey of police cars waiting for me."

"Maybe she's grateful to you for saving the pooch."

He grinned. "And maybe she's mad as hell and not going to take Aldo's crap anymore. That's more likely."

"Is that what she told you?"

"More or less."

No, that was exactly what she had told him. Every glance, every angry word had been layered with determination. "She was a little pissed about her dog."

"I can't blame her," Bartlett said. "Dreadful fellow, Aldo."

"You're a master of understatement."

"And apparently considerably more competent than you. You were so sure you'd get him this time." He gave him a sly glance. "But don't be upset. Every man meets his Waterloo."

"Shut up." He closed his eyes. "Just get me out of here. I need to sleep and then do some thinking. One step forward, two steps back. It's been a hell of a night."

"All may not be lost. Quinn may have caught Aldo."

"Then we'll know about it when we see the news tomorrow. Until then we'll assume the bastard got away."

"We're going to the lodge?"

"It's as safe as anywhere. Safer than staying here in town. Quinn is bound to have put out an APB on me."

"No doubt. It would be much smarter to move on."

"I can't move on. Aldo isn't going to budge from the area as long as Jane MacGuire is here." His lips tightened grimly. "And that means I have to dig in, too."

"No sign of either of them," Christy said. "We've scoured every acre of your property and the APB is coming up zero so far."

"Dammit."

"It's only been two days. How's Jane doing?"

"Cool as a cucumber."

"Toby?"

"He had to have stitches, but he'll be fine. He's fine now. He's lying on his dog bed in Jane's room getting belly rubs and eating turkey."

"Has Jane finished the sketch of Aldo yet?"

"I'll go in and ask her. She's been working on it long enough."

"If she only saw him in poor light, it must be difficult to remember every feature."

"Everything about this is difficult. Jane has a memory that would make an elephant look bad."

"You think she's stalling?"

"I can't figure out why she'd stall. But what do I know? She's done some things lately that have boggled my mind. And don't tell me about teenagers again. 'Bye, Christy." He pressed the disconnect.

"I'm not stalling," Jane said from behind him.

He turned to see her standing in the doorway with the sketchbook in her hand. "It took you a hell of a long time," he said curtly.

She crossed the porch and sat down beside him on the top step. "I had to be careful. It was funny. . . . When I was drawing him, it was too clear. I saw every feature as if he were standing before me. But I'd only seen him for a few seconds and I didn't see how I could be that sure." She shrugged. "Anyway, I was afraid that I could get it wrong. So I let myself have plenty of time for second guesses."

"And you're sure now?"

She flipped open the sketchbook. "Aldo."

A square face, high forehead and a roman nose. His hair was long but slightly receding. His eyes were deep-set and dark and were glaring out of the sketch with an expression of boundless animosity.

"I know you prefer for the portrayals to be expressionless because no one goes around looking like Jack the Ripper. I tried. I really tried. I redid the sketch three times, but it kept coming out the same. I think it's because I know that whenever we're together, he's going to look like this."

He kept his eyes on the sketch. "And does it frighten you?"

"Sometimes."

"Then why the hell did you go traipsing off after him when you should have come to me?" He lifted his head and his gaze was as hard as his tone. "And why did you lie to me about Trevor?"

"It seemed the right thing to do at the time." She smiled ruefully. "And it didn't do any good. You saw right through me."

"I've known you and Eve long enough to read you. But it was damn hard to believe you'd gang up on me like that."

"And it hurt you."

"Damn straight."

She laid her hand tentatively on his arm. "We didn't gang up on you. It wasn't Eve's fault."

"You don't have to defend her. Silence is a statement of its own."

"She didn't want you to have to make a choice."

"I'm used to making choices. It's a hell of a lot better than not being given one." He looked back at the sketch. "I know you and Eve are so close you're practically joined at the hip, but I thought we had a relationship too."

"We do." Her voice was uneven. "When I came to you, it was hard for me to get used to having— I never knew my father. I had no brother. I'd never trusted anyone in my life. Not really. Eve was easy. She was like me. You were different. It took time, but I came to . . . like you. I knew you'd never let me down."

"Then why didn't you come to me when you knew what that bastard was doing to Toby?"

"He was my responsibility. I had to make the decision."

"You're seventeen years old."

She nodded. "But don't you think some people are born old?"

"You mean old souls?"

She shrugged. "I don't know about that. That sounds a little wacky. I just never remember feeling like a kid."

And he couldn't remember a time when she'd acted like a kid. The closest she'd come was when she was tearing across the hills with Toby. "That's pretty sad."

"No, it's not. It's just the way things are. I bet Eve feels the same way."

He smiled slightly. "Ah, your role model."

"I couldn't have a better one."

His smile faded. "No, you couldn't." He covered her hand that still lay on his arm. "But both of you could be a little more trusting."

"I'll work on it." She squeezed his hand.

"But you're on your own with Eve. It should help that you know she's in your corner."

"With a hell of a lot of reservations."

She shook her head. "Did you ever wonder why you stayed with Eve all these years?"

"No, I love her."

"But it must have been very difficult to love someone like Eve. She'll tell you herself how scarred she is."

His gaze narrowed on her face. "What are you getting at?"

"I just think you hate anything easy. It bores you silly."

"You're crazy."

"You love Eve. You like me. I rest my case." She stood up. "I'm sorry I lied to you. I'll try not to do it again. Good night, Joe."

"Good night."

She stopped at the door. "Have you heard anything about Trevor?"

"I don't know if I should discuss him with you. I'm still pissed." He scowled. "No word about his apprehension. Christy told me this morning that there may be a report coming in soon from Johannesburg. Something popped up on their computer database."

"Will you let me see it?"

"Maybe."

"Ignorance is dangerous, Joe. Isn't that what you've always told me?"

"You should have thought about that when you kept us in the dark."

"Joe."

He was silent a moment. "Okay." He got up and moved down the stairs. "I'm going for a walk. I need to release some nervous energy. Tell Eve I won't be long."

Her gaze went to the woods. "Be careful."

"I'm not the one who has to be careful. That's the pot calling the kettle black." He paused. "The woods are crawling with officers, Jane. No one is going to try to get to you right now."

"You're probably right." She pulled her gaze from the line of trees. But as she turned and opened the screen door she repeated, "Be careful."

SEVEN

"Jackpot," Christy said when Joe answered the phone the next morning. "We've got a fix on Trevor."

"Talk to me."

"He was born in Johannesburg thirty years ago and his name is Trevor Montel, not Mark Trevor. His parents were planters who were killed by guerrillas when he was ten. He was placed in an orphanage and was in and out of trouble until he ran away at sixteen. The reports of the teachers were definitely mixed. Some wanted to toss him into jail and throw away the key. Others wanted to give him a scholarship and send him to Oxford."

"Why?"

"He's brilliant. He was something of a phenomenon. One of the finest minds his teachers had ever run across. Mathematics, chemistry, literature. You name it, he aced it. His test scores went off the charts. Genius territory."

"Hence the card counting."

"That's his most well-known profession. You know about his years as a mercenary and there were several years after that when we have no info on him. Then he started to do the casino circuit and he's also been known to do a little smuggling and deal in ancient artifacts. He was picked up in Singapore once for trying to remove a valuable Tang Dynasty vase from the country. He talked his way out of it but not before they booked him on suspicion. We seem to have a lot of suspicion and no convictions connected with Trevor. He's either been treading very cautiously or he's as smart as they say."

"Smart. There was nothing cautious about the way he conned his way into my home. We have to look for a connection between Trevor and Aldo. Did Aldo's sketch bring any response?"

"Not yet. Too bad you couldn't get fingerprints."

"No chance. He even wiped them off the dog collar. What about the volcanic ashes?"

"They've narrowed them down to Krakatoa in Indonesia, Vesuvius, or Montserrat."

"Sweet. That's not what I call narrowing. Talk about opposite ends of the earth."

"They're working on trying to refine the tests. According to the lab it shouldn't be this difficult. Every volcano has its own signature tephra."

"Tephra?"

"Unconsolidated fine-grained pyroclastic material."

"Ash."

"Yeah, I'm beginning to sound like the lab guys, aren't I? God help me. Anyway, the glass-shard particles have their own signature. The volcano from which they're taken can usually be pinpointed. In fact, it's possible for scientists to tell from which hole in the volcano the tephra was taken."

"Then what's the problem?"

"Mixed signals. They're puzzled."

"Great."

"I'm pushing them. They'll get there."

She paused. "I know this must seem to be taking forever, Joe. I'd hate every minute of delay if I were in your shoes. I just want you to know that everyone in the department is with you and working at top speed."

"I know that. Thanks, Christy."

After he hung up he went to the window and looked out at Jane sitting by the lake. Toby was lying at her feet. The sun was shining, the sky was blue, the lake was clear and placid. The scene should have been peaceful.

It wasn't.

"She's waiting." Eve had come to stand beside him at the window. Her gaze was on Jane. "She's been spending hours down there by the lake for the last two days. She says she's just enjoying the sunshine. But she's waiting for him."

He nodded. He'd also noticed the slight tension of Jane's body, the almost visible air of expectancy. "Aldo?"

"Or Trevor." Eve shrugged. "Or both. Since she won't admit she's waiting for anyone, we're not about to find out. I don't know how she thinks they're going to get near her." She added grimly, "If they do, I'll personally strangle every one of those men on stakeout."

"You'd have to stand in line," Joe said. He looked away from Jane. "Christy called with some info on Trevor. I'll fill you in."

"Good." But Eve's gaze remained on Jane. "I know how she feels," she whispered. "I'm waiting for them too."

Charlotte, North Carolina

She wasn't perfect, but she'd have to do.

Aldo cruised slowly behind her as she walked down the street watching the sway of hips in her short skirt and fur-trimmed jacket. He knew her hotel room was five blocks away because he'd watched her take two of her tricks there this evening. He'd waited until she was far enough from it to make it reasonable for them to drive rather than walk. Once in the car it was always much easier for him.

He accelerated, pulled over to the curb beside her, and rolled down the window. "Cold night, isn't it." He smiled. "But you look like you could warm any man. What's your name?"

She moved toward him and leaned her elbows on the window. "Janis."

This close he could see that she was even less perfect than he had thought. She bore only a slight resemblance to the true thing. Her skin was acne marked, her eyes were too close together, and her cheekbones were not nearly as defined as Jane MacGuire's.

But he could make do with the woman even though he might ordinarily have questioned if she was worth the kill. Now that the search was over he didn't have to be so selective. He pulled out the hundred-dollar bill he'd stuck in the visor. "Do you have a place we can go?"

Her eyes widened. "On Fifth Street." She opened the car door. "I can show you a good time, but I don't do kinky stuff. No whips or ropes."

"No whips or ropes. I promise." He locked the door as she settled on the passenger seat. "Janis is a pretty name but do you mind if I call you Cira?"

* * *

Joe hung up the phone and turned to Eve. "A woman was found in a ditch on the side of the road outside Charlotte, North Carolina. No face. Same MO as Aldo's other victims."

"Charlotte? That's hundreds of miles from here. Has he moved on? Should I be relieved?"

"No, it may be a copycat." He grabbed his jacket. "Anyway, I'm on my way to make sure. I'll call you from Charlotte. Don't let Jane leave the cottage. I'll tell the guys on stakeout I'm leaving and to keep sharp."

"But it could mean he's decided Jane isn't worth the risk?"

"Maybe. Don't count on it."

She watched him run down the steps and stride toward the squad car. No, she couldn't count on anything but she couldn't help but have a faint stirring of hope. Charlotte was miles away and in another state. Perhaps the bastard was showing sense and knew they wouldn't let him touch Jane. Christ, that would be wonderful. It was terrible to be this relieved at someone else's misfortune.

The phone rang.

"Hello."

No answer.

The person on the other end hung up.

Just a wrong number, she told herself as she replaced the receiver. People got them all the time. It was rude to just hang up without saying anything, but not unusual. It could have been one of those computer-generated sales calls that had gone awry.

It didn't have to be Aldo.

He was in Charlotte or somewhere near there. He'd lost interest in Jane and moved on.

Not here. Pray God, not here.

"It's possible," Joe said when he called that evening from Charlotte. "It has all the same signatures as the other cases. Ashes found near the body. Young woman. No face. She hasn't been dead for more than forty-eight hours. Very provocative attire. Signs of sexual intercourse. She could be a prostitute. CLTPD has set the Vice Squad on questioning some of the hookers in the area."

"Are you coming back tonight?"

"Probably not. I'm going to hit the computer and check the local Vice mug book to see what I can come up with. It might be quicker than questioning pimps and hookers."

Eve shivered. "To see if any of them look like Jane."

"It would narrow the field. No copycat would know the women had similar facial characteristics. How's Jane?"

"Fine. The same."

"And you?"

"Impatient as hell."

"Me, too. Let me get to work so that I can get back there." He paused. "I miss you. This is the first time I've been away from you for more than a few hours in years. I'd forgotten how empty I feel when I'm away from you." He didn't wait for her to answer. "I'll let you know when I find out something." He hung up.

She slowly pressed the disconnect. She missed him, too. He'd only been gone nine or ten hours and she was experiencing that same emptiness. Jesus, he was gone that long on cases here in town. She was being stupid.

"Was that Joe?" Jane stood in the doorway. "Is it a copycat?"

"He's not sure. It could be the real thing.

They believe the victim could have been a hooker. Joe's staying over to check the mug books." She moved toward the kitchen. "I'm opening a can of tomato soup for supper. Do you want to make some grilled cheese sandwiches?"

"Sure." Jane wrinkled her nose. "He's looking for my face. Right? It's really depressing how many people must look like me. I guess everyone wants to think they're an original." She opened the refrigerator and got out the cheese. "Maybe I should think about plastic surgery."

"Don't you dare. Your face is unique. Everyone is unique. Who should know better than me? Do you know how many faces I've reconstructed?"

"I don't want to guess." She began making the grilled cheese sandwiches. "You know I never actually saw the Caroline Halliburton reconstruction, just the photo. You must have thought she looked a lot like me."

"Yes. But there were differences. Your lower lip is fuller. Your brows are more arched." She studied her. "And no one has a smile like yours."

Jane laughed. “But you never have your reconstructions smile.”

“Exactly.” She poured the soup into a pot. “So you’re unique.”

“And so are you.” Jane’s smile lingered as she shook her head. “I was kidding about the plastic surgery.”

“I know.” She turned the flame down. “But it must be annoying to think you’re one of a—”

The phone rang.

“I’ll get it.” Jane turned away from the stove.

“No!” Eve hurried to the wall phone. “I’ll answer. You watch the cheese sandwiches.”

“Okay.” A slight frown wrinkled Jane’s brow. “Whatever you say.”

“Hello.”

“Susie?” It was a woman’s voice.

Relief surged through Eve. “No, you must have the wrong number.”

“Not again? This is the third time. There must be a crossed line. I’ve been having all kinds of connection problems reaching my daughter, Susie. Sometimes the call doesn’t even go through.” She sighed. “I must have some kind of bad phone karma. Sorry to bother you."

"That's okay. I hope you reach her." Eve hung up and turned back to the stove. "Wrong number."

"The way you jumped for the phone I thought you might have thought it was Joe again. Everything's okay with him, isn't it?"

"He wants to come home. Otherwise he's fine."

And she was fine too. That other call must have been a genuine wrong number just as she'd supposed. She smiled luminously. "Are those sandwiches done? I'm starved."

Janis Decker.

He'd almost missed her.

Joe leaned forward, his gaze on the photo on the monitor. She bore only a faint resemblance to Jane but it might have been enough for Aldo. Age twenty-nine. Picked up for prostitution three times in the last five years.

"Find something?" Detective Hal Probst of CLTPD was looking over his shoulder.

"Maybe." He pressed the button to print

out the report. "Will you ask the Vice boys to circulate this and see if they can find anyone who knows anything about her? It might be smart to check her fingerprints against the victim's."

"No problem. I'll have them get on it right away." Probst took the sheet from the printer. "The sooner we get some action going, the better. This case is a little too gory for our fine local politicians. They're going to be on our ass big-time. I wish you'd kept this joker in Atlanta."

"She may not be the one." He rubbed his eyes. "Four hours of staring at this computer screen may be making me see double."

Probst tilted his head, studying the mug sheet. "She does look a little like that reconstruction that appeared in the newspaper."

"Emphasis on 'little.' " Joe leaned back in the chair. "If it's our man, he wasn't choosy this time. How soon can you have the fingerprint match?"

"A few hours. It will take longer to get a report from Vice but we'll—" Probst's cell phone rang. "Probst." He listened. "Okay, I'm on it." He looked at Joe as he hung up.

"We may have another set of prints to match up. There's a report in from Richmond PD. Some hikers found the body of a woman near a lake outside of town."

Joe stiffened. "Same MO?"

Probst nodded. "Far as we can tell. No face."

"Richmond, Virginia," Eve repeated. "That's not far from Washington. He's moving up the coast." And away from Atlanta, she added thankfully to herself. "When was she killed?"

"Within the last twenty-four hours."

"You're going there?"

"I have to follow the trail. There are indications that he may be getting reckless. He wasn't careful when he picked Janis Decker and he left us fingerprints to work with. Reckless men make mistakes. They stumble and if you're there you can reel them in." He paused. "Unless you'd rather I come home. If you're nervous, say the word."

"Of course I'm nervous. That doesn't mean you have to come running back here.

I can take care of Jane." She added fiercely, "You get that bastard."

"I'll get him. I'll call you when I find out more after I get to Richmond."

She drew a deep breath as she hung up the phone. Charlotte and now Richmond. Each city was a giant step away from Atlanta, away from Jane. She moved out onto the porch and sat down on the porch swing beside Jane. "Nice night."

"You're in a good mood."

"I shouldn't be. There was another killing in Richmond. Same MO. Joe's on his way there now. He thinks Aldo may be getting careless."

"I hope he's right." Jane looked out at the lake. "He's crazy, you know. I could see it that night. I know most serial killers have a screw loose, but they have a sense of self-preservation. I don't believe Aldo does."

"Then he should be easier to catch."

"I said crazy, not stupid." She patted Eve's hand. "But Joe will get him either way. He's not about to let that twerp get the—"

The phone rang.

"Dammit, I was just getting comfortable."

Eve groaned. "What do you bet it's our lady looking for Susie?"

"No bet." Jane chuckled. "How many times has she called?"

"Four times this afternoon." She sighed. "I shouldn't be so impatient. I'm sure it's not her fault and she's always very nice."

"Sit still. I'll get it." Jane jumped up and headed for the door. "Be right back."

Eve leaned back. It was good to sit here with the cool wind brushing her face and the harvest moon shedding a glow over the lake. It brought back memories of other nights when she and Joe and Jane had sat here and talked and laughed before they went to bed. She had never taken that precious intimacy for granted, but perhaps she'd not valued it as much as she should have. Dear God, she wanted those times back. She closed her eyes and listened to the night sounds.

She heard Jane come back a few minutes later and opened her eyes to see her sit down in the porch swing beside her. "Susie's mama?"

Jane nodded, her gaze fixed on the lake. "Who else?"

EIGHT

Be casual. Stroll at a leisurely pace, Jane told herself.

Eve was working on a new reconstruction this morning, but that didn't mean she might not be watching Jane out the window. The early stages of reconstruction weren't nearly as demanding as the final ones and Eve was feeling as fiercely protective of Jane as a lioness with her cub. Jane moved at a lazy pace to the thick thatch of trees a few hundred yards beyond the log where she usually sat, sank down, and leaned her head back against an oak tree. She knew she was in full view of Mac and Brian in the squad car and Eve in the cottage as she lifted her face to the sun.

Leisurely. Do everything with deliberation and leisure.

She felt about as leisurely as if she were sitting on a live grenade.

"Talk fast." She tried to keep her lips from moving. "I'll give you five minutes before I start screaming."

"You're bluffing." Trevor chuckled from the depths of the shelter of shrubbery behind her. "You wouldn't have told me about the drainage pipe if you'd wanted me caught. You just want to get the upper hand. I understand. I knew you'd be a superb poker player."

"I don't play poker."

"It doesn't matter. The concept is the same. But you really should learn it. I'll teach you."

"I don't want you to teach me anything. And you don't know zilch about me."

"Yes, I do. Even if I hadn't had the opportunity of studying you long range, I'd know you. Some people you just have instincts about."

She couldn't deny that truth since she'd had that same feeling when she'd first met Trevor. "Why did you call me?"

"The same reason you didn't tell Eve that

I was the one on the phone. I thought it was time we got together. It was too dangerous to wait any longer. He's going to pounce anytime."

"He killed a woman in Charlotte and another in Richmond. Eve thinks he may have crossed me off his list."

"No, she doesn't. She's too wary. Wishful thinking. He's not giving up on you. He used the killings to draw Quinn away and convince the ATLPD that maximum surveillance for you isn't necessary."

"Joe didn't leave me without protection."

"I got to you."

"Because I chose to let you. How much did you pay that woman to make those phone calls for you?"

"Not much. She only had to keep calling until you answered instead of Eve. I told her it was a Romeo-Juliet thing and she had a romantic heart. It's always safer to rely on emotion rather than bribery."

"And what do you want from me?"

"I want you to go to Quinn and tell him I want to make a deal. If he'll let me work with him on catching Aldo, I'll turn myself in afterward."

"Why go through me? A con man like

you should be able to handle his own deals."

"I agree. In fact, it goes against the grain for me to rely on anyone else. But time is of the essence and Quinn's instinct is to resist anything I say. You're smart and you can do the groundwork for me. I'll take over from there."

"Joe doesn't make deals."

"Try him. This isn't his usual case. He has a vested interest in keeping you alive. I'd bet he'd be willing to overlook a small fish like me to get Aldo."

"He's not sure you are a small fish. You may be a barracuda."

"If I am, I don't go around killing helpless women or torturing dogs. But just in case I'm wrong, do you have a cell phone?"

"Yes. Eve gave me one for my birthday."

"You've got my cell phone number. Program it in your phone so that you can reach me by speed dial. I'll never be very far from you."

"You're offering to protect me? I don't want your protection. I want information. That's all I ever wanted from you."

"And if I tell you what you want to know,

you'll walk away and close me out. That's not going to happen."

"Then if you don't give me what I want, why shouldn't I yell and have them throw you in jail?"

"I didn't say I wouldn't give you information. I'll tell you enough to help you without making my presence superfluous." He was silent a moment. "But as a gesture of good faith, I'll let you ask me two questions right now."

"You want a question? Tell me why Aldo is killing all these women who look like me."

He hesitated. "To go into that right now wouldn't be to my advantage. Ask something else."

"Well, you struck out on that one. Okay, if you want to catch Aldo, why didn't you cooperate with Joe instead of trying to con him?"

"Quinn wants to nab Aldo and then put him behind bars."

"And you?"

"I want thirty minutes alone with him."

"And then you'll turn him over to Joe?"

He was silent. "Quinn will get him . . . eventually."

"Dead." His intent couldn't be more

clear but it didn't shock her. "You want to kill him."

"He'll have to die. I can't risk him getting free. Neither can Quinn. He'll come after you again. He'll never stop."

"And you're so concerned about me." Her tone was skeptical. "Bull."

"I've no desire to have you murdered."

"But I'd be a fool not to realize you're willing to use me to get Aldo. You consider me expendable, don't you?"

He didn't answer directly. "I've had you watched for weeks. I've had reports on every move you've made. I know how special you are, Jane."

His voice was soft, persuasive, almost seductive, and it was having an odd mesmerizing effect on her. Even though she couldn't see him, it was as if he were standing before her. She could sense the intensity, the charisma, the intelligence that was more attractive to her than those wonderful good looks. "Stop conning me. How much could you know from a report?"

"Enough. I would have come and done the surveillance myself but I didn't dare. I had to maintain perspective. I knew I wouldn't have a chance."

She felt heat touch her cheeks that had nothing to do with the sunlight. Jesus, he was good. He was playing on her emotions like a master musician, moving her, stirring her, making her believe every word. Put a stop to it. "You didn't answer me. You consider me expendable."

He didn't answer immediately. "I'd deeply regret anything happening to you."

That was what she needed. The answer furnished a cool splash of reality to temper her physical response to him. "Not enough to give up your agenda and dive in and help Joe."

"It will help Quinn to work with me. No one can help him more. I know Aldo inside out. Sometimes I think I can read the bastard's mind. I've almost caught him twice. I would have gotten him the other night if I hadn't had to worry about your blasted dog." He paused. "I have to leave now. These woods are crawling with Quinn's police buddies. I took a big chance coming back here."

"Wait. You said I could ask two questions."

"You've already asked more than two."

"Not really. They were all related."

He chuckled. "You're quibbling. I should have known. Okay, ask your question."

"The ashes. Joe said the lab couldn't identify where they originated. You know, don't you?"

"Yes. But I believe I should keep that as an ace in the hole."

She made a rude sound. "You seem to be stalling on all fronts. Maybe you're bluffing. Maybe you don't have anything to barter."

He was silent. "Vesuvius. Satisfied?"

Her heart leaped. "Then Aldo's from Italy?"

"The ashes are from Vesuvius," he repeated.

"The lab said they could be from either Montserrat or Indonesia."

"Aldo mixed the ashes from the three volcanoes to throw off the investigators but the majority of the shards are from Vesuvius. Call me after you've talked to Quinn."

"He said that sometimes scientists could tell in which hole particular ashes originated. Do you know that location?"

No answer.

He was gone.

She waited a few moments and then

rose to her feet. She could feel the excitement surge through her as she started back toward the cottage. She had to talk to Eve and then call Joe. It was clear why Trevor had chosen to go through her to get to Joe. He'd known she'd try to convince him. He was right. For the first time in days she felt as if things were going to happen, that she could reach out and do something, accomplish something. All she had to do was bring Trevor into the picture and it would start a chain reaction.

Vesuvius . . .

"Vesuvius?" Joe repeated. "It could be another con. Dangling a carrot to make us think he knows more than he does."

"Suppose we assume he's telling the truth and have Interpol explore the possibility that Aldo's career began in Italy," Eve said. "It couldn't hurt."

"The hell it couldn't. It would waste time we don't have. That bastard is running around killing women and we can't lay a finger on him."

"No clues in the Richmond murder either?"

"Ashes."

"Then it is him," Eve whispered. "Maybe Trevor is wrong. Maybe he's forgotten about Jane."

"And maybe he's right. The captain is already making noise about cutting down the security around Jane since the threat to her seems to be lessening."

"You can't have it both ways."

"I know that, dammit." He was silent a moment. "Tell Jane to pick up on the extension."

Eve motioned to Jane, who was sitting on the couch across the room. She nodded and picked up the receiver. "I don't think Trevor's lying, Joe. I wouldn't have told you about his offer if I hadn't believed him."

"He's proved he's an expert at deception."

"I thought it was worth a shot. Now stop growling at me and tell me what you're going to do."

"I don't make deals with crooks."

"That's what I told him. He said he thought you might make an exception to get Aldo. Naturally, he expected me to try to persuade you." She paused. "I was going to do it. I decided that I had to leave it up to you."

"How generous."

"But, if it means anything, I think Trevor could be the key to getting Aldo. And I think you believe that too."

Joe was silent a moment. "And what would you do if I said no deal? If Trevor called you, would you go running?"

"I wouldn't run. I'd think about it."

"And then you'd go."

She didn't answer for a moment. "Aldo hurt Toby, Joe. He *hurt* him. And it was my fault."

"God in heaven."

"I'm sorry if it makes you angry, but I'm not going to lie to you again."

"It does make me angry. I'm mad and frustrated and I want to kick someone."

"What are you going to do, Joe?" Eve asked quietly.

"I'll let you know when I do." He hung up.

Jane made a face as she replaced the receiver. "What do you think the chances are that he'll deal with Trevor?"

Eve hung up. "How do I know? It's his decision, but you did everything you could to influence it."

Her eyes widened. "What do you mean? You heard me. I left it entirely up to him."

"Supposedly. But you put the threat of danger to you very cleverly into the mix. You pushed all the right buttons." She met her gaze. "You handled him with the skill of Henry Kissinger. I was surprised."

"I'd never 'handle' Joe." Jane was genuinely upset. "I'd think you'd know that, Eve."

"Maybe not intentionally. But when I was studying your face while you were talking to him, it was almost like watching a stranger." She shrugged wearily. "Or maybe it's my imagination. You said all the right things. Perhaps I'm seeing things that aren't there." She got to her feet. "I'm going to bed. If Joe calls back, I'll let you know what he decides."

"Thanks." Jane was still gazing at her with a troubled expression. "I'd never do that to Joe. I hate being finessed myself. I was just being honest."

"Then forget I said anything. I'm so tired and stressed right now I'm probably seeing little green monkeys." Eve started toward her bedroom. "Good night, Jane."

* * *

"It was like watching someone else."

Jane shivered as she went out on the porch after Eve disappeared into her room. Her conversation with Joe, the words she'd chosen had been spoken totally without conscious thought. It was as if she'd been on automatic.

Yet she'd known at the time that they were exactly the right words to lead him down the path she wanted him to follow. It was as if she'd been doing it all her life. It had seemed perfectly natural and she hadn't even realized she was doing it until Eve had confronted her with it. Her first instinct had been rejection and denial, but now she wasn't so sure she hadn't tried to manipulate Joe. And what kind of person did that make her?

Toby whined and pawed at her leg.

She bent down and patted his head. "It's okay, boy."

He sensed she was disturbed and was trying to comfort her. She needed comforting. She hated lies and deceptions and she'd been dealing in both of them lately.

Jesus, and they'd come so easily. . . .

Then accept that she was imperfect and capable of manipulation and be on the alert. She was the one in control of her actions and she must be careful never to hurt Joe or Eve. It was scary to know that she'd not even realized what she was doing.

Forget it. It wouldn't happen again.

But damn Aldo for placing her in this position where she'd had to admit to herself that she was capable of trying to twist even these people she loved into the way she wanted them to go.

Annapolis, Maryland

The bar was crowded but that was good for him. It lessened the chances of anyone remembering one man sitting by himself at the bar. He'd made sure his facial disguise and clothes were nondescript but the key was always to blend into the crowd.

Though it was difficult to blend into a crowd consisting mainly of Annapolis cadets, Aldo thought. He'd have to make sure no one saw him watching the girl playing darts across the room. Although it was difficult not to watch her when she was doing her best to attract attention. In her cadet uniform and short haircut, Carrie Brockman appeared both mannish and loud. Laughing, whistling, kidding the other players. A noisy, boisterous extrovert.

Not like Cira, who need only walk silently into a room to rivet everyone's eyes on her.

It seemed almost sacrilegious that this woman possessed a few of Cira's features and yet none of her charisma.

Not like Jane MacGuire.

Don't think about Jane MacGuire. He mustn't compare her to this woman or he wouldn't be able to do what was necessary. The act with the woman in Richmond had made him feel like a cheat and that mustn't happen here.

"Another drink?"

It was the bartender.

"Yes, please." He made a face. "I need it to face these kids. Every time I come up here to see my son I go home feeling a hundred years old. How do they do it?"

The bartender chuckled. "Youth." He set another bourbon in front of Aldo. "It ain't fair, is it?" He turned away and strode toward a cadet who was hailing him at the end of the bar.

But youth didn't have to be crass. It

could be full of grace and fire and elegance.

Like Cira.

He flinched as he heard Carrie Brockman laugh shrilly across the bar. He welcomed the response.

Yes, let him feel disgust. It would make her death much more satisfying.

Richmond, Virginia
4:43 A.M.

The call woke Joe from a sound sleep.

"You said you wanted to know if we had anything come in on the wires," Christy said. "A female cadet was found at a rest stop outside Baltimore three hours ago. No attempt to disguise her identity other than the removal of her face. They ran fingerprints and they came up with Carrie Ann Brockman, age twenty-two, a cadet at Annapolis."

"Shit."

"He's getting bolder. This corpse wasn't more than eight hours old and he made practically no attempt to hide the body in the bushes at the rest stop. He dumped her and the ashes and took off. Arrogant as hell. Thumbing his nose at us?"

"Maybe."

"If he's getting this careless, you'll be able to pounce soon. You're heading for Baltimore?"

Another city, another step, leading him farther and farther away from home.

You can't have it both ways, Eve had said.

Take a chance that Trevor was telling the truth or take a chance that Aldo was going to be stupid enough to walk into his hands? Either way he could be screwed.

So rely on instinct.

"No." He swung his feet out of bed. "You monitor what's happening in Baltimore. I'm going back to Atlanta."

"He told me to set up a meeting with Trevor." Jane slowly hung up the phone. "He's coming home, Eve."

"Thank God." She studied Jane's expression. "You're not acting pleased. Why not? This is what you wanted."

"I know." Her teeth closed on her lower lip. "And I still think it's for the best. It's just . . . I feel as if I've set something in motion and it kind of scares me."

"You should have thought of that when you let Trevor use you to bring Joe back."

She stiffened. "He didn't use me. I don't let—" She smiled. "You were trying to get a rise out of me, weren't you? Tit for tat. I didn't intentionally try to use Joe."

"If I thought you had, I'd be giving you more than a few verbal jabs." She turned away. "When and where is this meeting?"

"Joe wants it no later than tomorrow here in the woods across the lake. I told him I wanted to go with him."

"So do I."

She nodded. "Mac and Brian won't follow us as long as Joe is with us." She grimaced. "He told me to make it clear that any amnesty toward Trevor ends when Joe gets his hands on Aldo. And he said he'd see Trevor in hell before he'd turn a prisoner over to him."

"You couldn't expect any other reaction. Trevor may not deal."

"I think he will. He usually asks more than he thinks he can get. He takes what he can and then works on finessing the rest."

"Really?" Eve tilted her head. " 'Usually'?

How the devil do you know what he usually does?"

"I don't. I mean . . ." She had spoken without thinking, her mind on the meeting tomorrow. "Of course I don't. How could I? But everyone gets impressions and he definitely leaves a strong impression."

"That he does," Eve said. "And evidently a particularly significant one on you."

"But that may be good. It's always good to have a grasp of the character of the people you have to deal with."

"If you're not wrong."

She nodded. "Absolutely." But she wasn't wrong. Not about Trevor. Her every instinct radiated that certainty. "But Joe won't rely on my 'impressions.' He's very good at forming his own opinions."

"Tell me about it," Eve said dryly. "And he's not going to give Trevor an easy ride."

"Trevor was in Rome four years ago," Christy said when Joe answered his phone while he was driving home from the airport that night. "He was under suspicion of smuggling artifacts found near an aqueduct in northern Italy. No arrest."

"Any link to Aldo?"

"Not so far as we can find yet." Christy paused. "I'm glad you decided to come home, Joe. It's better."

He went still. "Why is it better?"

"You belong here."

"And you can't talk? The captain wants to tell me herself? Let me do some guesswork. The captain is withdrawing most or all of the protection they've given Jane. They consider it not necessary since Aldo has clearly moved on. When are they taking the guys off her?"

"Tomorrow."

"Everyone?"

"They're leaving you, Mac, and Brian."

"Better than nothing. I was half expecting it." And Trevor had told Jane that Aldo had planned on it happening. "Thanks for giving me a heads-up, Christy."

"Like I said, it's better that you came home."

"I agree."

"I'll let you know when we find out more from the Italian police about what Trevor was doing in Rome."

"Do that." He hung up.

And tomorrow he'd be asking Trevor that same question, he thought grimly.

"Where the hell is he?" Joe scowled as his gaze circled the forest surrounding the glade. "He's thirty minutes late."

"He'll be here," Jane said. "He promised me."

"And Trevor's promise probably isn't worth the breath he used to give it."

"I'm hurt." Trevor strolled out of the forest. "After all, a man is only as good as his word. At least, that's what all the philosophers say. Personally, I believe that's a narrow—"

"You're late," Joe said curtly.

"I had to do a little scouting. I was making sure that you hadn't decided that a bird in the hand . . ." He grimaced. "I seem to be full of trite phrases today. Forgive me." He turned to Eve and Jane. "It wasn't that I didn't trust you, but Quinn is much more ruthless and unpredictable. He's a good deal like me."

"I'm nothing like you."

"I beg to disagree." He smiled. "But then I have the advantage of having made a study of your character. That's why I thought you might be willing to cooperate." He held up his hand as Joe started to speak. "Oh, Jane told me that you're not going to hand me Aldo's head on a platter. At least, not at present. I'd bet you'll change your mind before this is over. You're very protective of your family."

"Information," Joe said.

"I need certain assurances," Trevor said.

"And I need answers. Talk."

"I'm not going to be unreasonable. I'd like to have an active role in finding Aldo and park myself at your cottage, but I know you don't want me underfoot. So all I want from you is a promise that you'll let me stay here close to Jane. And that you'll call me if Aldo gets close to her." His lips tightened. "I'll probably know, but I can't take the chance."

Joe was silent.

"He's not asking much, Joe," Jane said quietly. "Less than I expected."

"I'll make up my own mind. I know where you stand."

"Where do I stand?" Jane asked. "You tell me. I want to live and I want Aldo. If you think that puts me in anyone's camp but yours, then you're mistaken."

Joe glanced at Eve.

She shrugged. "It's your job on the line. I'll go along with your decision."

"Well, that's a first."

She smiled. "Until I decide it's a wrong decision."

A little of his grimness disappeared. "That's better. I was afraid you were sick." He turned back to Trevor. "It's a deal. And if I change my mind for any reason, I'll give you warning. That's all I promise."

"It's enough," Trevor said. "I didn't expect much more."

Eve glanced at Jane. "Ask for the moon and settle for whatever you can get? Is that standard operating procedure with you?"

Trevor grinned. "You never win if you don't go for the high stakes." He turned to Joe. "Ask your questions."

"Where is Aldo?"

"I don't know. If I did, I'd be on his trail. If his last victim was in Baltimore, I'd judge that he'll go farther north to hit again. He'll want to seem to establish a pattern that will lead away from Jane."

"You're so sure that he'll double back? Why?"

Trevor's gaze shifted to Jane. "Because she's perfect," he said softly. "And he knows it. He's found her."

"Maybe that's only your opinion. Those other women looked—"

"Found who?" Jane stepped forward to face Trevor. "Who does he think he's found? And why does he want to kill her?"

Trevor smiled. "You asked me that before. Actually, I expected that to be Quinn's first question too."

"Tell me."

"He's looking for a woman he thinks turned his father against him and was then responsible for his death."

"Did she?"

"Maybe."

"So he hates her."

"And desires her. Sometimes the lines blur when you're insane."

"He wants her so much that he tries to destroy her image wherever he finds it?" Joe shook his head. "He's a butcher."

Trevor nodded. "But he had sexual intercourse with the first few victims. He probably had hopes he'd actually found her and sex was the ultimate humiliation. But then he realized that it was a big world and there were many women who had some resemblance. He felt bound to kill them, destroy the likeness, but he had no desire to have sex with them. Since they weren't really her, it was only a duty."

"Duty," Jane repeated. "Why?"

"Because they looked like her and mustn't be allowed to escape," Trevor said. "He couldn't bear to have anyone who resembled her left alive. They had to die."

Jane shook her head. "That doesn't make sense. Those women . . . They came from all walks of life. If he followed them, hunted them, he'd have to know something about their history. He must have known they couldn't be the woman who seduced his father."

"According to his way of thinking there was a chance."

"Bull. And if Aldo was so clever about tracking down all those women with her face, my face, why didn't he investigate?" She gestured with one hand. "Why not go to the police or hire private detectives and find the right one?"

"It would have been difficult."

"Not as difficult as killing eleven women on the chance of getting the right one."

"Yes, it would."

"Why?" She was shaking, she realized. She didn't want him to answer. What the devil was wrong with her?

He gazed directly into her eyes. "Don't be afraid. I'll take care of you."

"I don't need you to take care of me. Just tell me why he couldn't find her."

"Because Cira's been dead for over two thousand years."

She felt as if she'd been punched in the stomach. At first, only the name he'd spoken was clear to her. "Cira . . ." she whispered. "Her name is Cira?"

Joe grunted with disgust. "A two-thousand-year-old corpse? What the hell are you trying to pull, Trevor?"

"Wait, Joe," Eve said, her gaze on Jane's face. "Let him talk."

"He's scaring Jane, dammit."

"I can see that. Let him talk."

Jane scarcely heard them. "Cira?" Her hands clenched into fists. "He's looking for Cira?"

"Cira who?" Joe asked.

"No one knew her last name." Trevor's

gaze never left Jane's face. "She was only Cira. Cira the magnificent, Cira the divine, Cira the enchantress."

"Cut to the chase," Eve said curtly. "We're losing patience. How could a two-thousand-year-old corpse kill Aldo's father?"

"Sorry." Trevor pulled his gaze away from Jane to smile at Eve. "Actually, Cira wasn't really responsible. His father killed himself when he set off an explosion to seal off the tunnel."

"Tunnel?" Eve repeated.

He nodded. "The selfish bastard wanted everything for himself. He sealed the entrance, but he wasn't good with explosives and blew himself up too."

"Where did this happen?"

"Northern Italy," Joe said. "Four years ago. Right?"

"Close," Trevor said. "You've been busy, if you traced me that far. It was four years ago and the job was supposed to be in northern Italy. But something more interesting popped up."

"Aldo?"

"No, Aldo was in the shadows back then. Aldo's father, Guido."

"What was his whole name?"

Trevor hesitated before answering, "Guido Manza."

Joe swore. "Dammit, you've known Aldo's last name all this time and you've never told the police? Some of those women might be alive now."

"I didn't know what the bastard was doing until he left Italy and went to England. I thought he was just running from me until I saw the photo in the *Times* of that woman he killed in Brighton. I made the connection as soon as I saw the resemblance and started backtracking."

"Why would he run from you?"

He didn't answer. "And what good would a name do Scotland Yard? He was using fake ID and there was no way of using his friends or family to get to him. Aldo was a loner."

"Descriptions. They could have run photos of him in the newspapers."

"Aldo wanted to be an actor. He studied costume and makeup in Rome before his father jerked him away to the excavation. That's one of the reasons why he was difficult to trace when he started his killing spree. He's an expert at disguise. He's an expert at quite a few things. He's really brilliant."

"You're making excuses."

"No, I'm giving you reasons." He shrugged. "But you're right. From your point of view I did everything wrong."

"Because you wanted to catch Aldo yourself," Jane said.

"Of course. I told you. He has to die."

The matter-of-factness of the words sent a chill through Jane. He was right, he'd said those words before but in this moment they seemed more real, more frightening. Before she'd been excited, challenged, confident. She didn't feel confident now. She felt shaken, as if her entire world had been sent spinning.

"Why?" Joe asked.

"What?" Trevor's gaze was on Jane's face again. "Oh, because he deserves it. Why else?" He turned away. "She's had enough. Take her back to the cottage. I'll contact you later."

"I want to know—"

"She's had enough," Trevor repeated over his shoulder. "You'll get your answers but not until she's able to absorb them."

"I'm fine," Jane said. She was being stupid. Get a grip.

"Yes, you are," Trevor said. "But there's no immediate urgency. You need time to digest what I've told you."

"You haven't told me anything. This tunnel, where is it?"

He was striding away from them. "Later."

"Where is it? You tell me *now*."

"Don't get upset. I've no intention of keeping secrets. Well, perhaps a few. But that isn't one of them." He'd already reached the trees. "Herculaneum."

NINE

Cira.

Dead over two thousand years.

Herculaneum.

"Go lie down." Eve's worried gaze was on Jane's face. "You're white as a sheet. Maybe Trevor was right to tell us to get you home."

"Stop fretting. There's nothing wrong with me." She gave her the ghost of a smile. "And Joe doesn't think he was right." She glanced at Joe, who'd been on the phone with the department since they'd arrived back at the cottage, giving Christy the info Trevor had divulged about Guido Manza. "He hates delays. He doesn't like to be teased and then have the rug yanked from under him. He likes everything laid out in crystal-clear order." She made a face. "And you can't say that anything Trevor told us was clear-cut."

"It was clear enough to upset you." She paused. "You nearly went into shock when Trevor mentioned that name." She repeated it slowly, "Cira. And the tunnel was a little too coincid—"

"I don't want to talk about it." Jane turned quickly away. She had to get out of here. She was holding on to her composure by main force. "Maybe I am a little tired. I'll go rest until it's time to fix dinner."

"You can't run away from me, Jane. I'll let you delay but not bury whatever is bothering you."

"I know that." She headed down the hall. "But it would help if I knew what was bothering me. Right now, I'm all mixed up."

"You're not alone. Trevor dropped a bomb and then just walked away. It's no wonder Joe's upset."

"Herculaneum . . ." She frowned. "It's familiar, but where the devil is Herculaneum?"

"Italy," Eve said. "It was destroyed by the Vesuvius eruption at the same time as Pompeii."

"Weird." Jane opened her bedroom door. "I'm sure Trevor won't leave us hanging long. I'll talk to you later." She leaned back against the door as she closed it behind her. Dear God, her knees felt like spaghetti. She hated to feel this weak.

And there was no reason for it. It could be a coincidence.

Yeah, sure. Cira was such a common name.

Then what other explanation? She was dreaming about a woman who'd been dead two thousand years? She immediately rejected the thought. There was nothing ancient about the thinking processes of the Cira she knew. She'd never even questioned that Cira was not a present-day woman. Every thought, every instinct were ones that Jane understood perfectly.

Too perfectly?

That's right, question every memory and impulse. That was the way to really go around the bend. She didn't even know the story behind the woman Trevor called Cira. Who knows? Maybe she'd picked up some weird vibes from Aldo that filtered into her dreams.

But Aldo hadn't even appeared on her

radarscope until weeks after the dreams had started.

So maybe she was psychic after all. She'd heard of long-distance telepathy.

She was really reaching, she thought in disgust. Next she'd be seeing aliens or those little green monkeys Eve had mentioned. There had to be an explanation, and however weird or pragmatic, it just had to be faced and handled, and everything would be okay.

And that was what Cira would have done.

No, that was what she, Jane, would do. Cira was a dream and had nothing to do with reality. She was already beginning to feel better, stronger. All she'd needed was a little time to get over the shock and realize that this was nothing she couldn't control.

She straightened and headed for the bathroom. She wasn't about to curl up in bed and "rest." She'd wash her face and then she'd hit the computer and see if she could find any historical reference to a Cira in Herculaneum. It was entirely possible she'd run across information, maybe just a line or two that she'd absorbed and then forgotten and later reprocessed in those dreams. If that didn't work, she'd call the reference library downtown and see if they knew anything or could tell her where else to look. Before Trevor had thrown that bombshell she'd accepted those dreams with curiosity and fascination but she couldn't do that any longer. If there was any fragment of reality connected with Cira she had to know about it and how it was connected to her.

Two hours later she sat back and gazed in frustration at her computer. Nothing. And the reference librarians had not been able to access anything about Cira either. Okay, don't wig out. There had to be an answer. She just had to find it.

And the only knowledgeable source on Cira appeared to be Trevor, blast him.

Cira *and* Aldo.

She tried to quell her impatience. Keep busy. Go cook dinner. She'd always found if you concentrated on doing the little things right, the big things usually fell into place too.

So call me, Trevor, I'm ready for you.

* * *

Hot.

Smoke was beginning to creep through the rocks.

Antonio was just ahead, moving swiftly.

Go faster. Keep from coughing. He mustn't know she was following.

He was gone!

No, he must have just disappeared from view around a turn in the tunnel.

She mustn't lose him. She was committed and there was no turning back.

She started to run.

Don't lose him. Don't lose him.

She turned the corner.

"Can't we go the rest of the way together?" Antonio was outlined against the glowing rocks.

She skidded to a stop. "You knew I was following you."

"I knew there was a good possibility. You're smart and you don't want to die." He held out his hand. "Second chance, Cira. For me and for you. We both know second chances don't come along very often. We can make this work." He grimaced. "If we get out of here in time."

"I don't want a second chance with you."

"You loved me once. I can make you love me again."

"You can't make me do anything. I choose. Always."

"That's what I've always said. But I'm willing to give in . . . a little. For you." He coughed. "The smoke is getting worse. I'm not standing here begging. No woman is worth dying for. But you may be worth living for."

"It's the gold you want. And you can't get the gold away from here without dealing with Julius."

"Maybe not under the usual circumstances, but the world is ending tonight. There's a chance Julius may end with it. Or that we can find a way to escape to someplace he'll never find us."

"And you can be emperor," she said sarcastically.

"Why not? I'd be a magnificent emperor."

"In some primitive village hiding from Julius?"

"It wouldn't be primitive long if we were both there."

He was exerting that charisma that had first drawn her to him and the force of his personality was almost overpowering. She mustn't be seduced by him. He was too dangerous.

But he was also beautiful as a god and possessed a reckless, wicked charm that made the danger seem worth risking.

"Don't give me all your trust," he said. "Take it one step at a time. Just let me get you out of here."

She looked down at his outstretched hand. She could take his hand as she'd once taken his body.

No, she'd never be that foolish again.

"One step at a time," he said softly.

"If you wanted to get me out of here, why didn't you just let me follow you?"

"Because we'll need each other before we reach the end." He stiffened as a rumble shook the earth. "Make up your mind, Cira."

"I told you that—"

The earth beneath her feet broke apart and she looked down into hell!

She was falling, dying. . . .

"Antonio!"

Jane lunged up in bed, her heart beating so hard she thought it was going to leap from her chest.

Fire.

Liquid, molten fire.

She was falling. . . .

No, she wasn't falling. She took a deep breath and then another. That was better. She swung her feet to the floor and stood up.

Toby sat up and looked at her inquiringly.

"Yeah, it happened again. No fun, huh?" she whispered. She glanced at the clock. Three thirty-seven in the morning, but there was no way she could go back to sleep. Cira had taken care of that. Or her weird psyche or whatever. "Let's go out on the porch. I need some air."

Night with no air. Heat. The earth exploding beneath her feet.

She grabbed her robe and her phone that she'd put on the nightstand before she went to bed. "Be quiet now. It's the middle of the night. You don't want to wake up Eve or Joe."

Toby's tail thumped happily on the wood floor and the knocking was far from quiet.

"Get up, silly."

He leaped to his feet and the thumping stopped but his tail kept wagging. He streaked down the hall and reached the door before her.

The air was cool and fresh against her cheeks as she sat down on the top porch step. She could see the dull gleam of the patrol car down the road and waved to Mac and Brian. Their headlights blinked on and then went dark again.

Lord, the air felt good. She filled her lungs and the clean, soothing sensation made her almost heady with pleasure.

Night with no air . . .

Toby whined as he settled beside her.

"It's okay," she murmured as she stroked his head. "Only a dream. Nothing bad . . ."

Then why was she so terrified?

The world is ending tonight.

Not her world. Forget it. The dream had probably been triggered by Trevor's words and had no basis in—

Her phone rang.

She stared at it with no surprise. Why else had she taken it with her? It was Trevor and that was no surprise either.

"Are you alone?" he asked.

"If you don't count Toby."

"I wouldn't dare not count Toby." He paused. "How are you?"

"Fine. I was fine when you left us. You didn't have to use me as an excuse to bolt."

"Jane."

She wasn't being honest and they both knew it. "Okay, you freaked me out."

"I know and it surprised me. It wasn't the reaction I expected."

"What did you expect?"

"Curiosity. Interest. Maybe a little excitement."

And that was exactly the response she would have experienced if he hadn't mentioned Cira. He'd gauged her well. "Then obviously you don't know me as well as you think you do. The only thing you accomplished by leaving us yesterday afternoon was to irritate Joe and give him a chance to get on the phone and try to substantiate what you told us about Guido Manza."

"And did he do it?"

"Not yet. He shouldn't have to do it that way. Help him, blast it. You made a deal."

"You weren't ready. And you're the one who's important to me."

"I'm ready now."

He was silent a moment. "I think you are. I wish I could see your face. I'd like to be sure."

"Be sure. Who is Cira?"

"She was an actress in the theater in Herculaneum in the years before Vesuvius erupted and destroyed both Herculaneum and Pompeii in—"

"Then why did Aldo think she killed his father?"

"The tunnel that Guido blew led to Julius Precebio's library near his villa outside of Herculaneum. It contained several bronze tubes containing scrolls, jewels, and statues that had been preserved by the lava flow the night Herculaneum was destroyed. Julius was evidently a wealthy citizen of the city and completely enamored with Cira. A good many of the scrolls were devoted to praising her talents."

"Acting?"

"And other more intimate accomplishments. It seems that to be Cira's lover was a coveted honor among the elite of Herculaneum. She picked and chose who was to occupy her bed. She was born a slave and managed to work and scheme her way to freedom. Then she started to climb the ladder. Some called her a prostitute, but she—"

"They had no right to call her a prostitute," she said fiercely. "She had to survive and sometimes men only understand what they can use and possess. You said she was a slave. How could she be expected to— Do you know how hard it must have been for her to survive?"

"No." He paused. "Do you?"

"I can imagine. Beatings and starving and—" She stopped, realizing that her reaction was far too extreme. "Sorry. I've always hated people who condemn first and try to understand second. Or maybe don't try at all."

"You're taking this very personally."

"I have reason. I assume this woman had my face. You can't get more personal than that."

He nodded. "Touché. And, yes, she did look like you. There's an amazing resemblance."

"How do you know?"

"The library had several statues of Cira. Julius evidently commissioned some of the finest artists of his day to create likenesses of her."

"And you saw them? You only mentioned Aldo and his father being in the tunnel. You were there in the library?"

"Yes."

"That was brief. It won't fly, Trevor. I don't want bits and pieces. I want the entire story."

He chuckled. "You want it all. You have more than a physical resemblance to Cira. She wanted it all, too."

"How do you know?"

"I read some of the scrolls. I was stuck there at the site for weeks and I had to have something to do while I waited for them to find the pot of gold at the end of the rainbow."

"Pot of gold?"

"Julius mentioned a chest full of gold that he'd given to Cira to get her to stay with him for a few more weeks. It was supposed to be hidden in a room in one of the tunnels and only he and Cira knew where it was. She'd found another lover and was about to leave him and he was desperate."

"It's the gold you want."

Don't remember Cira's words to Antonio. Concentrate on today, Trevor, Aldo. "Those scrolls must have been in ancient Latin. How did you translate them?"

"I was motivated. And I had the services of a scholar Guido had hired after he discovered the library. Actually, I put him in touch with Pietro Tatligno. Pietro was smart as a whip and had an almost childish enthusiasm. He was more interested in a historical find than he was in the money Guido promised him. The scrolls were preserved in the bronze tubes. But Pietro still had to be extremely careful when he was handling and transcribing in order not to damage them. He made Guido pay a fortune for the equipment to preserve them."

"But you weren't concerned about the incredible historical find."

"I like money. I appreciate historical artifacts, but in the end I've noticed that even museums use them to barter. Besides, I don't believe Cira would want her possessions stared at by strangers."

"My, what an incredibly convenient belief."

"But true. I found myself developing a very personal feeling for Cira during those weeks. We all did. It may even be that Guido never intended a double cross when he brought me to the site. He and his son became obsessed and didn't want to share."

"The gold?"

"Not really. It wasn't long before I found out what was most important to them. Guido was completely obsessed with finding Cira's remains. When he was a young man he'd run across a statue of Cira in the ruins of the theater and spent the rest of his life trying to find her."

"Were there any stories in the newspapers about it?"

"No, I told you, he was completely obsessed. He talked about her as if she were a living woman even before we found the scrolls. Believe me, he didn't want anyone to discover anything about Cira before he did."

She felt a surge of disappointment. For a moment she'd thought she'd found a possible way she could have learned about Cira. "And Aldo was obsessed with her too?"

"In a different way. He became very quiet whenever his father was talking about her but he was pretty easy to read. She was alive for him too. But he didn't want her alive, he wanted her to stay dead and buried forever."

"Why?"

"Then the torment might someday be over."

"Torment?"

"Picture Aldo at five years old when his father discovered the bust of Cira. His father was his whole world, and then to have Guido be so focused on a dead woman that he totally ignored Aldo's needs would be devastating. Enough to send him insane."

"Then why was he helping his father to find her?"

"He was firmly under his thumb. And maybe he wanted to find the gold, too."

"Did you find it?"

"No, but that doesn't mean it wasn't there. He'd barely gotten started picking his way through the rocks when he decided he didn't want to share. He had to be very careful. The walls of the tunnels were weakened by the volcanic explosions and they couldn't go more than a few feet a day or risk a collapse."

"And in the meantime you sat and read scrolls?"

"Physical labor wasn't part of our deal."

"What was your deal?"

"I was in Milan working on another project when Manza contacted me."

"Smuggling."

"Well, yes. Anyway, Manza said he'd located an ancient find that would net all of us millions. He'd excavate the artifacts and I'd smuggle them out of the country and find buyers for them. He'd been on an archaeological dig near Herculaneum and stumbled on some ancient letters that led him to Julius's estate located some distance from the city. He didn't mention the bust of Cira. I was pretty skeptical. There have been digs at Herculaneum since 1750. I was sure every site would have been discovered."

"But you went anyway."

"I was interested. Manza had worked on excavations in Herculaneum for years. Aldo had spent half his childhood running around in those tunnels that had been dug down to the old city over the centuries. There was a chance Manza had struck it rich. Anyway, I figured it couldn't hurt. I was wrong. I ended up on my ass in a hospital for two months."

"How?"

"Guido decided not only to blow the

tunnel but everyone connected with the deal. He planned on closing the entrance and then going back later when he wouldn't have to either share the booty or leave anyone alive who'd know he'd found Cira's remains."

"And you were in the tunnel?"

"Me and Pietro and six laborers he'd hired in Corsica. I was the only one who managed to crawl out of that hole. Only because I was on my way out when he blew the tunnel. I had a broken leg and it took me three days to wriggle through those rocks to daylight. I found Guido dead at the cave entrance."

"No one else survived?"

"They were deeper in the tunnel. The charge literally blew them to bits and then buried them. He didn't want to destroy the library so the charge was less powerful near it."

She shivered. "All those deaths . . ."

"Aldo evidently came by his homicidal tendencies naturally. Although I'd never heard anything about Guido being particularly lethal before this job. He'd been a professor of archaeology in Florence before he started peddling artifacts."

"And where was Aldo when you got out of the tunnel?"

"Gone. He'd obviously made a half-hearted attempt to drag his father out of the debris and then just covered him with a blanket and got the hell out of there."

"Not a very caring good-bye."

"He cared. In his weird, twisted way. It was pretty clear Aldo had a screw loose from the moment he showed up at the site. He was completely absorbed in his computer and muttered a lot about destiny and reincarnation, besides being involved in some pretty sicko stuff. He was also nasty, sadistic, and bullied the workers whenever he got the chance. But around his father he'd cave if he raised an eyebrow."

"And you're sure he blamed Cira for his death?"

"More importantly, Aldo blamed her for the life he had been forced to live because of her. He and his father had taken a statue of Cira out of the library and loaded it in their truck. It was gone. But I found next to the body the statue Guido had discovered when Aldo was a boy. It had been placed on a rock above his head and cleaved in half with an ax."

"Couldn't it have been the explosion?"

"No, the bust's features had been hammered off."

"Like he removed all those features of the women he killed," she whispered.

"I didn't think much about any symbolism at the time. I was mad as hell and all I wanted to do was to get my hands on Aldo. It was too late for Guido, but not for Aldo. I didn't know any of those other workers but I liked Pietro. He was a good guy and he didn't deserve to die. But, by the time I made it to the nearest town, my leg was infected and I was too busy fighting to keep them from amputating it to worry about anything else."

"You told the people at the hospital what happened?"

"Hell, no. I would have ended up in jail, and I have an excellent sense of self-preservation. When I was released, I went back and buried Guido, camouflaged the site, and then went after Aldo."

"But you didn't find him."

"I told you he was smart. He made himself invisible and disappeared. Every time I got close to him he vanished. It was frustrating as hell. And then I saw the photo of the victim, Peggy Knowles, in Brighton."

"Cira."

"It made sense. He and his father were both obsessed with her, and that symbolic smashing of the statue was pretty clear. He blamed Cira for both his father's death and for his miserable childhood. Maybe the shock of his father's death sent him over the edge and he began to think of her as a living presence, as his father did. Or it could be the first kill in Rome was because he accidentally stumbled over a woman who looked like Cira. Then when he realized there were others, he went on the search for her."

"You think he believes in . . . reincarnation?"

"Who knows? He's nuts. I'd say there's a good chance it's all mixed up in his head. We know he's been searching the world for anyone who looks like her and made it his life's mission. He can't tolerate anyone living who even resembles Cira. Since she died two thousand years ago, his belief in reincarnation seems to be the most likely answer. Which came first, the chicken or the egg?"

"And he thinks I'm this reincarnation?" She made a rude sound. "No way. I'm not a carbon copy of anyone. It's bad enough to look like this Cira. Inside, I'm all me."

"You don't believe in the possibility of reincarnation? There are millions of people who do."

"Then good luck to them. I'm the only one who accepts credit or blame for what I do. I'm not about to moan and whine and say it's all because of some woman who bit it two thousand years ago."

"You're very emphatic."

"Because I mean it. I'm sick to death of hearing how Aldo is going after me because of my face. I'm more than a face."

"You're preaching to the choir. I knew that the moment I saw you." He paused. "And Aldo isn't only going after you because you look like Cira. He probably believes you have her soul."

"Then he's going to find out he's wrong. I'm not like her. Not really." Her hand tightened on the phone. "And I don't know what's going on, but I'm the one who has to deal with it, not Cira."

"We have to deal with it," he corrected. "We're in this together."

He was wrong. Comforting words, but she had a gut feeling that in the end it wouldn't be that way. All her life she'd been alone. Why should this be any different?

No, that wasn't right. Why had she even had that thought? It was Cira who'd been alone all her life. She, Jane, had Eve and Joe. It was frightening that she'd had that instant of confusion. It must be all this stupid talk of Cira and reincarnation. "Don't think I won't call loud and clear. Now tell me about Aldo. All you've said is that he's nasty, sadistic, and was studying acting when his father sent for him to come to Herculaneum. That's a weird career choice for a beast like him."

"Not so weird for someone who's not got all his marbles. Split personality, paranoia . . . He could be anyone he liked the minute he got on the stage."

"You said he was brilliant. In what way?"

"Computers. He did all of his father's research. That's one of the reasons Guido wanted him at the site. He had him exploring every map on the Internet to see if any tunnel excavated in Herculaneum was possibly connected to Julius's."

"Were there any?"

He shook his head. "Guido was disgusted. He'd hoped that he might be able to make the excavation easier. No luck. And he made his disappointment in him very obvious to Aldo. He treated him like an idiot, made him check and recheck to make sure he wasn't making a mistake. It was pretty clear that was how he'd treated him all his life. If Aldo hadn't been such a bastard, I would have felt sorry him."

"I wouldn't." Her mind was puzzling over something else. "I don't understand how Aldo could have been able to flit from country to country without being caught. Did he have money?"

"Not when he left Herculaneum. But he did have one of the statues of Cira he took from the library. He sold it to a private collector in London. That's how I traced him to the U.K. I heard about it from one of my informants. The statue was priceless and even on the black market he would have enough money to buy as many false documents as he needed and have enough to support himself for a good many years."

"So he used Cira to kill all those women."

"In a manner of speaking. Do you need to know anything else?"

"I have one more question to ask." Her lips twisted. "Were you more angry with Aldo because he killed all those people or because he tried to cheat you of the gold?"

He was silent. "Interesting question." But he wasn't answering it.

"I have to warn you I'm telling Eve and Joe everything you've told me. And that means that there will probably be investigators all over that site at Herculaneum. Someone else will find that pot of gold in those tunnels."

"They won't find it. Those tunnels are very well hidden. They went undiscovered for all those years and that blast sealed the entrances to the tunnel and I did the rest. I covered any trace of excavation. When this is over I'll still have my chance . . . if I want it."

"Oh, I think you'll want it."

"My, how cynical. You think my mercenary streak dominates my life? Maybe you're right. And maybe you're wrong. Did it occur to you that I knew you'd tell Quinn and was willing to take my chances? So it could be that I'm more bloodthirsty than greedy. I'll call you tomorrow and you can tell me if Quinn has any more questions. Sleep well, Jane."

He hung up before she could answer.

Sleep well? Fat chance, she thought as she hung up the phone. Her head was spinning with the overload he'd given her to digest that filled her with fear, panic, and defiance. Then don't try to absorb it. Let it sink in and don't force it. One step at a time.

Antonio had said that, she remembered. He'd held out his hand and told Cira to trust him. But Cira hadn't taken his hand. She hadn't had time before the earth had opened and she'd seen the molten—

Forget the dream. Remember reality. If it was reality that Trevor had told her and not lies. He wanted the gold.

No, Antonio had wanted the gold. Once more, dream and reality had blended, becoming one for the moment. It mustn't happen again.

Toby sighed and rubbed his head on her lap.

"Okay, we're going inside." Jane got to her feet. "What a nag you are." She paused, gazing out at the forest. Was Trevor out there watching her? It was an odd coincidence that he'd called her as soon as she'd come out on the porch. He'd asked her if she was alone, but he might not want her to know how closely he was watching her. She was feeling a little claustrophobic from all the restrictions and scrutiny, and he was very perceptive.

He *was* there.

She lifted her hand in a mocking salute and went into the house.

TEN

Trevor smiled ruefully as he watched the door close behind Jane.

He should have known she'd know he was watching her. They were on the same wavelength and had been since that first moment she'd walked into the cottage.

Or maybe before. At least, as far as he was concerned. He'd studied everything about her since the moment Bartlett had brought him that photo in the newspaper. It was natural that he'd feel this sense of empathy.

Or was it?

His smile faded. Of course it was natural. He was no psycho like Aldo. He'd been fascinated and intrigued by Cira, but it had no connection with what he was feeling for Jane. She was little more than a child and he was no cradle robber.

But Cira had been only seventeen when Herculaneum had been destroyed. She'd been the mistress of at least three important men of the town and carved a career that shone like a star in the darkness of that age. She'd packed decades of living into her short life.

Jesus, Cira wasn't Jane MacGuire. It was a different culture and a different time. So stop making comparisons and close out the thought of Jane as anything but a possible victim.

"How did she take it?"

He turned to see Bartlett standing behind him. "As well as could be expected. She'll be better once she has a chance to mull everything over and come to terms with it. She's already halfway there."

"And then what?"

"Then we do what we've been doing since you found that photograph of her." He gazed at the cottage, remembering how she'd looked sitting on that step with the dog beside her. Young, slim, vulnerable, but, strangely, radiating strength. "We wait."

Pittsburgh, Pennsylvania

His latex gloves were bloody.

Aldo looked down at his hands with distaste. He hated using gloves, but it was better than touching these unworthy ones. When he had the time to make a true selection he never covered his hands. He enjoyed the feel of warm blood on his skin. But, again, time was short and this woman bore only a slight resemblance to Cira.

These kills provided no pleasure, he thought in frustration.

He bundled the woman up in a blanket and watched the blood seep through the wool. Good. The blood would attract instant attention when he dumped her body behind the Red Lobster restaurant where he'd picked her up. Otherwise he would have used a tarp to wrap her.

He could feel the joy tear through him as he lifted her and put her in the van. The last one. The trail was far enough away from

Jane MacGuire to throw off suspicion. The police were always eager to wash their hands of their failures. Joe Quinn and Eve Duncan would probably not be fooled, but they'd be alone.

He could go back to Cira now.

Joe turned away from the phone. "Lea Elmore. A waitress at the Red Lobster in Pittsburgh. Found this morning behind the restaurant. No face. Ashes in the blanket in which she was wrapped."

"A Jane look-alike?" Eve asked.

He nodded. "According to her photo ID she's a little closer than the ones he killed in Richmond and Charlotte."

She shook her head in bewilderment. "How is he finding them when he's moving so fast? I could understand if there was a reasonable length of time between the kills, but they've barely been forty-eight hours apart. He can't just stumble on these women." She glanced at Jane. "Did Trevor say—"

"No," Jane answered. "I told you everything he told me. But he seems to have done a lot of guesswork and putting together the pieces. Maybe he did figure it out. Do you want me to phone him? He said to let him know if Joe had questions."

"Joe?" Eve asked.

"Go ahead. I'll take any help I can get." Joe's tone was absent as he moved across the living room to stare out the window. "Though that's not high on the priority list at the moment."

"What are you looking at?" Eve followed him to the window.

"Nothing." His lips tightened. "Not a damn thing."

"What do—" Her gaze had followed his. "The patrol car is gone."

"Right." His cell phone rang. "And I'd bet that's Mac Gunther to tell me why." He listened for a moment. "I understand. No, I can't let you do that. It's okay, Mac." He hung up. "The captain pulled Mac and Brian off surveillance. He apologized and said he'd be glad to come back on his own time and work a double shift if we needed him."

"The department is doing exactly what Trevor said Aldo would try to make them do," Eve said numbly. "He wants us alone and unprotected."

"Then he screwed up," Jane said fiercely. "We're not alone. We've got each other. Stop looking like that, Eve. He's not going to win." She turned to Joe. "The department thinks Aldo has forgotten me?"

Joe nodded. "This last kill cinched it for them." He looked at Eve. "But Jane's right, we don't have to be alone. I'll call a private security agency and get men out here. It just means the department is out of it."

"Then do it," Eve said. "Now."

"I will." His gaze went to the window again. "It's time we called in all the help we can get." He was silent a moment before turning away from the window and starting to dial his phone. "I'll get Matt Singer's security team. They're good. Jane, you call Trevor and tell him to get up here. He says he wants to protect you? Well, let him put his ass on the line instead of hovering out there in the woods like a damn chipmunk."

"Chipmunk?" Trevor repeated when he walked into the cottage an hour later. "Really, Quinn. You could have at least compared me to a more interesting and lethal animal. A cougar or wolf would have been nice."

"Or skunk," Jane murmured. "Skunks are interesting."

Trevor gave her a reproachful glance. "I'm here to lay myself open to murder and mayhem and all I get is abuse." He turned back to Joe. "From what Jane said, I understand your fellow law-enforcement associates have jerked the rug from beneath your feet?"

"It's no more than I expected," Joe said. "They play the percentages and, if Aldo follows the usual serial killer profile, the odds are against him coming back once he's moved on."

"Should I be flattered you're paying more attention to my warning than the odds?"

"No, I'm paying attention to keeping Jane safe and to hell with the percentages." He looked him in the eye. "So tell me what you can do that makes it worth my while to keep you close to Jane."

Trevor's smile faded. "For one thing just my presence here is a minor deterrent. Aldo knows me and he'll be a little more cautious about moving on her."

"Only a little cautious?"

"Take what you can get. Sometimes a hesitation can save a life. You should know that." He added crisply, "And I gather you've arranged other protection for Jane. You could let me handle the day-to-day co-ordination of the security team. I know something about reconnaissance and sentry detail."

"So I've heard."

"It would keep me from under your feet and out of your hair. And that would free you to work more closely with your department to track Aldo." His voice was soft but emphatic. "And I guarantee no one would sleep on their watch if I was in charge. When are they supposed to get here?"

"In a couple hours."

"Then I'm just in time to break them in right, aren't I?"

Joe studied him for a long moment and then nodded slowly. "But remember these are private citizens, not mercenaries. No rough stuff."

"I'll be gentle with them." Trevor smiled. "As gentle as you'd be if you found them slacking. You SEALs are always prone to discuss and persuade rather than take violent action."

"You son of a bitch." But Jane could see his lips twitching. "That was a long time ago."

"Not that long." He turned and started for the door. "Oh, by the way. I'm posting someone of my own out front to guard the cottage. His name is John Bartlett and he'll try to be unobtrusive."

"You said Bartlett was on the case before. But why the hell should I just accept him on your say-so?" Joe asked.

"You shouldn't. Check on him with Scotland Yard. But you'll find he has a motivation that's a recommendation in itself."

"What motivation?"

"His ex-wife was Ellen Carter. She was one of the first women killed by Aldo in London. He couldn't stand living with her, but he still loved her. Having her burned to death made him very upset. So upset he was willing to put up with me to have a chance at finding Aldo." He glanced back over his shoulder at Jane. "He's the one who found your photo in the paper. He's had a vested interest in you since he brought that clipping to me. He found out everything he could about you and Quinn and Eve. He's not exactly bodyguard material, but I wouldn't let him close to you if I didn't think he'd be the best man for the job. He won't let anything suspicious get past him. But if you don't want him, send him back to me."

"I will."

But he didn't hear. He'd already left the cottage and was going down the steps.

"He was doing everything he could to try to control the situation, wasn't he?" Jane asked. "You'll have to watch him."

Eve looked at her in surprise. "I thought you wanted us to bring him in."

"I did. I still think it's a good idea." How could she explain the dichotomy of her feelings for Trevor? While part of her had been amused and admiring as she had watched Trevor insinuating himself into the fray, she'd still had the impulse to step between him and Joe and Eve. She had never lost the awareness of the volatility and danger that had struck her from the first moment she had met him. "Just watch him, Joe."

"Ms. MacGuire?" The man who had knocked on the door smiled. "I'm John

Bartlett. I was the one who did the background research on you and your family. And later I had the honor of watching you myself to make sure you were safe. I feel as if I know you already."

"I imagine you do." Bartlett definitely wasn't what she had expected. He was plump, no more than five foot seven, with rosy cheeks, thinning brown hair, and huge blue eyes that were looking at her with a sort of troubled innocence that reminded her of . . . someone.

His expression clouded at the dryness of her tone. "I know I violated your privacy. I only meant to help. And I don't mean to be intrusive now. I'll try not to bother you. But Trevor thinks I can help in guarding you—" He made a face. "Well, not really guarding you. That denotes a certain talent for violence I don't possess. That's Trevor's forte and he does it well. But there are other ways I can help."

"And what are they?"

"I've got great skills of observation." He added earnestly, "I promise nothing and no one will get past without my noticing."

Winnie-the-Pooh, she realized suddenly. He reminded her of Winnie-the-Pooh. That same wide-eyed, cuddly frankness. "That's very comforting."

He nodded. "It's one of my better qualities. It's not very exciting but being comforting isn't bad. I've got three ex-wives who'll give testimony to that." His expression was suddenly shadowed. "Two ex-wives. Ellen isn't around to give anyone recommendations anymore." He started to turn away. "I just wanted to let you know I'd be on the job."

"Wait."

He turned to look at her.

"Would you like a cup of coffee?"

"No, thank you." His smile lit his plump face with a kind of boyish radiance. "You're very kind but I've got to go on duty now."

She was smiling too as she watched him go down the steps.

"Was that Bartlett?" Eve came to stand beside her.

"I think so." She shook her head. "Or maybe it was Peter Pan or Winnie-the-Pooh."

"What?"

"Why don't you go see for yourself? Take him a cup of coffee." She added solemnly, "He was on duty and wouldn't come in."

Eve watched as Bartlett picked up a pebble and sent it skimming across the lake. "Maybe I will." She turned and headed for the kitchen.

For the rest of the day Jane didn't see Trevor except at a distance. He seemed very busy and intent as he talked to Singer and his men. In spite of Joe's cautioning, she couldn't see any signs that Trevor was being overbearing with any of the security team. There was no question that he was in charge but he appeared to be handling them with respect and humor.

It was fully dark when he drove up to the cottage. He spoke for a moment to Bartlett before he got out of the SUV, his arms loaded with catalogues and packages. "I brought your mail," he said as he climbed the porch steps. "I checked for it earlier. Does it come late in the afternoon every day?"

She nodded. "About four." She set her computer aside and held out her hand for the bundle. "Thank you. But you didn't have to pick it up."

"Yes, I did. Your mailbox is three miles

away on the main road. I wanted to make sure that there weren't any surprises. Since Aldo was camped out in the woods he probably checked out your mailbox occasionally. It's what I would have done. You never can tell what will come in handy when you're on the hunt." He sat down beside her on the swing. "But there didn't seem to be anything to worry about. Most of it's for Eve."

"It's usually that way. Eve's very famous and she has a lot of requests for her services. And she wouldn't like you going through her mail."

"Like I said, I didn't want any surprises."

"What did you expect? A cobra in the mailbox?"

"No, that wouldn't fit Aldo's pattern. But Julia Brandon was killed by poison gas. There are ways of making an envelope deadly."

Her mind jumped immediately to the aftermath of 9/11. "Anthrax?"

"Or something else. I didn't think it likely he'd want to rob himself of the pleasure of a close-up kill, but he's not always predictable."

"You seem to be doing a pretty good job

so far. Poison gas . . . That's the only one who died like that, isn't it? Drownings, incineration, smothering. For a serial killer he doesn't seem to be consistent in his methods. They usually have a weapon of preference, don't they?"

"He's consistent. Each one of those deaths occurred to the citizens of Herculaneum during the eruption. He's killing Cira over and over in every conceivable way she could have died that night."

"My God."

No air. Hot. Hot. Hot.

"Are you okay?" Trevor's gaze was narrowed on her face.

"Of course I am." She looked out at the lake. "How did Cira die?"

"I don't know. Every scroll in the library concerned Cira's life, not her death."

"Then maybe she didn't die at Herculaneum. There were survivors, weren't there?"

"Yes."

"Then she could have been one of them."

"I'd think a woman like Cira would have been heard from in the years after the disaster if she'd lived. She was no shrinking violet."

"Maybe she had a reason to disappear."

He was silent a moment. "That had a note of desperation. You really want her to have survived, don't you? Why?"

"Don't be silly. I'm not desperate about anything. She just didn't deserve to die in that tunnel."

"Tunnel?" He was gazing at her oddly. "Why should she have died in a tunnel? She had a fine home in Herculaneum."

"Did she? I must have been thinking about the gold in the tunnel." She changed the subject. "I just remembered that Joe wanted to know if you'd figured out how Aldo found all those women with Cira's face. You said one woman's photo was in the newspaper and I guess he could have stumbled on one or two of them, but not all. And he was moving so fast in the past few weeks that he couldn't have just gotten lucky."

He shook his head. "I've been concentrating more on getting Aldo, not the whys and wherefores. But tell Quinn I'll work on it."

"Good. You won't be alone. Joe may figure it out before you do. He doesn't like to ask for help."

"He didn't. You did it for him. Did Bartlett come by and introduce himself?"

"Yes, he's very unusual. How did you get together with him?"

"I was backtracking after I saw that photo of Peggy Knowles and questioned all the families of the victims I ran across. Bartlett was on Ellen Carter's list. I was pretending to be from Scotland Yard at the time. I'm pretty good and no one else was suspicious. But Bartlett is a hell of a lot smarter than he looks. He followed me back to my hotel and pulled a gun on me."

"Bartlett?"

He smiled. "He surprised me, too. He was scared to death but he was determined. His hand was shaking so badly that I thought I'd better talk fast or he'd shoot one of us by accident."

"Why didn't he call the police on you?"

"Because he wasn't happy with the way the investigation had been going. He loved Ellen Carter."

"He said he had three ex-wives."

"She was number two. Bartlett stays

close to his wives even after they divorce him."

"Why would they divorce him? He seems . . . sweet."

"He has a talent for choosing the wrong partners. Some men marry the same type of woman over and over. He has no problem acquiring wives. Women seem to melt and want to take him home. Didn't you?"

She nodded. "And Eve's taken him lunch and coffee today. And she had to leave a reconstruction she's working on to do it."

"See?"

"Well, evidently you weren't immune either."

"You're right." His lips twisted ruefully. "He's stubborn as hell and he wouldn't leave me alone after he knew that I was trying to find Aldo. He quit his job as an accountant and he's been with me ever since."

"I like him."

"All women—dammit, I like him, too." His gaze went to Bartlett. "But he drives me crazy. I'll probably have to rope, tie, and drag him away or he'd stay out there all night. He was happy as hell he could do something constructive to help you."

"Sweet."

"And you're melting, too." He sighed as he got to his feet. "I'll take the mail into the house."

"I can do it."

He glanced at the computer. "You're busy. What are you doing?"

"Homework. I like to work out here on the porch."

He made a face. "Homework. I keep forgetting how young you are. Maybe it's Freudian." He headed for the door. "Make sure no one picks up the mail every day but me."

"Tell that to Joe."

"Quinn is willing to let me do the donkey work. He knows I'm not dumb enough to step on his toes. We're gradually coming to an understanding." He opened the screen door. "It's Eve I'm worrying about."

"Because she doesn't melt around you like she does Bartlett?"

"Because she's a mother protecting her cub. Talk about unpredictable." He glanced over his shoulder. "Are you going to tell me why you want so badly for Cira to have survived that volcano?"

He obviously hadn't been deceived and

wasn't about to let it go. Well, she wasn't about to confide in him. "Since everyone seems to be equating the two of us maybe I just want her to have come out on top. It would be a good sign."

"Yes, it would." He studied her expression and then shook his head. "But I don't think that's it. . . ."

"Think what you like."

"I always do." He paused. "But I need to know. I need to know everything about you. It's safer for both of us."

"Why?"

"He'll use any secret, any memory, any feeling that will draw you to him. He's done it already once with Toby."

"I made a mistake. I won't do it again. And I'm not about to bare my soul to you. You've taken it upon yourself to learn entirely too much about me on your own."

"Yes." A sudden smile lit his face. "And it was my pleasure. It's still my pleasure." He went into the cottage.

She had to force herself to look away from that door. Sweet Jesus, he was handsome. Most of the time when she was with him she was only aware of that magnetic personality and the sense of wariness it brought her. But in that last moment it had hit home what a beautiful man Trevor really was.

Beautiful? Trevor would not have been pleased. Where had that word come from?

Beautiful as a god.

Cira had been thinking of Antonio when those words had sprung to her mind. Antonio, intelligent, cynical, and totally charismatic. Antonio, who had seduced and dazzled and betrayed her. But in the end had he also tried to save her, or was that another deception?

What difference did it make? She was treating a dream as reality. And if this was some kind of psychic connection she'd made with Aldo, she'd evidently embroidered and enhanced it on her own. She was rooting for Cira every step of the way and Aldo certainly saw her as a villainess.

And what about Antonio?

Maybe she had to have a hero to save Cira. Though he was more of an antihero.

Like Trevor.

She stiffened. Cira's view of Antonio was remarkably like Jane's opinion of Trevor. And from that first moment she had felt a strange familiarity with him. She'd even told Eve he reminded her of someone.

Antonio?

She couldn't even remember what Antonio looked like. Cira was seeing him, not her. Cira was feeling the tempest of resentment, bitterness, hope, and love.

Love? Did Cira still love Antonio?

Oh, to the devil with it. What difference did it make? There was a chance she'd never have another dream about Cira. It had been several nights since she'd had that nightmare in which the ground had cracked beneath Cira's feet and she stared into molten fire.

Lava. When she'd known about the tunnel at Herculaneum and the woman who'd lived and died there.

But Trevor had already told her that the ashes were from Vesuvius and her imagination might have made a mental leap to an active volcano. How did she know what tricks a mind could play? These blasted dreams of Cira had completely shaken her confidence. At first, as she'd told Eve, she'd been able to view Cira and her struggles with curiosity and excitement as if she were reading a novel. It had been interesting and she'd looked forward to the next installment and trying to figure out exactly what was happening to her. That was no longer the case. After what Trevor had told her, she was flailing in the dark, trying to find her way. She was caught, held captive, and she was dreading going back into that tunnel.

"Stay away, Cira," she whispered. "I have enough on my plate. Don't come back."

ELEVEN

Molten lava yawning before her feet.

"Jump!" Antonio held out his arms. "Now, Cira. I'll catch you."

Jump? The crack was too wide and getting wider every second.

No time. No other choice. She leaped across the crack. The heat seared her legs even as her feet touched the opposite ledge.

It crumbled beneath her!

Then he was yanking her upward and forward in one movement.

"I've got you." Antonio's hands grasped her forearms and they were stumbling backward.

Another rumble.

"We've got to get out of this passage." Cira glanced over her shoulder.

The crack was widening, gaping.

"You said you knew the way," Cira gasped. "Prove it. Get us out of here."

"Only you'd be stubborn enough to wait until you saw the gates of hell to say that to me." Antonio grabbed her hand and started at a dead run down the tunnel. "The crack seems to be going across the tunnel. We can't go back, but it's not following us."

"If it doesn't cause the roof to cave in when it tries to devour the other wall."

Heat.

The lava behind them was gobbling what little air was still in the tunnel.

"Then we'd better be out of this branch of the tunnel before it happens. There's a turnoff just ahead that should lead us to the sea."

"Or to Julius."

"Shut up." His hand tightened with bruising force on hers. "I'm not taking you to Julius. If I'd wanted you dead, I'd have taken his money for your face when he offered it two weeks ago."

"My face?"

"When you told him you were leaving and

wouldn't give him back the gold, he asked me to kill you."

"What's that got to do with my face?"

"He said he'd commissioned a dozen likenesses of that wonderful face and didn't want anyone but him to possess it. Not even you. He wanted me to kill you and take my knife and remove your face and bring it to him."

She felt sick. "Madness."

"I agree. And, as I have a fondness for that face, I declined his offer. But it meant I had to leave Herculaneum for a few days. There was a good chance he would have put a price on my head as well. He knew I was your lover. It was why he thought I might have a chance of killing you."

"If you could have gotten past Dominic," she said fiercely. "Dominic would have cut your head off and served it to me on a silver tray."

"That was why Julius resorted to bribery. Everyone knew how well guarded you were. Where is Dominic? He should be here with you."

"I sent him home to the country."

"Because you didn't want Julius aiming

his arrows at him. That's what bodyguards are for, Cira."

"He served me well. I didn't want him— I can take care of myself. Shouldn't we have reached the end of the tunnel by now?"

"It winds around. Julius didn't want to make getting out of the villa too easy."

"And how do you know how to get out?"

"I made it my business. I spent many nights in these tunnels while we were together. It would hardly be intelligent to steal the gold and then not have an escape hole."

"Bastard."

"I was willing to share."

"My gold."

"There was enough for both of us. I would have earned it. I would have provided safety and treasured you as much as the gold."

"I'm to believe you? Good gods, what nonsense you're—"

Rumbling.

Rocks tumbling around them.

A sharp stone pierced Cira's skin. She felt the warm blood pouring down her arm.

"Hurry!" Antonio was jerking her through the tunnel. "The structure of the tunnel's weakening. It could go any moment."

"I am hurrying. What a stupid—" Another rock struck her cheek.

More pain.

More blood.

More pain.

More pain . . .

"Wake up. Stop moaning, dammit."

Blood . . .

She opened her eyes. "Blood," she gasped.

"Wake up."

"Antonio . . ."

No, it was Trevor standing above her beside the porch swing.

Of course it wasn't Antonio. . . .

"I'm awake." She tried to catch her breath. "I'm fine." She sat up and rubbed her eyes. "I must have dozed off. What time is it?"

"Only a little after midnight. I saw you curled up in the porch swing when I took over for Bartlett an hour ago. But you were sleeping so soundly I thought I'd let you sleep until you stirred." His lips tightened. "But that was before you started whimpering. It was damn disconcerting. You're not a person given to whimpering. What the hell were you dreaming?"

Rocks flying, blood, pain.

"I don't remember." She arched her back to ease the stiffness. She must have been curled in that fetal position for hours. Or maybe not. How long did a dream last? "Is everything okay?"

"No problems. The security team is sharp. I just have to remind them to keep sharp. Boredom is our worst enemy." He was frowning. "You don't have to be afraid."

"Of course I do. I'd be an idiot not to be afraid."

"Scared enough for it to give you nightmares?"

"Everyone has bad dreams."

"Not about blood." He paused. "And not about Cira."

She stiffened. "I take it I was doing more than whimpering. What did I say?"

"I couldn't make out very much. I think you said, 'Watch out, Cira. Rocks. Too late.' When you woke, you were talking to someone named Antonio." He gazed directly into her eyes. "And, if you know what I'm talking about, then you do remember that nightmare."

"And you should have waked me right away and not eavesdropped."

"You have to admit that it's natural that my attention should be caught by Cira's name."

"I don't care if it's natural. You shouldn't have eavesdropped."

"Granted." He was silent. "What were you dreaming?"

She looked away from him. "What you'd expect me to dream since you told me about her. Tunnels. A volcano erupting. A woman running for her life."

"Is this the first time you dreamed about her?"

"No."

"When did it start?"

"None of your business." She rose to her feet and picked up her laptop. "We've let you inveigle yourself into our lives, but keep your hands off my dreams, Trevor."

"If I can."

"What the devil is that supposed to mean?"

He shrugged. "I'm having trouble not being drawn into every aspect of your life.

Believe me, I've tried to keep my distance. It's not working."

"Try harder." She took a step toward the door. "I don't need you to confide in. I have Eve and Joe. If I want to talk about Cira or anything else, it will be with them."

He held up his hand in surrender. "Okay. Okay. I hear you." He stood looking at her as she opened the screen door. "If you change your mind . . ."

"I won't. Why should I?"

"Curiosity." He smiled faintly. "Did it ever occur to you that you're not the only one who dreams of Cira?"

Her gaze flew to his face. "What?"

"Why the surprise? She seems to dominate all of us. I started dreaming about her years ago after I read those scrolls."

She moistened her lips. "What . . . kind of dreams?"

He shook his head and said softly, "You tell me your dreams, I'll tell you mine."

"And you'll probably make up yours."

He chuckled. "O ye of little faith." He started down the steps. "If you decide you want to talk, you know where I'll be."

"I won't want to talk. I don't care about

your blasted dreams." She slammed the screen door behind her.

But she did care, dammit. He had known that little alluring tidbit would intrigue her. Someone else who dreamed of Cira?

If it was the truth.

And she wasn't about to lay herself open to possible ridicule just to satisfy his curiosity.

And her own curiosity, blast his soul.

Dahlonega, Georgia
Three days later

Eve Duncan.

Joe Quinn.

Mark Trevor.

Aldo closed the lid of the laptop computer and leaned back with a sigh of contentment as he stared at the printout. He knew enough now to launch the plan into action. What a pity Cira's enemies had not had access to the Internet. Information would have been a formidable weapon to bring her down. She had been soft in many ways. About that bodyguard she had saved from execution. About the street child she had taken into her home. All Julius would have had to do was to find her weak spot and capitalize on it to kill the bitch. And information was always the key.

Maybe Julius had killed her. But if he had killed her, he hadn't prevented her from remaining a presence, able to torment and destroy. He should have wiped her from the face of the earth.

As he would do.

He'd cleared the path to Jane MacGuire as much as he could. Now he would reconnoiter, find out the obstacles, and then he'd be ready to move with all due ritual.

He smiled as he looked at the suitcase across the motel room.

Green fire. Lovely deadly fire.

Are you waiting for me, Cira?

"Mail," Trevor announced as he came up the steps. "Bills, a postcard from Eve's mother from Yellowstone. Two FedEx boxes. One for Eve and one for you."

"I hope you enjoyed the postcard." Jane set aside the computer. "You're learning a little too much about us."

"There can't ever be too much." He smiled. "And I didn't read the postcard, just the signature. Eve's package is from a university in Michigan. Your package is from a Mail Boxes Unlimited in Carmel, California. Do you know anyone in Carmel?"

She nodded. "Sarah Logan. She and John live on the Seventeen Mile Strip. She gave me Toby."

"So of course she's a very good friend, indeed. Come on inside and we'll open the packages."

"I can open mine here."

"No, you can't. You don't open anything. I checked the box out and it seemed okay but you can never tell."

"What?" she lifted her brows. "No bomb? No anthrax?"

"Not funny. As a matter of fact, I had Quinn get me a portable scanner to detect the presence of a bomb."

"Why? A bomb is a modern weapon of destruction. They didn't have them in Herculaneum."

"Right. But a volcano explodes and so does a bomb. It's a very tenuous linking but I'm not taking any chances. As for anthrax, I don't think so. But he may have found some other volcano-related powder, that's why I'm opening it." He opened the door. "Coming?"

She rose to her feet. "It's not unusual for Sarah to send me presents. She has to travel all over the world and she picks up toys for Toby and little surprises for me and Eve."

"Nice lady. Let's see what she sent this time."

He was holding the door open for her and it was clear he wasn't going to give her the package. She shrugged and preceded him into the house. "I won't argue. But you said yourself that you thought Aldo would want a close kill."

"I'm not the one who'd bear the consequences if I was wrong." He smiled at Eve, who was working on a reconstruction in her studio across the room. "Mail, Eve. Your mother is enjoying Yellowstone."

"You said you didn't read her postcard," Jane said dryly.

"I didn't. From what I understand, everyone enjoys Yellowstone. I must go sometime. Where do you want your mail, Eve?"

"On the coffee table." She held up her

clay-coated hands. "If I handled it now, I'd mess it up and wouldn't be able to read it."

"How's the reconstruction going?"

"Pretty good. I've done the measuring and I'm starting the molding. But I never know until the final stages."

"That's what you told me." He began to separate Eve's mail on the coffee table. "Interesting stuff . . ."

Jane gazed at the two of them in bewilderment. She hadn't realized until this moment how at ease they'd become with each other during these last days. She'd seen him talking to Eve on occasion and even having a cup of coffee with her when she'd taken a carafe down to Bartlett, but Eve seemed perfectly accepting of Trevor now.

Eve turned back to the pedestal. "Did Jane get anything?"

"A package. She thinks it's from Sarah Logan."

"Again? She just sent her a leash from Morocco a few weeks ago. . . ." Her hands were moving, sculpting, and her tone was absent. A moment later Jane knew she was completely absorbed in the work and no longer with them.

"Where's Quinn?" Trevor asked as he finished stacking the bills.

"At the precinct. Christy set up a conference call with Scotland Yard and the Rome police to discuss Aldo." Jane gave him a cool look as she sat down on the couch. "And the local Italian police have found no trace of any tunnel in the countryside outside of Herculaneum. And no villa belonging to a Julius Precebio."

"I told you they wouldn't find it."

"Because you did your best to hide it. When this is over, you're going to have a lot of questions to answer."

"Hmm." Trevor was tearing the strip on the FedEx box. "I'm duly intimidated."

She scowled. "You are not."

"No, but I'd hate to disappoint you." His smile faded as he opened the lid. "There's another package inside." He moved away from the couch on which she was sitting to the screen door. "It's small, velvet, and doesn't look like it would contain a dog toy for Toby. I think I'll just open this on the porch."

She tensed in spite of herself. "Stop it. Aren't you overreacting?"

"Perhaps." He looked in the FedEx box. "No note."

"Maybe it's in the velvet box."

"Possibly." He dropped the FedEx box and slowly opened the blue velvet box.

"What is it?"

"A ring."

"Jewelry?" Relief surged through her as she jumped to her feet and followed him across the room. "Let me see it."

"In a minute." He was holding the ring up to the light.

"Now." The ring was a broad band of intricately carved gold and the stone it held was a brilliant pale green, too pale to be an emerald, probably a peridot. "Do you think Sarah would send me a Borgia poison ring or something?"

"No." He held the ring away from her. "But I don't believe this ring is from Sarah. Why don't you call her while I look it over?"

Her gaze shifted from the ring to his face and what she saw there made her eyes widen. "Why?"

"Call her," he repeated. "If it's from her, it will give you the opportunity to thank her. I'll stay here and wait for you."

She hesitated, tempted to refuse and

confront him. Then she went inside, picked up her phone, and dialed Sarah in Carmel.

Trevor was standing underneath the porch light when she came out of the house five minutes later.

"She didn't send it," Jane said flatly. "She didn't know anything about it. Aldo?"

He nodded. "My guess."

"Why would he send me a ring? That's a peridot, isn't it?"

"I don't think so. It's similar and most people would mistake it for a peridot."

"Then what is it?"

"It's a vesuvianite."

"What the devil is that?"

"When a volcano erupts the tephra sometimes forms a glasslike substance that can be polished and refined to resemble fine gems. You may have seen helenite, the dark green stone that became popular after the Mount Saint Helens eruption."

"But this came from Vesuvius?" Her gaze was fastened in sick fascination on the ring in his hand. "I was joking, but could it be some kind of poison ring?"

He shook his head. "I examined it. It's

exactly what it appears. He obviously didn't mean to kill you."

"It's beautiful. . . . Why would he want to give me something this beautiful?"

"How does it make you feel?"

"Angry, confused."

"And afraid?"

Was there fear at the core of her emotions? She only knew she felt chilled and shaken. "It's only a piece of jewelry."

"That's disturbing the hell out of you."

"And that's what he wanted. He wants me scared and panicked." She reached out and touched the gold of the ring. It was warm from Trevor's touch but it didn't pierce the chill surrounding her. "And he wants me to know he's not forgotten me."

Trevor nodded. "It's a mind game."

"Bastard."

"If he knows he can't touch you yet, it will probably get worse. A little long-distance torment will be very satisfying to him."

"Do you think he's watching me?"

He shrugged. "Not from anywhere close. I'd guarantee that, Jane."

"And I can guarantee he'll want to see if sending me this . . . thing made a sniveling wreck of me. What kind of satisfaction can he get just from imagining the upset?" She could feel her anger growing by the minute. "Oh, no, he'll want to see that he's hurt me."

"Possibly."

"No, certainly." She snatched the ring from his palm and jammed it on her index finger. "So let's let him see it doesn't mean a damn thing to me."

He threw back his head and laughed. "I should have known. Aldo may have been carrying this bauble around for years but don't you think Quinn will want the ring to try to run a tracer?"

"He can take a photo." The ring felt heavy and tight on her finger, like a python curling around its victim. But she wasn't a victim and she'd prove it to him. Her anger remained but it was now mixed with exhilaration and excitement. "I'm wearing it."

His smile faded. "You're liking this a little too much. What do you have in mind? A little goading to stir the tiger?"

"He's not a tiger, he's a slug. And what do you care if I goad him? It might bring him out into the open."

He was silent a moment. "You're right. It might do that, if he doesn't pounce and tear you to bits." He started down the porch steps. "And, strangely enough, I would care if that happened."

"But you're not trying to talk me out of it."

"No, but then I've always been a son of a bitch. Do what you like. I'll be there for you."

"Sarah just called me." Eve had left her studio and was standing in the living room when Jane walked into the cottage a moment later. "She was concerned. She said you didn't sound like yourself. What's this about a ring, Jane?"

Jane held up her hand with a hint of bravado. "A present from Aldo. A vesuvianite. Pretty, isn't it?"

Eve stiffened. "Don't be flip. What's happening?"

"So much for him forgetting about me and going on to bigger and better kills."

"Sarah said it was mailed from a Mail Boxes Unlimited in Carmel."

"He's not in California. He'd want to see if the ring had the right effect." Her lips tightened. “He probably hopes I’m cowering under the bed.”

“You seem very certain.” Eve crossed the room and took her hand. “It looks Byzantine.”

“I’m sure it’s supposed to look Roman. But what can you expect? He probably took what he could get. Vesuvianite can’t be that readily available.”

“Then it should be easier to trace. Take it off.”

“No.”

“Jane.”

“No.” She pulled her hand away. “I’m wearing it. He’s not going to think he’s scared me. I’ll wear it and I’ll flaunt it as if it were only a pretty bauble a lover had given me.”

“Lover?”

“That’s what Cira would do.” She smiled recklessly. “He thinks I’m Cira? Well, I’ll act like Cira. She’d never let a murdering bastard make her cringe. She’d face him and taunt him and find a way to bring him down.”

“Would she?” Eve’s gaze was narrowed on her face. “And how do you know that, Jane?”

"That's how Trevor describes her." Jane shook her head. "No, I won't lie to you. I *feel* it."

Eve was silent a moment. "Or did you dream it? You never told me the name of the woman in your dream. Was it Cira?"

Smart, savvy Eve. She should have known that the empathy between them was so intense that she'd sense what was going on in Jane's mind. "Yes." She rushed on, "But that isn't— For all I know, I'm picking up Aldo's view of her or maybe Trevor's. It could be I read something sometime and I just don't remember doing it. Or maybe I am having psychic flashes. It's not likely, but I'd rather think that than that I'm nutty enough to believe I know Cira because of a dream."

"I think you're protesting too much," Eve said. "You don't have to make explanations to me. I thought we'd settled that issue." She glanced down at the ring again. "Take it off."

"I told you that—"

"I know what you told me," Eve said curtly. "And I know it's waving a red cape at a bull. Take it off."

"He'll think I'm afraid."

"I don't care."

"I care." She could feel her throat tighten as she looked at Eve. Lord, this was hard. "I love you, Eve. I never want to do anything that will make you unhappy."

"Then take it off."

She shook her head. "You're wrong. We can't give in to him. I might even be able to draw him out and into making a mistake if I annoy him enough. Otherwise, if I take one step back, he'll take one step forward. And I won't be backed into a corner where he can hack my face off." She saw Eve flinch and she hurried on, "I'm sorry. But that's what he wants. He wants me scared and on my knees. We can't give him that."

"I'm not going to give him you either. Why don't—" Eve closed her eyes and drew a deep breath. "I'm wasting my time." She opened her eyes and added wearily, "And maybe you're right. I don't know. But I do know if you're going to wave that ring under Aldo's nose we're going to make sure that you're as safe as you can be." She headed for the phone. "I'm calling Joe. Take that ring off, get the digital camera, and take pictures of it so that he can try to locate who sold it to Aldo."

"Eve—"

"I'm not angry with you." Eve picked up the phone. "I'm just tired and frustrated and I want this maniac caught before he drives all of us crazy." She smiled. "And, no, I'm not saying you're crazy. Obstinate, opinionated, yes. Now go take those photos."

TWELVE

"You're wrong, Jane," Joe said curtly. "You're playing his game."

"No, I'd be playing his game if I hid the ring away." She met his gaze. "And you know it. You just don't want me to take chances. There's an opportunity here. If I was anyone else, you'd admit it." She held out her hand. "Do you think I want to wear it? It makes me sick to my stomach. But it's the right thing to do." She tossed the packet of photos down on the coffee table in front of him. "There are enough photos to start a search for the seller. Trevor said that he may have gotten the ring in Italy years ago."

"We'll see." His lips twisted. "As far as

we know he didn't give any of the other victims jewelry. If he's been carrying it around that long evidently you're considered special."

She made a face. "If I'm special, it's because I'm not a victim. And I won't be."

"We hope," Eve said.

"Think positive." Jane moved toward her bedroom. "I'm going to bed now. If I stay here, you'll try to argue me out of it and that's not going to happen. It will only be hurtful. Good night, Joe."

"Running away isn't going to stop me from—" He muttered a curse as her bedroom door closed gently but firmly behind her. "You talk her out of it, Eve. She listens to you."

"I tried," Eve said quietly. "She's not listening to anyone now. She thinks she's right and she's sticking to it."

"She's only a kid, dammit."

"Really? I believe we had this discussion weeks ago and you were telling me that she's never really been a kid and that was okay."

"That was before we knew Aldo was on the scene. It's not okay now."

"Too late." Eve's faint smile was sad. "We

might have had a chance of bringing a little springtime into her life before this happened, but not now. She's changed."

"She's just gotten more obstinate."

Eve shook her head. "She's formed. I've been watching it happen. She reminds me of one of my reconstructions. I work and I work and I know somewhere beneath my fingers everything is there but it's not ready to come out. Then all of a sudden, it all comes together."

Joe was looking at her with a frown and she tried again. "It's like placing a fine piece of pottery in a kiln. When it goes in, it's soft and still malleable. When it comes out, everything has been burned away but what it is and is going to be forever. Aldo did that to her." Her lips tightened. "May he burn in hell."

"I'll second that." Joe looked down at the photos. "He may not be close enough to her to know she's flaunting that thing."

Eve raised her brows.

"Okay, wishful thinking." He picked up the photos. "I'll fax these to the department and get busy on trying to backtrack that package from that Mail Boxes Unlimited in Carmel."

"She's right, isn't she? Much as we hate it, it's an opportunity."

He nodded as he headed for the fax machine. "Yes, dammit, she's right."

The lamplight made the pale green vesuvianite flash and sparkle like the cold edge of a knife. Aldo liked knives, Jane thought.

Don't look at it. Don't think about what he did with those knives.

She turned out the light and tucked her hand beneath the covers. It didn't help. She could still see it burning, glittering in her mind's eye.

Then accept it. She'd made the decision and she had to live with it. She took her hand from beneath the covers and let it lie on top of the counterpane. Aldo had handled this ring. He'd touched it and looked at the glowing stone and thought about how it would disturb her. She could almost see him smiling and fondling it.

Well, it's mine now. And I won't let it be anything to me that I don't want it to be. So screw you, Aldo.

She closed her eyes and willed herself to go to sleep. She would not dream of Cira and she would not dream of Aldo. Close them out, rest, and gain strength and determination.

No, don't sleep. Think. Go over everything she knew about Aldo and find a way to bring him down. She was tired of hiding and letting him think he could terrorize her. The situation had to change. She had to make a move.

Sorry, Eve. . . .

The next morning Bartlett, as usual, was standing in front of the cottage. He smiled gently as Jane walked toward him. "Good morning. I hear there was a little disturbance with the mail last night."

"A little. Where's Trevor?"

"With Matt Singer double-checking security. He should be here soon. You can reach him by cell phone if it's important."

She shook her head. "I want to talk to him face-to-face."

"I see. Well, I'll be glad of your company while you're waiting." His gaze went to her hand and his smile faded. "Trevor is right, you really shouldn't be wearing that."

"Trevor didn't try to stop me."

"I know. He said it was up to you. It didn't surprise me. Though I was disappointed."

"Why?"

"I like him. But I'd like him more if he'd admit that he isn't as hard as he pretends."

"I don't believe there's much pretense about it."

"That's because he's extremely good at it."

"Like the time he was pretending to be from Scotland Yard investigating your wife's death? Evidently he didn't fool you."

He smiled. "Almost. But I knew he wasn't a policeman when I followed him to Claridge's. Policemen don't usually have the funds for elite accommodations."

"But smugglers and con men do?"

"Exactly. And after I became acquainted with Trevor I realized my best chance of getting Ellen's killer was with him. He had dedication." He added gravely, "Dedication is important."

"So is honesty. How many times has he lied to you?"

"Only the one time. He is honest in his own way."

She shook her head. "I don't understand

that kind of honesty. It's either one way or the other."

"Black or white? I'm afraid Trevor is definitely in the gray areas. But that's better than being black, isn't it? A man of his capabilities could be a superb villain. It must be a great temptation to him."

"He told me how much he liked money."

He nodded. "So he says."

"You don't believe him?"

"Oh, I believe he likes it. He grew up poor and had to fight his way. But there are easier ways to acquire money when you're as brilliant as Trevor. He doesn't have to walk a tightrope. I think he got a taste of it when he was a kid and over the years it's become an addiction."

"Is that why he's after Aldo? Not the gold, just the thrill of the chase?"

"No, I think it's a little more personal than that. Did he tell you Pietro Tatligno was a mercenary with him in Colombia?"

Her eyes widened. "No, he just said he was an antiquities scholar."

"And a very brilliant one, but he sowed a few wild oats before he gave up the military life and went back to school. Evidently he and Trevor became very good friends and it was Trevor who brought him to Guido Manza."

"You're saying he's after Aldo because of guilt?"

"Trevor would deny it. He says guilt is nonproductive." He smiled. "He might even tell you he was after Aldo because Aldo double-crossed him."

"He did say Pietro didn't deserve to die."

"Ah, maybe he's getting close to admitting the truth." He shook his head as he looked down at her ring. "It's very pretty, isn't it? It's a terrible thing to use beauty to bring fear."

"It only brings fear if you let it. It's only a ring."

"And she's not about to let it," Trevor said from behind her. "I take it Quinn wasn't able to persuade you to shed it."

"No." She turned to watch him come toward her. He looked wired, restless, and she was again aware of that barely contained energy he exuded with every movement. "It's my ring. My choice."

"True." He stopped before her. "But since I'm not as ethical as Quinn I might try to manipulate circumstances to make your choice be my choice."

"Joe's honest but he's not above doing that, too. So maybe you're more alike than you think."

He grimaced. "Don't tell him that. He wouldn't be flattered. He's a straight arrow and I'm nowhere near straight. I prefer the path untraveled and most of those are as twisted as a snake's back."

She nodded. "Twisted. That's why I came out to talk to you."

"I told her that she could call you and you'd come," Bartlett said.

"Anytime." He stared her directly in the eye. "Anywhere."

She felt . . . strange. Breathless. She glanced hurriedly away. "Easy to say. You couldn't have been more than a mile down the road."

He smiled. "But you still didn't phone me. Because you preferred to quiz my friend, Bartlett, about me?"

"I'm touched." Bartlett beamed. "Do you know that's the first time you admitted I was your friend? How encouraging."

Trevor shook his head resignedly. "Do you know he really means it? You can't fight it." He took her arm. "Come on, I have to get out from under his shadow. All that sweetness and light makes me look bad in comparison."

"It shouldn't," Bartlett called after them. "I did my best to make you appear to advantage. It was quite difficult."

"I don't doubt it." Trevor glanced down at her as they moved down the path. "Did you laugh in his face?"

"No, I wouldn't hurt his feelings."

"Perish the thought. Are you going to be in line to be wife number four?"

"I didn't come down here to talk about Bartlett." She stopped and turned to face him. "And you know it. So why are you trying to keep me from saying what I mean to say?"

"Maybe I'm enjoying myself. From the moment I met you it's all been tension, defensiveness, and suspicion. I like to see you like this."

"Like what?"

"Sort of soft. I don't give myself credit for any change of demeanor but I've always been one to take advantage of any break I'm given."

"I'm not soft. I don't pretend to be."

"Most people have a soft side. You show

yours to Eve and Quinn and Toby." He wrinkled his nose. "And now to Bartlett."

"That's different."

"And that's what I'm saying. Refreshing." He held up his hand as she started to speak. "Okay, I can see you're growing impatient. Fire when ready."

"You said that Aldo was a computer genius. When you were hobnobbing together in Herculaneum how much did you find out about his surfing habits?"

"Internet surfing?"

"What else?"

"First, we weren't hobnobbing. Second, why the hell do you want to know?"

"I'm not sure. Something keeps nagging at me but it's not clear yet. I'm sure you weren't bosom buddies but you were both computer geeks. You had that in common and you were isolated together in the tunnel. You must have communicated on some level."

"What are you digging for?"

She shrugged. "Everyone has favorite Internet sites they go to almost every day. I know I do."

"So do I." He was frowning. "You want to know what sites are Aldo's favorites?"

"Do you know?"

"Probably. As you said, we had that in common and I admired his expertise. We didn't share information but I did watch him occasionally."

"Can you remember?"

"It's been a long time."

"Can you remember?"

He nodded slowly. "That entire period is pretty well carved into my memory. What do you want from me?"

"I want you to make a list of all his preferred sites."

"I may not remember all of them, Jane."

"Well, whatever you do remember. Anything."

"Why?"

"It's a starting place. I don't know where else we can go. I was lying in bed last night and trying to think of any way to get to Aldo before he got to me. But I don't know anything about him. Not really." She made a helpless gesture with her hand. "There's so little . . . He's nuts. He thinks I'm Cira's reincarnation, and he uses computers. I picked the most concrete thing to work on."

"And how do you intend to use it once I

rack my memory and furnish you with the info you need?"

"I told you. I'm not sure yet."

He studied her expression. "You may not be sure but you have an idea where you're going with this. I could hold out and force you to share."

"And I'd resent the force and you'd have the devil of a time getting me to cooperate with you for the foreseeable future."

"That's true." He smiled. "I just thought I'd bluff a bit. I don't like being left in the dark but I'll be patient. I know I'll be the first you'll tell when it all comes together."

"Why?"

"Because you realize I'll help you. I won't argue. I won't try to keep you from sticking your neck out. If you have a chance of getting him, I'll let you run the risks." He paused. "Even if it means taking you away from Eve and Quinn and that blanket of protection they've wrapped around you."

She was disappointed, she realized in surprise. Why? It was what she'd expected, what she needed from him. "Good. When can you have the list for me?"

"Tonight. Is that soon enough?"

"It will have to be." She turned away.

"And I'm going to be busy this afternoon anyway."

He stiffened. "Doing what?"

"I'm going to the mall and then to have a pizza at CiCi's."

"What the hell? And you think Quinn will allow that?"

"Not without a fight. But he'll let me go in the end. He won't want to miss the opportunity of drawing Aldo. I'll ask Eve to go with me and Joe will have Singer assign someone to follow us."

"I suppose I don't have to guess why you've decided that you have to go shopping and are ignoring the fact that Domino's delivers?"

"He'll consider a crowded mall safe and a restaurant will give me a chance to display his little gift." She lifted her hand so that the sunlight caused the stone to blaze with color. "He has to see me. I have to push him. I have to make him angry and uncertain. He's killed twelve women that we know about, and never been caught. That must make him feel confident, even godlike. He probably thinks all he has to do is wait for an opportunity and he'll chalk up number thirteen." She smiled without mirth.

"But we have to make sure thirteen is his unlucky number. Catch him off balance and keep pulling the rug from beneath him until he topples."

"And you think flashing that ring is going to help?"

"It's a start. If it doesn't shake him, I'll make sure it irritates him."

"I'm sure you will." He was silent a moment. "I'd enjoy seeing you in action. I may have to go along and watch."

She shook her head. "You have work to do. And I don't want him to see me under any obvious surveillance. It's much more effective to seem to have only Eve with me to show him how little he matters."

"He wouldn't see me."

"I thought you were going to let me take my own risks."

He shrugged. "It's not as easy as I thought. I'm working on it."

"Work harder." She started toward the cottage. "You stay here."

She was flushed, radiant, beautiful.

And triumphant.

Aldo tried to suppress the anger that

burned through him while he watched her laughing with Eve Duncan as they crossed the parking lot toward the restaurant. Now the bitch was gesturing, every motion causing the ring on her hand to glitter.

It had been the same in the mall. She had been glowing, every feature of her face animated and so alive it had been like a slap in the face to him.

She was taunting him not only with his gift but with her living presence.

She wasn't afraid. The ring had meant nothing to her; the implied threat had brought only laughter.

He could feel the rage break free and tear through him. How dare she? Couldn't she see that her time had come and he was the sword that was going to stab her to her black heart?

Keep calm. She would learn. Every slight would be revenged in time. He'd carve that smile from her face.

Bitch!

But he couldn't tolerate the knowledge that she had been so scornful of him, that she'd dared to treat him as if he were of no importance. He couldn't sit here and let her do that. He had to show her. He had to make her realize with whom she was dealing.

"Satisfied?" Eve asked Jane quietly as she drove up the road toward the lake cottage. "You look like a truck ran over you."

"I feel like it." Jane leaned back in the seat and closed her eyes. "I never imagined being this cheerful would be such a strain. I'm exhausted."

"So am I," Eve said dryly. "But I'm tired from glancing discreetly over my shoulder."

"Very discreetly." Jane opened her eyes and smiled. "Thank you for that. It wouldn't have done me any good to show how uncaring of Aldo I was if you were looking worried."

"I know that." She parked the car in front of the cottage. "And I wasn't about to go through all this stress for nothing." She turned and looked at Jane. "Was it for nothing? Do you think he was watching?"

Lord, I hope he'd been there, Jane thought wearily. "I don't know. A few times I felt as if . . . Maybe. It was worth a try."

"Once," Eve said. "Joe and I went along

with you but you'll have a battle if you decide to make this a daily outing."

Jane nodded as she got out of the car. "Definitely not daily."

"That's a little noncommittal," Eve said. "I meant a permanent end to—" She stopped. "Okay, let's be reasonable about this. If you continue, you'll form a pattern of behavior and the last thing you want is to be predictable. That can be fatal."

Jane smiled. "I agree. We won't be predictable."

Eve relaxed. "I'm glad you said 'we.' You're getting a little too independent for Joe and me. It scares us."

Jane shook her head. "I came to you and asked you to come with me, didn't I? I don't want to be independent if it means closing you out. I was too much alone when I was a kid. It sucks."

Eve chuckled. "Yes, it does." She took Jane's arm and climbed the porch steps. "As you put it so delicately. It sucks big-time." She looked out over the lake. "Pretty sunset. I never get tired of them. They soothe the soul."

Jane shook her head. "Not for me. I take

a lot more soothing than a sunset. But you do the job just fine."

"Do I?" Eve looked at her uncertainly. "You never showed me you needed soothing."

"Because you were always there. You didn't have to do anything." She opened the screen door. "Do you want me to help with dinner?"

Eve shook her head. "I'll make a salad and sandwiches later when Joe comes in."

"Then I'll get my computer and sit out on the porch and do some homework." She went down the hall toward her bedroom. "Don't bother to fix me anything. I'm not hungry after that pizza. I didn't taste much of it, but it filled me. . . ."

She'd barely opened the computer when her cell phone rang.

"Whore. Bitch. Prancing and wriggling like the prostitute you are. Are you proud of yourself? Do you really think you proved anything by wearing that ring? It meant *nothing* to me."

She froze.

Aldo. His words spewing rage, ugliness, and malice.

Don't fall apart. She should have realized he'd be able to find her cell number. Don't let him see the shock and fear. "It meant nothing to me either. Just a little trinket. Why shouldn't I wear it? I'm sorry you're so disappointed."

"It's from your mountain, the one that killed you. Doesn't it bring back memories? I hope you choke on them."

"I've no idea what you mean. And do you believe I'd actually let you keep me penned up in this cottage? I'll go where I please. Do you know I got a compliment on this ring from the waitress at CiCi's? I told her it was given to me by a man who followed me around like a lost puppy. We both laughed about it."

"Lost puppy?" She could hear the rage vibrating in his voice. "Do you realize how powerful I am? How many women with your foul face I've slaughtered?"

"I don't want to know." She paused. "Why are you calling me now, Aldo? You've never done it before. I think you lied. I did manage to get under your skin."

"It meant nothing," he repeated. "I just

decided there was no reason to withhold myself from you. It may be a long time before I take your life. Months. Years. I don't care how long it takes now that I've found you. As long as I watch you, guard you, you'll never get away from me. But I deserve the pleasure of getting closer to you, hearing your voice, listening as you become more and more afraid. It's my right."

"And it's my right to hang up on you."

"But you won't do it. You'll keep on talking because you're hoping I'll tell you something that will lead Trevor and Quinn to me. And every word you say gives me a burst of pleasure."

She felt sick with revulsion. He meant it. She could hear the feverish excitement mixed with the anger in his tone. But he was right, she had to take advantage of the opportunity. "Just who do you think I am?"

"I don't think, I know. You're Cira. I thought I'd buried you in that tunnel but I realized after I killed that woman in Rome that you were too strong not to be able to be born again. I knew I had to search until I found you."

"You're certifiably nuts. I'm not Cira, I'm Jane MacGuire."

"With Cira's soul. And you know it. Why else did you attach yourself to a forensic sculptor like Eve Duncan? You knew I'd come to destroy that hideous face and you wanted to make sure that it survived. It won't survive. Do you know how many times I woke up at night and watched my father staring at you? I can't remember him ever touching me with affection but he'd stroke that damn bust like it was a woman he loved. I tried to destroy it when I was ten and he beat me until I couldn't walk for a week."

"Am I supposed to feel sorry for you? He should have drowned you at birth."

"He probably thought the same thing. I was just an encumbrance to him after you came into his life. But now I'll get my own back. So enjoy your feeling of triumph. Sit in that cottage surrounded by all those people you've duped to do your will. You'll rot there, bitch." He hung up.

She couldn't move to turn off her phone. She felt as if she'd been scourged, beaten. Dear God, he was brimming, frothing with hatred. The poison was all-consuming and paralyzing.

Get over it. Aldo wanted her to feel this

weak and helpless. Think about what he said and try to find something positive in all that ugliness. She forced herself to turn off the phone and lean back in the swing.

Positive?

My God.

"Mail," Trevor said as he came up the steps an hour later. "Nothing for you but a letter from— What the hell is wrong with you?"

"I'm okay." She wasn't okay, but she was better. She wasn't surprised that Trevor had noticed how disturbed she was. She felt as if it were written in every line of her expression. That was the reason she hadn't wanted to go inside and face Eve. She added haltingly, "It's not been an easy day."

"It was your choice to flaunt that blasted ring in Aldo's face." His gaze was searching her expression. "But I didn't expect this reaction."

"Neither did I." She tried to smile. "And I guess I shouldn't complain. Actually, I suppose my little jaunt was a complete success. I was trying to goad him to make a move and I certainly accomplished that aim."

"What?"

"Aldo called me." She looked down at the phone still in her hand. "About an hour ago."

"Holy shit. What did he say?"

"He was angry. He didn't like the fact that his gift didn't seem to bother me. It was . . . ugly." She moistened her lips. "He was muttering about me having Cira's soul and how he hated— My God, he hates my face. He's on some kind of mission to rid the world of it. You were right, he was killing her in effigy with all those other murders."

"But he didn't call any of the others to chat," he said grimly. "And he didn't squander pretty trinkets on them."

"None of them made him as angry as I did. I've been sitting here trying to think of something constructive that could come out of this but it's hard. One thing, he's going to phone me again. He believes it's his just reward. On the negative side, he said he could wait a long time to kill me, that he was in no hurry. He wants to break me, make me afraid." Her hands clenched into fists. "Well, *I'm* in a hurry. I can't take much more of this."

"We made progress today. He called you."

"It's not enough. He meant what he said. He'll wait until he's wrung every bit of pleasure from the situation." Her lips tightened. "He was . . . foul. I've never touched anything that ugly. He . . . made me afraid. I can't let that happen again."

"We can have Quinn check phone records to try to trace him."

She nodded. "I thought of that. But I doubt if he'd have called if he hadn't thought it was safe."

"We'll try anyway."

"Of course." She straightened on the swing. "We'll do everything we can. I'll talk to Joe and Eve later tonight."

"Not now?"

"I don't want them to see me like this—not now." Talking to Trevor had eased the sick fear that Aldo had engendered, but she had to move away from it, drown the memory of that call for a while. Her glance went to the envelope still in his hand. "You said I had a letter?"

He didn't speak for a moment and then smiled faintly. "Yes, from Harvard. Did you apply there?"

He was letting her slide away from the subject, she realized with relief.

"Yes, I applied for early acceptance." She took the letter without opening it. "Maybe I've been accepted." She tossed it down on the porch swing. "That would be nice."

"Your enthusiasm is astonishing."

"I'm not sure I want to go to an Ivy League school. But Joe went there and he liked it. Where's my list?"

He reached in his pocket and handed her a slip of paper. "This is all I can remember and he may not go to these sites anymore."

"And he may." She glanced over the list. "Two of these are Italian Web sites. One English newspaper . . ."

"He went to Oxford for two years. He liked to keep in touch."

"And this one in Florence, *La Nazione.* Is that a newspaper too?"

He nodded. "He grew up there. Most people keep an eye on their hometowns. He also went to another newspaper site in Rome, *Corriere della Sera*."

She pointed to another site. "And this one?"

"*Archaeology Journal*? It's a weekly

magazine and practically the professional bible of modern-day archaeology."

"But he was an actor. It was his father who was the archaeologist. He probably skips this one now."

"No, there are often articles about Pompeii and Herculaneum. He has a vested interest."

She'd gone on to another site. "This one's in Rome, too. Another newspaper?"

He smiled. "No, one of Italy's premier porn sites. Very explicit, very kinky. You can bet he's still interested in visiting that one occasionally."

"What kind of kinky?"

"I was curious, too, when I watched him bring up the site so I checked it out. They specialize in sadomasochism and necrophilia."

"Raping dead people?" She shivered. "Creepy."

"And it confirmed my belief that Aldo was not a nice fellow."

"You said he didn't rape any of the victims after those first women he killed in Rome."

"That doesn't mean he's not interested in sex. Maybe he didn't consider any of the others worthy. Or these days he may get off on the kill itself."

She moistened her lips. "Those women he raped. Was it before or after he killed them?"

"After."

"Sick."

"No question. Do you need to know anything else?"

"I'll let you know." Her tone was abstracted as she went over the list. "I may be able to figure out the rest. I can go to a gateway site and get a rough translation."

"Then I'm dismissed?"

"For now."

"And am I going to be allowed to know what the hell you're planning on doing with it?"

She glanced up. "Oh, yes. I'm going to need you."

"I'll take comfort in that." He turned to leave. "I don't imagine you admit you need many people."

"No."

"Can you give me a time estimate?"

She shook her head. "I have to think about it and do some research."

"And you have to recover a little from Aldo's verbal assault."

"I'm already recovering." It was the truth, thank heavens. The distraction had diluted the emotional impact of Aldo's venom. "It was stupid to become upset. After all, his call was actually a victory. And it clarified his attitude and intentions."

"And I'd judge it also clarified your attitude and reinforced your determination to move at light-speed."

"It didn't take much reinforcement."

"No, you're at full throttle." He lifted his brows. "I can't wait to see where you're going with it."

"Neither can I," she said dryly. "I just hope it's not a blind alley."

"Then there's usually a way to backtrack and find your way out."

Heat. Night without air.

Run. Falling rocks. Pain.

"I don't want to backtrack." Her lips tightened. "I need to go straight ahead and run over that bastard if he gets in my way."

He gave a low whistle. "I'll vote for that." He started down the steps. "And I'll furnish the bulldozer to do it. Just say the word."

She didn't answer, her gaze once more on the list.

Trevor shook his head ruefully as he moved down the path toward Bartlett. She was so intent, she'd closed out the call from Aldo and she'd probably already forgotten Trevor. Not good for a man's ego.

What the hell. He couldn't apply any of the usual man-woman rules to his relationship with Jane.

He'd better not.

"She's excited." Bartlett's gaze was fixed on Jane. "She looks like you gave her a present."

"In a manner of speaking. Not a box of chocolates or a bouquet. A list of Aldo's Web sites."

"I see." Bartlett nodded gravely. "Much more valuable than a box of chocolates and she's not one to appreciate sweetness."

"Maybe she's not had the opportunity to really sample it."

Her head was bent over the list and he could see the tenseness, the taut, slim elegance of her body as she reached for her computer. She did everything with a natural grace that was as unconscious as it was a delight to watch. There was youth without the awkwardness of youth. Grace and fire. She burned like a candle in the—

"No, Trevor."

He glanced at Bartlett. "What?"

Bartlett was shaking his head, his expression troubled. "She's too young."

"Do you think I don't know that?" He tried to pull his gaze away from her. God, it was hard. "It doesn't hurt to look."

"It might. She's not a statue and she's not Cira."

"No?" His lips twisted. "Tell that to Aldo."

"I'm telling you." Barlett frowned. "And I shouldn't have to tell you. You could hurt her."

He smiled recklessly. "She'd deny it. She'd say she was far more likely to hurt me."

"But you know that's not true. Experience counts, and she's seventeen."

He turned away. "Why are we even talking about it? I told you I wasn't going to do anything but look."

"I hope not."

"Count on it." He went down the path.

"I'll come back and relieve you in an hour. She spent all afternoon taunting Aldo and he's mad as hell. I want to be around if he decides to pounce."

THIRTEEN

"You've been watching me all evening. I feel like a bug under a microscope." Eve turned away from the reconstruction on the pedestal before her to look at Jane. "Is something wrong? Are you still upset about that call from Aldo?"

"A little." She made a face. "You can understand it would stick in my mind."

"That goes without saying. It's been worrying me since you told me about it."

"But you'll be able to forget it once you get deep enough into your work. That's a blessing, isn't it?"

"Work is always a great healer." She frowned. "Have you been concerned that you're interfering with my work on this reconstruction?"

Jane shook her head. "I was just wondering if you were almost finished."

"Tomorrow. I might have finished tonight if you hadn't decided on dragging me out this afternoon."

"You didn't object."

"And I wouldn't again. Keeping you alive is more important than identifying this poor dead girl."

"What are you calling her?"

"Lucy." Her hands moved over the skull, carefully measuring the space between the eyes. "The Chicago police think she may be a child that's been missing for over fifteen years. Her parents must be going through hell."

"Like you."

Eve didn't deny it. "At least I can give other parents back their children. I suppose that's a form of closure."

"Bull. Very noble but it doesn't keep you from hurting."

"No." Eve smiled faintly. "May I ask why you're so interested in my work tonight?"

"I'm always interested. It's kind of creepy but it's part of you."

"The creepy part."

"You said it." Jane grinned. "I wouldn't dare. So Lucy is winging her way back to Chicago tomorrow?"

"Probably." Eve lifted her brows. "Is it important that she be finished quickly?"

"Maybe. I've been sitting here and thinking. . . ." Her gaze focused musingly on the skull. "How does she . . . feel?"

"Touching her face?" She was silent, thinking about it. "Not creepy. I've done it so long that it's difficult to describe."

"Pity?"

"Yes, and anger and sadness." She gently touched Lucy's cheek. "And a deep, deep urgency to bring her home. Home has always been so important to me. There are so many lost ones out there."

"I've heard you say that before. Do you really think that her soul is somewhere wandering around and that she cares about being brought home?"

"I don't know. Maybe. But I do know I care." Eve smoothed the clay at Lucy's forehead. "Now go to bed and let me work or I'll never get her finished."

"Okay." Jane stood up. "I was just curious."

"Jane."

Jane glanced back over her shoulder.

"Why now?" Eve asked. "You've never been this curious about my work before."

Jane turned back to face her. "I've never been brought this close to the possibility of my own death before. It's bound to make you wonder what's out there for us."

"Right now, the only thing out there for you is a long and happy life."

"Don't worry. I'm not being gloomy and pessimistic. I don't know why all this came tumbling out of left field. I was sitting here watching you and thinking about something completely different when it occurred to me . . ." She paused. "Cira is one of those lost ones. Nobody seems to know what happened to her. She probably died in that eruption."

"Two thousand years ago, Jane."

"Does time make a difference? Lost is lost."

"No, I guess not. It's just that it takes away the personal, familiar factor."

"No, I don't agree." She reached up and touched her own cheekbone and traced the line to her temple. "I'm taking this very personally. She had my face."

"And it bothers you that she's one of the lost ones?"

"I don't know. Maybe she wasn't lost at all. Maybe she wasn't killed. Maybe she lived to be a hundred with her great-great-grandchildren all around her."

"It's possible."

"Yeah, but I've been asking myself, what if you're right and lost souls have a passion to come home? What if these dreams I've been having have been her way of telling me that she needs to be found and brought to a final resting place?"

"Is that what you think? I have to point out that it's a totally unrealistic conclusion."

"Because it's your duty." She was silent a moment. "I'm not sure what's real anymore and I don't believe you are either. It makes as much sense as thinking I'm picking up psychic vibrations." She grimaced. "But it would help if I had a little guidance. Perhaps you should ask Bonnie what's happening to me."

"Is that a joke?"

"Not an unkind one. She rules your world and that's fine with me. Just thought we'd put her to work." She moved down the hall.

"Forget it. We'll work everything out for ourselves. But try to finish Lucy tonight."

She booted up her laptop as soon as she reached her bedroom, and went immediately to the Archaeology Journal site. Very dry stuff. It was hard to believe a sicko like Aldo would be interested in it. No articles in the current issue about Herculaneum.

She tensed, drew a deep breath, and accessed the porn site. She'd glanced through it earlier but she had to be sure. . . . After five minutes she had to get out of it. Horrible. It seemed impossible that anyone could relish this kind of obscenity. Forget it. Go on to the next site. They were all forming a picture of Aldo that was growing clearer by the minute.

She finished the last site on Trevor's list at 3:42 A.M. and leaned back and tried to suppress her growing excitement. Would it work?

Chancy at best. Success would depend on many factors, including the elusive power of luck.

Well, they were due for some good luck, dammit.

She reached for her telephone and began to dial.

The sun was shining through the windows and bathing Eve and Joe in clear light as they sat at the breakfast table. Warm. Loving. Serene. So different from Aldo's dark world that Jane had been delving into last night.

Jane stood looking at them for an instant, hesitating. Stop it. You've made up your mind. Now go for it.

"Good morning." She strode toward them. "I didn't hear you come in last night, Joe." She went to the refrigerator and took out the orange juice. "Were you late?"

"Yes." He took a sip of his coffee. "But you should have heard me. I saw the light under your door."

"I was busy." She poured her juice. "How's Lucy coming, Eve?"

"Finished." Eve smiled faintly. "As you ordered, little madam."

"You know I wouldn't—" She broke off as she met Eve's knowing gaze. "Busted?"

"Busted. What are you up to?"

"I had to make sure your decks were

cleared." She lifted her glass to her lips. "I'm going to need you." She turned to Joe. "And you, too."

"I'm honored not to be left out," he said dryly. "Are you going to let us into your confidence or are we supposed to guess?"

"I would have talked to you before but I had to be sure. . . ." She moistened her lips. "I was confused. There were too many lost pieces and I had to fill in the blanks. Otherwise you'd blow me out of the water. I couldn't let that happen."

"What the hell are you talking about?"

"We can't sit here and wait for Aldo to come after me. I thought maybe I could find a way to draw him out in the open. But after talking to him, I realize it's going to take something pretty strong to make him lose his cool. He'll just sit and wait and I can't take that. We have to go after him."

"We *are* going after him," Joe said sharply. "Why do you think I've been spending eighteen hours a day at the precinct? We're gathering information, we're sifting evidence, we're collating. We'll get there."

"And it's driving you crazy. That's not the

way you like to operate," Jane said. "You want to go after him, too."

"It's safer this way."

"He's not in any hurry. He thinks he's found Cira and he's willing to wait for his opportunity. It could take years of cat-and-mouse. I'm not giving him my years. I want to live them to the hilt." She turned to Eve. "I think I know a way to bring him out in the open, if you'll help me."

"How?"

At least they were listening. "Wait just a moment." She headed for the front door. "I called Trevor last night and told him to come here." She gestured to Trevor, who was standing outside talking to Bartlett. "We'll need him."

"You told Trevor about this before you talked to us?" Joe asked.

She shook her head. "That wouldn't have been fair. He just knows that I'm ready."

"Ready for what?" Joe asked.

"Easy," Eve said quietly. "Listen, Joe. She's trying to tell us."

"It could work," Jane said. "I know it could work." She turned to Trevor, who had just come into the room. "Tell Joe that we haven't been conspiring behind his back."

Trevor shrugged. "I came because I got the royal summons. I gave her the list she wanted and she sent me on my way."

"What list?"

Trevor nodded at Jane. "Over to you."

"Aldo is a computer geek. It's the one interest Trevor found he had a passion for other than his acting. Trevor gave me a list of the sites he noticed Aldo frequenting most often."

"Give it to me."

"I will. After I finish." She turned back to Eve. "But Aldo's overwhelming passion is his desire to revenge himself on Cira."

"You mean on all her look-alikes."

"It's still Cira in his mind."

"So?"

"What if he had a chance to revenge himself on the real Cira?"

Eve frowned. "What?"

"As well as skeletons there were bodies found almost perfectly preserved at Pompeii and Herculaneum. What if he found out that they'd unearthed an anteroom off the theater at Herculaneum and discovered the skeleton of a woman who'd been killed the day of the eruption?"

"Cira?"

Trevor gave a low whistle. "Holy shit."

"Trevor, you said there were several statues of Cira commissioned by Julius. Considering how famous she was, it wouldn't be too unlikely that there would be one of her found in the anteroom of the theater where she died. Wouldn't mention of a statue immediately pique Aldo's interest?"

"Absolutely."

"Of course, we couldn't announce the discovery right away. We'd have to leak the information to make sure it was believable."

"How?" Eve asked.

"Use the Web sites I furnished her," Trevor said. "Three were newspapers. One was an archaeology magazine. I believe she's hinting that I do a little manipulation of the content."

"And you're so good at that," Joe said sarcastically.

"He might need your help," Jane said. "We wouldn't want him to be caught and have them issue a retraction. But if you could have the local police quiet any protests from the publisher we'd be safe."

"And why would he go after the bones of a dead woman when he could go after you?" Eve asked.

"He smashed a statue of her in effigy even before he started killing those women. He told me he thought he'd destroyed her when he blew that tunnel. But he's lived with her image too long, she's still alive for him." She paused. "And when I was talking to him I realized why. It's her face. Whenever he sees a face that resembles hers, it triggers memories and then it triggers the killings. He can't stand even the chance of seeing her face, having it exist somewhere in the world. What if we rubbed his ugly mug in that phobia? What if we made Cira a household name? What if he couldn't pick up a newspaper or switch on a TV without seeing Cira? What if she became as famous as Nefertiti?"

"Jackpot," Trevor murmured.

"I hope." She grimaced. "And one of his favorite Internet sites is a porn site dealing with necrophilia. It's not unreasonable to assume he'd jump at the chance to humiliate her in that way."

Eve shuddered. "It's difficult to believe he could—" She shook her head. "What a beast."

"But we have to make sure it's a temptation he can't resist." Jane paused again. "We've got to make it a doubleheader."

Eve stiffened. "Go on."

"I have to be there. Cira and I have to be together."

"No!" Joe said.

Eve was studying her expression. "Why?"

"Because I'm not certain the draw of Cira present isn't stronger than Cira past. But if we're together, then he'll feel he can gather us both in one swoop. He can destroy Cira's remains once and for all and kill me."

"And he'll consider it a threat that Jane is going to the place where Cira's bones were found," Trevor said. "After the reconstruction it would magnify the story and get more publicity, more faces in the media."

"Reconstruction," Eve repeated slowly.

"I didn't mention it to him," Jane said quickly. "He just followed my line of thought."

"And now I'm following it," Eve said. "Elaborate."

"You're the key. You'd be the final threat to turn Cira into a world-famous image if you did a reconstruction on the skeleton."

"Go on."

"How many times have you been invited to do a forensic reconstruction by foreign governments and museums? It wouldn't be too far out to have them come knocking on your door to verify that the skeleton is Cira's."

Trevor nodded. "And that you'd go, considering the fact that Aldo will know I told you that Cira was his motivation."

"And we all know what your motivation is, Trevor," Joe said dryly.

"And you should be glad it's so strong," Trevor said. "You'll be going into my territory and you'll need all the help you can get."

"Your territory?"

"The art of the con." Trevor smiled. "A very big, complicated, twisted con."

"And you're looking forward to it."

"You bet your life." He said to Eve, "But Jane's right, it will all revolve around you. There has to be a thread of truth in any lie to make it believable and you're our thread."

"Should I be flattered?"

"Do you think I'm stupid? I know better than to try to butter you up. I'm just stating the way I see it."

Eve was silent a moment. "You think it will work?"

"I think it has a chance. Jane's hit on a way to use Aldo's obsession. Providing it's presented to him in the right way."

"And that's your job?"

"I can't think of anyone more qualified."

"Neither can I," Jane said. "That's why you're here."

"It sounds damn chancy to me," Joe said.

"I don't care what it sounds like," Jane said. "As long as it gives us a chance to draw Aldo out of the shadows."

"And exactly what are we going to do once we get the bastard's attention?"

Jane shook her head. "We'll have to play it by ear and work it out. But no matter how difficult it is to find a way to trap him, we're still a step ahead. We'll have the advantage as long as he thinks we have something he wants. He wants Cira and he wants me. He'll be playing on our ball field and there's a chance we can catch him in a mistake if we can make him frantic enough." She couldn't read Joe's expression, dammit. She added persuasively, "It's what you were trying to do when you were following him to Charlotte and Richmond, wasn't it? Only this will knock him off-balance. It will give us a chance and, in the end, it will be safest for me."

"Bullshit."

"Okay, then it will put an end to this nightmare. This standoff with Aldo could last for years if we don't do something." She turned to Eve. "Help me."

Eve stared at her and then slowly shook her head. "Don't push me. This whole idea scares the hell out of me. I need time." She rose to her feet. "Come on, Joe. Let's take a walk by the lake and talk."

"Eve . . ."

"I said you'll have to wait." Eve shook her head ruefully. "In some ways you're so grown up, but you still have the impatience of youth. Nothing you say is going to change my mind. Joe and I will set the pace and do what we think is right." She headed for the door Joe was holding open for her. "We'll let you know."

Jane's hands clenched into fists as she watched them go down the steps. "Why can't they see it's the right thing to do?" she muttered. "It's so clear to me."

Trevor smiled. "God, they're right. You

are still a kid. I'm profoundly glad for this moment of revelation. I needed it."

"What?"

"Never mind. It's clear to me, too. It's a good plan and we can keep you safe if we work at it. So they should come around to our way of thinking." He opened the door. "Let's go out on the porch and wait for them."

"Okay, it's a go," Joe said when he and Eve came up the steps an hour later. "But you don't do anything, go anywhere, without consulting with us first. It's a team effort or we pull the plug."

Relief surged through her. "I've no intention of going off on a tangent by myself," she said. "The whole basis of the plan is that it will take cooperation from all of us."

"And that's why we're agreeing to do it," Eve said. "It's the only way we can be sure that you won't strike out on your own."

"Very perceptive," Trevor murmured.

"You know I wouldn't want to do that," Jane said.

"But you're not saying it's not a possibility." Eve shook her head. "I know you. Do you think I couldn't see it coming?"

"I wouldn't do it willingly." Jane shrugged. "Anyway, it's a moot point now." She turned to Trevor. "How do we start?"

"Slowly." He smiled as Jane gave him a frustrated glance. "Patience is golden."

"Patience sucks." She scowled. "And I'm getting sick and tired of everyone thinking that dragging your heels is a sign of maturity."

He chuckled. "I was waiting for that." He turned to Joe and Eve. "I'll need some information from both of you. I've put on a pot of coffee. Let's have a powwow." He opened the door and gestured. "I've had a few thoughts while we've been standing around here waiting for you. I want to get started." He glanced at Jane. "And maybe I'm a little impatient myself."

Jane could see that in his expression. Impatient and eager and excited. She could almost forgive him for being patronizing.

Almost.

"How very immature of you." She sailed ahead of him into the house.

* * *

Eve didn't wait for Jane to finish pouring the coffee before she was questioning Trevor. "Let's have it. What do you need to know?"

"Do you have any contacts with any of the forensic departments in Italy?"

"No. I've done some work with the forensic team in Dublin but not anywhere else in Europe."

"Any work on ancient skulls?"

"I was sent an Egyptian skull that was believed to be Nefertiti's."

"Was it?"

"Forensics said that she was probably related but the reconstruction didn't look like the statue."

"But the job still furnishes you with the necessary qualifications. Nefertiti . . . That's very good." Trevor took the cup Jane handed him. "Who requested your help? The museum? The government?"

She shook her head. "The archaeologist in charge of the dig. He was an American and I'd done some work on a skull he'd found in a Navajo site in Arizona."

"What's his name?"

"Ted Carpenter."

"Where is he now?"

"I have no idea. But I doubt if he's in Herculaneum."

"So do I. That would be too lucky. But archaeologists are a rare breed and they're pretty close-knit. It's possible you could persuade him to contact one of the archaeologists who are doing work at Herculaneum."

"And?"

"A little truth for the big lie?" Jane sat down on the arm of the couch.

Trevor nodded. "Aldo is bound to check up on any story that has to do with Cira. If we announce that an archaeologist has made the find and is inviting Eve to do the reconstruction, we have to be able to make sure he'll substantiate the story."

"And how are we going to make this announcement?" Joe asked.

"Carefully. Over a period of weeks."

"How many weeks?" Jane asked.

"Whatever it takes."

"Estimate."

"Three . . . maybe. If everything falls into place." He turned to Joe. "I'll have to take off for Herculaneum today to pave the way. There are all kinds of problems lurking in Jane's neat little scenario. For one thing, excavation around the theater is controlled by the Italian government. Can I count on you to keep me out of jail if the Italians get too interested in my poking around?"

"I'll work on it," Joe said. "Though a few days in jail might do you good."

"But it won't do Jane good. She wants things to happen in a hurry."

"What else?" Joe asked.

"I'm going to start dropping one-liners in the newspapers on Aldo's favorite sites."

"You're actually going to change the text?" Jane asked. "How can you do that?"

"It's not easy. I'll not only have to break into the site but I may have to reformat the pages."

"Without the newspaper knowing?"

"The papers are proofread before they're put on the Web and then scanned after they're on. If I wait five or six hours after they're posted, it's doubtful that anyone will notice the changes. After all, I'm not changing a story, I'm adding. They'll catch on eventually but we may have days before that happens."

"And when they do?" Joe asked.

"Then it's up to you." Trevor smiled. "Use

influence, muscle, or appeal to their greed. Hell, promise them an exclusive."

"To all three newspapers?"

"I would. It would be a difficult balancing act but that's what makes life interesting."

"And criminal," Joe said dryly. "This will take constant monitoring and we're not sure he even still reads those newspapers."

"It only takes one. If he sees anything about Cira in one newspaper, the chances are he'll go back to the others for verification." He frowned thoughtfully. "But *Archaeology Journal* is a different kettle of fish. I'm not going to be able to pull the wool over their eyes for long. It's an esoteric professional magazine and they're going to care about their reputation."

"So what are you going to do? Skip them?"

He shook his head. "We need them. It would be a tip-off if the magazine ignored a find like this." He shrugged. "I'll figure it out." He put his cup down. "And I'd better get started on the newspapers right away."

"How?" Jane asked.

"I'll start with the two Italian newspapers. That would be the most logical progression. Just a small paragraph in the back of the

Science section. The first will be an announcement about the new find but no details. Very cut-and-dried. The next will mention the theater and that the skeleton is that of a woman. We'll skip a few days and then give a few more details including the discovery of a statue in the anteroom."

"A tease?" Eve asked.

He nodded. "If I work it right, he'll be either tearing his hair or salivating by the end of the week."

"Wouldn't a find like this attract a lot more attention?"

"Not until the excavation site was secured. The last thing they want are thieves nosing around and reporters getting in their way. Aldo will know that from his experience with his father."

"But there must be excavations going on right now near there. The discovery of an anteroom to the theater would be a big deal. I can't believe that we could pull it off."

"I wouldn't be able to do it if the theater excavation wasn't what it is. There are tunnels all over the area down there. They were the primary form of access to reach the heart of the stage and seats of the theater.

Some were dug by archaeologists over the centuries and are charted. Others were dug by thieves, the robbers' tunnels that were used to steal artifacts from the theater. It wouldn't be too unusual that an anteroom might be discovered in one of the robbers' tunnels that had been ignored. But we need to contact someone who can both authenticate the find and cover for us."

"Then you want me to contact Ted right away?"

"It can't be too soon. Be persuasive."

Eve made a face. "That's not my style."

"Then do whatever you have to do. We need that contact in place as soon as possible."

"And what story am I supposed to tell him?"

"If he's a friend, tell him the truth, but he'll have to give another version to the archaeologist we get to authenticate. The entire truth would be too dangerous for us."

"So what should Ted tell him?"

He thought about it. "Tell him that Carpenter himself found the skeleton and statue in a tunnel north of the city but made the mistake of not getting permission from the government to dig. In order to keep in good with the Italians he's willing to share the publicity for a share of the profits. Aldo will assume it's Precebio's tunnel if there's a leak. That should make sense to him." He started for the door. "I'll be leaving for Italy tonight. I'll keep you informed when I do an insert, Quinn."

"How kind," Joe said. "I do hate to work in the dark. Though I can see how you might benefit from it."

"Another jab." Trevor smiled at him over his shoulder. "It might bother me if I didn't know you're looking forward to making this move as much as I am. Neither of us is good at spinning our wheels." He turned to Jane. "And we'll all be going full speed ahead to get you to Herculaneum. So chill. Okay?"

"No. It's not okay. What am I supposed to do?"

"You've done it. It's your plan. We're just implementing."

She shook her head.

"Okay, if you want something to do, go to the mall and taunt Aldo again. That should keep you at the front of his mind until I get some action on the Web sites going."

"No," Eve said firmly.

"Just a little. I'd bet once he's read the first articles in the newspapers, he won't be making any new moves on her. He'll be confused and uncertain about his next course of action."

"Maybe," Eve said. "It's bad enough that we're taking her to Herculaneum and staking her out for him."

"We're not staking her out. We'll figure some way to keep her safe there. That's my job. That's one of the things I'm going to set up as soon as I get to Italy. Your job is to keep her secure here until you get the magic invitation to come do your voodoo." He started down the steps. "The quicker you get your archaeologist to make his call, the quicker we can begin moving forward."

"No one asked me if I wanted to go to the damn mall," Jane said. "I'm not a kid to be kept busy on trivialities because I'm not allowed to do anything important." She took a step forward and confronted him. "I've no intention of taunting Aldo, Trevor. It would be overkill. Subtle is better. We want him to concentrate on Cira, not me. So I'll stay here and be bored out of my mind. But it better not be for more than three weeks."

He lifted his hand to his brow in a salute. "Aye, aye. I hear you loud and clear."

"And you call me and tell me what's happening."

"My pleasure." He smiled. "Every night. I promise."

"You'd better keep it."

"I will." He was walking quickly down the path. "I'd miss the sound of your voice berating me. . . ."

"Am I going with you?" Bartlett asked as he watched Trevor throw his suitcase in the rental car. "I don't speak Italian but I've found that doesn't make much difference if you want to communicate. I've always been able to make myself understood."

"I'm sure you have." Trevor got into the driver's seat. "No, you're not going. If I find I can't do without you, I'll give you a call. But I need you here to keep an eye on Jane."

"Quinn will do that."

"But he won't call me and report anything that looks suspicious. He'll try to take care of it himself."

Bartlett thought about it. “That’s true. Maybe you do need me here.” He sighed. “But it would be much more exciting to go with you. I have to admit life is much more interesting with you around.”

“And how many times have you told me how happy you’ll be to get rid of me and have your uneventful, comfortable life back?”

“Perhaps I’ve been corrupted. Oh, dear, I hope not.” Bartlett took a step back as Trevor started the car. “I’ll take this period to contemplate and evaluate your effect on me. In the meantime you can be sure that Jane will be as safe as I can make her. Take care.”

“You take care.” Trevor paused. “Don’t do anything foolish. If you see anything suspicious, call Quinn.”

“Certainly. See and report. I’m far too valuable to be sacrificed.” He turned back to the cottage. “And so are you. It would behoove you to be cautious.”

“Behoove? Good Lord, what a dated word.”

“I’m dated. It’s part of my charm. And I’ll thank you not to make fun of me.”

"I wouldn't think of it." He pressed on the accelerator and moved down the road. "Your army of female fans would come after me with machetes."

FOURTEEN

"It's not here," Jane muttered, her gaze glued to *La Nazione* on the computer screen. "Not a word."

"It's only been two days," Eve said. "I'm not sure what breaking into a secure Web site entails but I'd think it would take longer than that."

"Then why hasn't he called and told us he was having trouble? He said the prep work would only take three weeks."

"Tentatively. I believe you're the one who carved it in stone."

She made a face. "I did, didn't I? I just wanted to push him a little."

"I'd judge he didn't need any nudging.

He was running on all cylinders when he left here."

"Just so he didn't slow down without a—here it is!" She leaned forward, her body tense with excitement. "Just a tiny article at the bottom of page five."

"Where?" Eve came across the room and looked over her shoulder. "It's only four lines."

"It's just right. Enough to attract Aldo's attention and curiosity and not enough to be blatant." Jane exited the Florence site and went to the Rome newspaper. "If he'd put anything else in, it would have been suspicious."

"I'm sure he'd appreciate your approval."

"He wouldn't give a damn." Jane was scanning the articles. "But he is clever, isn't he? This must have been very difficult. . . . Here it is." She smiled. "It's got an AP byline to make it seem it was picked up from the Florence newspaper." She switched to the London *Times* site. After ten minutes she shook her head in disappointment. "Nothing."

"Give him a break. Two out of three isn't bad."

"I guess." She leaned back on the

couch. "At least he's making progress. Did you get through to Ted Carpenter?"

"He's in Guyana. I left a message yesterday. He hasn't called me back yet. I'll try again later." She shook her head as Jane started to speak. "Later," she repeated. "I'm handling this, Jane."

"Sorry. I didn't mean to step on your toes." Her lips twisted. "My problem is that I'm not being allowed to handle anything myself. It makes me crazy and tends to make me want to reach out and grab." She got up and moved out onto the porch with Toby at her heels. "I'm going to get some air. Let me know if you find out anything."

"I will." Then Eve called after her resignedly, "Okay, dammit, I'll call him back right away."

A radiant smile lit Jane's face. "Thanks."

"You're welcome. But don't you dare think you're manipulating me."

Jane shook her head. "Never." The door slammed behind her and she plopped down on the top step. At last things were beginning to happen. Not fast enough. But there was movement and action that gave her hope. She'd be happier if she could participate in that action but she could wait.

Maybe.

"Have you heard from Trevor?" Bartlett called from the path.

"No, have you?"

Bartlett shook his head. "I didn't expect it. When he gets in motion he's like a whirlwind. It's easy for him to forget me."

"Then why did you think he'd call me?"

"Because he thinks about you all the time. You don't forget what's always with you."

Jane made a face. "He thinks about Aldo, not me."

Bartlett smiled. "Perhaps you're right. I've been wrong before." He moved down the path. "But do tell me when he calls, won't you?"

If he called, Jane thought crossly. He'd promised her a call every night and he'd already broken his promise. Okay, he'd been busy and that activity had yielded rich fruit. But a promise was a promise and she was feeling strangely lonely. She'd not realized how much she'd become accustomed to the sight of him moving around the grounds, bringing her the mail in the evening, waving casually at her while he was speaking to Singer or Joe. He'd become a part of the pattern of her life and the pattern was now broken.

And it was a good thing. She didn't need any patterns that contained an erratic force like Trevor. Face it, her body seemed to respond the moment he came into view. She wasn't ignorant. She knew it was only sexual attraction but it was new to her and she wasn't sure how to handle it. He was too disturbing.

But one side of her nature liked the disturbance. The conflict was a challenge and similar to the way she'd felt when she was training Toby. Every moment an adventure, full of laughter and minor catastrophes. She found herself smiling. Trevor wouldn't be flattered at the comparison with her dog, and there was no way he'd tolerate training. Not that she'd want to get close enough to him to make the—

Her phone rang.

"Did you see the insert?" Trevor asked.

Her heart leaped and she had to steady her voice. "Yes. Why wasn't it in the English paper?"

"God, you're tough." His tone was testy. "Give me another twenty-four hours. I have to be more careful with the English press.

Unless you want it in the *Sun*. They'd have no problem if the story was sensational enough."

"Aldo reads the *Times,* not the *Sun.*"

"I was joking."

"Oh." She paused. "You did very well."

"She said with faint praise."

"You don't want my praise."

"Who said? I like stroking as much as anyone else. And since I'm limited to verbal in your case, I might as well take advantage of it." He continued on before she could answer, "Out of line. Forget I said it. Has Eve contacted Ted Carpenter?"

"Not yet. He's in Guyana and hasn't returned her call. She's placing another call." She stood up. "She might be finished by now. I'll go in the house and check."

"You're on the porch?"

"Yes, why do you want to know?"

"I'm a long way from there and surrounded by ruins and hucksters hawking their wares. It's nice to be able to picture you by the lake. Clean . . ."

She felt that sudden strange warmth that was becoming too familiar surge through her, and said quickly, "Eve's off the phone. Do you want to speak to her?"

"Yes."

"Eve." Jane handed her the phone. "Trevor."

Eve gave her a curious glance before she spoke into the phone. "I just hung up from talking to Ted. He says the man we need to talk to is Professor Herbert Sontag. He's been excavating Herculaneum for the past fifteen years and is well-known and respected by the Italian government. He's got his own little kingdom going there and is probably the only man who could pull off what we need done. Ted's met him several times at conferences and says he doesn't have many people skills but he's great at what he does. He said he'd call Sontag tomorrow and tell him the version of the story you concocted and ask for his cooperation." She grimaced. "Don't thank me too soon. Ted didn't sound encouraging. He wasn't sure Sontag would give us the time of day. He'll call me back as soon as he hears from him." She handed the phone back to Jane. "You'd better tell him to start thinking about another plan. This one's on shaky ground."

"Did you hear her?" Jane asked Trevor. "But we don't have another plan."

"I have a few ideas, but we'd better make this one work. I've devoted too much time and effort to it." He was silent a moment. "Sontag . . . I've heard the name but I don't know anything concrete about him. And, dammit, I've got to give names and places in the next articles and I can't mention Sontag without him willing to go along with us. Get back to me as soon as she hears."

"I will." She added deliberately, "I realize the importance of communication in situations like this."

"Was that another jab?" Trevor asked. "I've been a little busy for the last forty-eight hours. I haven't had more than two hours' sleep since I left Atlanta."

"What have you been doing besides hijacking Web sites?"

"Isn't that enough? No, I guess not. Oh, and while I was trying to break into those secure Internet sites, I had a thought about how Aldo could have found his victims. So simple. The Driver's License Bureau. Their files are well secured but a good computer hacker could get in and go through them and Aldo's an expert. He'd be able to get photos and addresses without a problem."

"And Aldo didn't start stalking me until I took my driver's test."

"I could be wrong, but you might have Quinn check out the possibility."

"I'll tell him right away."

"It may be closing the barn door after the horses have escaped but it's all I could come up with. Other than brainstorming on that subject, I've been scouting out places to set up Aldo. It has to be a place that he thinks he can access and yet one that we can booby-trap."

"Did you find it?"

"Not yet. But I've still got time. You gave me my three weeks."

"No, I didn't. I accepted your estimate. The sooner, the better."

He laughed. "In other words, don't sleep, don't rest, until I get the job done."

"I didn't say that. Just don't lollygag."

"I'll try not to." He paused. "What have you been doing since I've been gone?"

"Sketching, doing homework, playing with Toby, going out of my mind with boredom. The same things I did when you were here."

"I notice you're being careful to make

sure I know my presence makes absolutely no difference in your scheme of things."

"Maybe it makes a little difference. It irritates me that you're free to *do* something."

"I stand corrected."

"And at least you're somewhere different and interesting. I've never been out of the U.S."

"You're young. You have plenty of time to do your globe-trotting. And this town isn't all that fascinating."

"You have the experience to judge and compare. It would probably seem interesting to me. Tell me about it."

"I've barely scratched the surface and these tourist towns are pretty much the same until you dig deep." He laughed. "Cripes, what a play on words. I promise it wasn't intentional."

"I still want to hear about it."

He was silent a moment. "Because Cira lived here?"

"Is it so strange that I'm curious about the place where she lived and died?"

"No stranger than anything else connected with this muddle." He paused. "I'll make a deal. You tell me about those dreams, and I'll describe this town down to the last ruin. You can see it through my eyes."

"I'll be able to see it myself in three weeks."

"But I doubt if Quinn is going to allow you to traipse around the city."

That was true but she'd be darned if she gave in to him after resisting the temptation for the past weeks. "I'll find a way."

"Okay, I thought I'd try." He sighed. "It was only a bluff. Give me a day or so and I'll fill you in on the joys of ancient Herculaneum. Maybe that will shame you into being more generous with your confidences."

"It won't." Her mind was racing, trying to think of all the things she wanted to ask. "The theater. I want to know all about the theater at Herculaneum. All I could find on the Internet was a mention that it was famous. Nothing about Cira. Surely there has to be some mention somewhere if she was so famous."

"Two thousand years, Jane."

"Okay, then I want to know how she lived, the flavor of the time. . . ."

"Good God, I'm not a history buff and I'm going to have a few more things to do than—"

"Then do them. I just thought during your spare time you could— Forget it."

He sighed. "I won't forget it. I'll give you what you want. You'll have to forgive me if I put Aldo first in priority."

"I wouldn't forgive you if you didn't." Her hand tightened on the phone. "Do you think he's seen the articles yet?"

"It depends how often he checks these Web sites. That's why we have to keep the insertions coming and building in intensity. If something catches his eye, he'll go back and see if he can find other references. But, dammit, we have to have something in *Archaeology Journal* to authenticate."

"How soon?"

"Next week would be best. The week after if necessary. It doesn't have to be much. Just a short story and maybe a picture of the statue found with the skeleton."

"What statue? That's just part of the big lie. We don't have a statue of Cira."

He was silent. "I do."

She stiffened. "What?"

"I bought it from the British collector Aldo sold it to. I made him an offer he couldn't refuse."

"Why?"

"I wanted it." He hurried on, "Anyway, we have a statue to use in the *Archaeology Journal* article if they'll use it."

"I'm surprised you're willing to lend it. Isn't that dangerous for your plans of finding the gold? It's bound to attract more attention to Cira and her life. An article is one thing, but it's a visual-oriented world and a photo prods the imagination. Look at all that fuss the bust of Nefertiti caused."

"I'll take my chances. You can bet the place I choose to stage Cira's reconstruction won't be anywhere near Julius Precebio's tunnel."

"That goes without saying." Jane was silent, and then asked, "Why did you want it?"

"It was mine, dammit. It was my favorite bust of Cira and I negotiated with Guido for it as part of my cut. Aldo stole it. It was *mine*."

"The Italian government would give you an argument."

"It was mine," he repeated. "I'll call you tomorrow night at midnight. Good night, Jane."

"Good night." She hung up the phone

and stared thoughtfully out at the lake. Cira again.

"I wanted it. It was mine."

"Jane?" Eve called. "Are you through talking?"

"Yes." She turned and went into the cottage. "But he didn't tell me much more than we knew from checking the Web sites. He's worried about *Archaeology Journal* but he said he'd handle it."

"Then I'm sure he will. You can't fault his skill and dedication."

"It was mine. Aldo stole it from me."

"I believe the word's 'obsession,' not 'dedication,' " she murmured. "At any rate, he's going to call me back tomorrow night and maybe we'll learn more."

Dahlonega, Georgia
Two days later

Cira?

Aldo stiffened as his gaze flew over the words in the Florence newspaper. Only a few lines but they were enough to rivet his attention and take his breath away.

A woman's skeleton entombed and preserved for the ages.

He closed his eyes as fear surged through him in an icy tide. His worst nightmare.

If it was true. If the woman was Cira.

But it could be Cira. Found in an anteroom of the ancient theater, and what other actress had so many statues commissioned of her?

He opened his eyes, his gaze scanning the article. Be sure. Check all sources. He started jumping from site to site.

There it was again. Rome.

Maybe. Don't get too excited. This article referred to rumors of a find but no details. Nothing in *Archaeology Journal*.

Perhaps it wasn't true.

But if it was true then he had to face it. It wasn't only a bunch of fragile bones lying waiting for centuries to be laid to rest. It was that Medusa who had woven her death coils around his father. He had to break her. Use her. Humiliate her. Dominate her. Then crush her bones to powder so that no one would ever be able to resurrect her.

Then kill her abomination of an offspring

who had been taunting him only days before.

Keep calm. He could wait. He had time to make sure this skeleton was the true Cira. He could study and research and put all the pieces together. It could be a trap.

Or this might not be the disaster he'd first thought. It might be fate giving him his due. The final destruction of that bitch.

And it was his due, he thought fiercely. He could see himself going to her sarcophagus and looking down at her in triumph. Reaching out and touching her. It was such a clear picture that he started to shake.

Wait. Watch. There was no hurry.

No matter what was happening in Herculaneum he still had the other Cira in Jane MacGuire.

Jane didn't wait for Trevor to call her. At 10:45 P.M. the next evening she phoned him. "Sontag refused to cooperate. Carpenter said that he was pompous as hell and said that he couldn't compromise himself by admitting a connection with a find that wasn't his. He wasn't about to risk his sterling reputation with a hoax, and threatened to expose Carpenter if he tried to unveil his discovery. Carpenter thinks he doesn't want to share his little empire with anyone who might get more publicity than he does."

"Damn. Can Eve convince Carpenter to make a second try?"

"She's ahead of you. She was on the phone with him for an hour but it's no go. He said there's nothing more he can do with Sontag and he doesn't intend to talk to the bastard again. Evidently Sontag was pretty unpleasant."

"Yeah, so I've found out. Even his crew thinks he's an asshole. The student interns draw straws to see who's going to have to work with him."

"You've learned that already?"

"I wasn't about to sit on my hands and wait for Carpenter to come through for us if there was a possibility it wouldn't happen. I went out to the dig and did some snooping."

"What did you find out?"

"Other than he's not a wonderful human being? He loves publicity and has got an ego that's as big as all outdoors. He likes money and eats up admiration."

"Anything you could use?"

"Possibly. I'm doing a little background checking. I'll know soon."

"How soon?"

"I'll let you know when I do."

She stopped pushing. He'd made more progress than she could have hoped. "Anything else?"

"Not about Sontag. But I got a chance to talk to two of the students about the eruption. It wasn't hard when they're so excited about what they do. They live and breathe that day with every scoop of their shovels."

"Did they talk about the theater?" she asked eagerly.

"We didn't get that far. They were too absorbed with the eruption itself."

"I can understand that."

"But you're disappointed. I'm surprised. It must have been one hell of a blowup. First, the sun brightly shining and then the end of their world."

Night without air.

"Sun? I thought it happened at night."

"Did you? It blew at their seventh hour. But it must have seemed like night if anyone was in a tunnel. Or when the ash and smoke covered the sky. . . . Like I said, the end of their world."

"But I read that fewer than a dozen bodies were found in Herculaneum over all these years. Maybe most of them escaped."

"Recently more bodies have been discovered in a drainage ditch under the marina. There's a theory that hundreds tried to get to the sea and died on the beaches or in the seismic tidal wave that rushed back to engulf them."

"Dear God."

"But skeletons and bodies were almost perfectly preserved there also, which lends credibility to our story about the preservation of Cira's skeleton in the anteroom of the theater. I'm sure Aldo would know every detail he could find out about that eruption."

She had been so caught up in the vision of those poor people running in panic toward the sea that she'd forgotten about Aldo. "I'm sure he would, too. Since it seems to have dominated his life." She moistened her lips. "Then it could be true. She could still be buried there."

"Possibly. The scholars still don't have a

clue about what happened to all those people. The entire town was buried in volcanic matter over sixty-five feet deep. And the intense heat of the flow played tricks. Carbonizing some items and leaving others unscathed. In some houses wax tablets were actually left undamaged. It was freaky."

"But the scrolls in Julius's library weren't damaged."

"That tunnel was far outside town and in a different direction from Herculaneum. It wouldn't have received the full force of the flow. Besides, the scrolls were protected in bronze tubes."

"Did you see any sign in that tunnel that the earth had broken open and lava rushed in?"

"No, but we didn't get much past the library. As I said, it was slow going and Guido got greedy." He paused. "Why?"

"I was just curious." No, she couldn't pull off casual curiosity. Not if she wanted to find out what she needed. "Trevor, I *really* want to know about the theater."

"Because it's part of her."

"And I want to know exactly what those

scrolls told you about Cira. You were very vague."

"I can only tell you about her from Julius's point of view. And from the viewpoint of a few of the scribes he had writing his descriptions of her."

"Were they the same?"

"Not really. I believe the scribes did what all ghostwriters do if not reined in. They tell their own story, with their own impressions."

"What did they say?"

"I believe I'll leave that for another day."

"Bastard."

He laughed. "Such language for a youngster. Don't Quinn and Eve ever reprove you?"

"No. They don't believe in censorship and anyway it was too late to change me by the time I came to live with them. And you shouldn't call the kettle black."

"I'll keep that in mind. I'll call you tomorrow evening."

"What shall I tell Eve about Sontag?"

"That I'll handle it. Good night."

She went back inside the cottage after she hung up. "He said he'd handle it," she said to Eve. “Don’t ask me how. We probably don’t want to know.”

Eve nodded. “I wouldn’t be surprised. I just checked the Rome Web site. Tonight it mentions a leading British archaeologist who’s quoted as saying this may be the most exciting discovery since King Tut. If he’s going to handle it, he’d better do it damn fast. Sontag’s not the only archaeologist at Herculaneum, but he’s the best known and he’s going to be asked questions.”

“But a denial might not be a disaster. Trevor said that most archaeologists are secretive about their work.”

“Unless he opens his mouth about the phone call from Ted Carpenter.”

Jane shrugged. “Then I guess we’ll have to trust Trevor to come through. We don’t have much choice.”

Sontag’s office occupied the first floor of a small warehouse on the waterfront and was surprisingly luxurious. A low velvet couch and kilim carpet vied with an obviously antique desk for elegant prominence.

“Professor Sontag?” Trevor said. “May I come in?”

Herbert Sontag looked up with a frown. “Who are you? I’m busy. Speak to my assistant.”

“He seems to have stepped out. My name is Mark Trevor.” He came into the room and shut the door behind him. “And I’m sure that you wouldn’t want your assistant to hear our discussion anyway. We have some negotiating to do.”

“Get out.” He rose to his feet, his cheeks flushed with anger. “Whatever you’re selling, I’m not buying.”

“No, you don’t buy, you sell. And at a nice tidy profit. Of course, if you had the proper contacts you’d have done much better. I could have increased your take a hundred percent.”

“I don’t know what you’re talking about,” Sontag said coldly. “But if you don’t leave at once I’m calling the security guard.”

“Do you really want him to know about the Girl and the Dolphin?”

Sontag froze. “I beg your pardon.”

“An exquisite statue that survived the eruption. You discovered it eleven years ago here in the marina.”

"Bullshit."

"It's quite small and you must have had no problem keeping the find secret. From what I found out about you during that period of your career, you were much more hands-on. As soon as you thought there was a possibility of recovering something of value, you probably sent the crew away and excavated it yourself. But you evidently didn't have the proper connections to get as much money for the statue as it was worth because James Mandky is still chortling about how he cheated you."

Sontag was no longer flushed but pale. "You lie."

Trevor shook his head. "You know better. And I've no problem with you stealing an artifact or two. It's common practice among your less honorable brethren. When I heard you were very fond of the good life, it was almost a given that you'd pick up a treasure at some point and make it your own. After all, it's a hard life and a man deserves a few comforts."

"Mandky is as much a criminal as I am. He's a receiver of stolen goods. He'd never testify against me."

"Perhaps. But a whiff of scandal would

ruin your reputation and send you back to London in disgrace. I understand from Ted Carpenter that you're very protective of your good name." He smiled. "And I'm very good at dropping little tidbits in the newspapers."

"Carpenter." His lips tightened. "Are you trying to blackmail me?"

"Oh, yes. And it's ridiculously easy. I was hoping for more of a challenge."

He moistened his lips nervously. "You're saying that you'll forget my transaction with Mandky if I agree to pretend to find this skeleton?"

"And extend your full cooperation. I give the orders and you follow them. No questions, no arguments."

"I won't do it." He scowled. "I'll make the announcement but that's the end of it."

"Wrong." Trevor gazed directly into his eyes and his tone became hard. "Look at me and you'll see who you're up against. I've no problem with criminals since you might say I'm similarly inclined. But you're an amateur and I'm a professional and that makes you out of your league. You're in a corner and you'd better know when to fold. I don't give a damn about you if you get in my way. I'll ruin your career. I'll ruin this cushy life you've carved out. And if you piss me off, I may decide to put an end to your miserable existence. Are we clear?"

"You're bluffing," Sontag whispered.

"Try me." He headed for the door. "I'll call you in a few hours and tell you exactly what to say at the press conference you're calling this evening. Exactly. No ad-libs. No grandiose verbiage. Well, maybe a little grandiose. You've got to sound natural."

"I'm not promising anything."

"Promise? I wouldn't believe you if you gave me your word on a stack of Bibles. You'll do it because you realize that I mean every word I say."

"It won't work. My crew will know that lately I've done no excavating near the theater."

"That's why you hired a crew in Morocco and had them working in secret in the middle of the night. This was going to be your career's grand climax and you wanted to keep it to yourself until you could make your splendid announcement. Carpenter has generously agreed to stay in the background and only reap the monetary rewards. The glory is all yours."

"He did?" Sontag was silent, thinking about it. "It could sound plausible," he said cautiously.

"It will. Work at it." He opened the door. "I'll give you the details later."

Sontag.

Aldo eagerly scanned the article in the Rome newspaper. He vaguely remembered hearing about Herbert Sontag from his father and tried to recall what he'd said. Something about Sontag's larcenous nature and there being a possibility that they could work together. But it had never happened. His father had discovered the Precebio tunnel and hadn't had to bring in another archaeologist.

And now Sontag was back on the scene and boasting of this great find. No details. He was still making the discovery out to be this big secret. He hadn't named the actress found in the anteroom. Maybe he didn't know who she was yet. He'd only made reference to her beauty and the gold and lapis jewelry that adorned her. Another Nefertiti, he was claiming.

The phrase sent a chill through him. No,

more beautiful than Nefertiti, Aldo thought. Cira.

And that bastard Sontag was already trying to make her out to be this immortal icon.

No!

He drew a deep breath and tried to control himself. He checked the other newspapers. No more information. He pulled up *Archaeology Journal*. No mention of Sontag's discovery.

Relief surged through him. The weekly magazine was usually on top of every significant find and they hadn't made reference to even the first hints that had been dropped before Sontag's announcement. Maybe it was just Sontag trying to garner a little more publicity for himself.

Wait. Be wary. The stakes were too high.

Cira.

Jane was still looking at the report of the interview when Trevor called that evening.

"Sontag's interview is in *The New York Times*. How did you manage that?" she asked.

"I didn't. The minute the story became

real news and not a concoction, it was like a snowball going downhill. But that means we're going to have to move fast. There will be reporters buzzing around Sontag and there's nothing more dangerous than an inquisitive reporter."

"What about *Archaeology Journal*?"

"I'll get to it as soon as I can. I can't leave Sontag right now. He's getting a little too enthusiastic. He loves to see his name in print and he's already set up another interview for tomorrow. He's clever but he might make a slip that could land us in hot water."

"Where's the main office of the magazine?"

"It's a university press in Newark, New Jersey. Tiny and esoteric and damn important to us. Any sign of Aldo?"

"You know that Joe would have let you know if there had been."

"I hope he would." He paused. "I found out a little about your theater while I was hovering around that press interview."

"From one of Sontag's interns?"

"No, from Mario Latanza, a reporter from Milan. He had to do his homework when Sontag announced that the skeleton was almost certainly one of the actresses who performed at the theater. Latanza thought that since the actress appeared to be bejeweled and successful that she was probably the Herculaneum version of a musical comedy star."

"What?"

"Musical pantomime was the most popular form of spectacle other than chariot races and gladiatorial battles. Lots of nudity, broad graphic jokes, singing, and dancing. Satyrs chasing nymphs brandishing erect leather phalluses. If Cira was as well-known as Julius's scrolls indicate, then she was more than likely catering to that popularity."

"Musical comedy? I always think of ancient theater as being Greek or Roman tragedies. For that matter, weren't most of the actors men?"

"Not by the time Herculaneum's theater came into being. Women came into their own and they dropped their masks and faced the audience. It was a magnificent theater with marble walls and columns made with the finest materials available at the time. The actors and actresses became almost as popular as gladiators and were welcomed into the beds of the town elite and even an occasional emperor."

"And Cira was able to climb that ladder."

"She climbed as high as she could but there was a stigma connected with being an actress that she would never have been able to overcome. There were strict laws regulating the marriages of actors and actresses and isolating them from the rest of society."

"No wonder she tried to carve out a little security for herself."

"A chest full of gold was more than a little security. Particularly during that age."

"They treated her like a plaything, with no substance or rights," she said fiercely. "It was natural that she'd want to make sure that could never happen again."

"I'm not arguing. It was just a comment. I admire her. More now than ever. Hell, I don't even know how she ever got to be an actress. The performances were free and open to all citizens of Herculaneum. Except slaves. Cira was born a slave, and wouldn't have been permitted to even watch a play."

"And she worked and worked and rose to be a star, damn them."

He chuckled. “Yes, she did.” He repeated, “Damn them.”

Companionship. Warmth. Togetherness. This was even more potent than the physical magnetism he managed to exert over her. To hell with it, she thought recklessly. They were thousands of miles away from each other. It was safe to take more from him. “What else did you find out about—”

“That’s all. I was understandably more concerned about what Sontag was saying than I was about ancient history. More later.”

She smothered the disappointment. “Of course. Sontag was much more important. I’ll talk to you tomorrow night then.”

“Now that you’ve wrung me dry, you’re through with me?”

“I should be so lucky. You’re not a man who’d allow that to happen. I’ve got some thinking to do and I can’t do that while I’m talking to you.”

“Heaven forbid that I interfere with your ruminations. Good night, Jane.” He hung up.

She pressed the disconnect and leaned back in the swing, her mind whirling with images.

Slaves. Actors and actresses striding

flamboyantly through the streets of Herculaneum. Satyrs with fake phalluses cavorting on marble stages.

Aldo waiting in the shadows with his knife drawn.

No, that had nothing to do with the theater where Cira had made her magic.

Yes, it did. The images of past and present seemed to be merging, overlapping, she realized in panic.

Then stop it.

She drew a deep breath and cleared her mind of everything but Joe and Eve and this dear, familiar place where she had lived for so many years.

And Aldo.

Aldo was the real threat. Not something that happened centuries ago.

Okay, it was better, more clear.

And perfectly natural that she had been swept down into the whirlpool of images Trevor had drawn for her. Now it was over and she had to keep it at bay while she dealt with the problems Aldo presented.

And she had to deal with them. She couldn't sit here any longer and wait to be summoned to Herculaneum like the helpless slave Cira had been all those centuries ago. She was no slave and she had to *move*.

She reached for her laptop and flipped it open.

Joe was sitting on the couch when she came into the cottage two hours later, paperwork spread on the coffee table in front of him.

"Where's Eve?"

"She went to bed." He looked up and then stiffened as he saw her expression. "Any problem? I thought it was going well. What did Trevor say?"

"Not much. He's busy. But he said we have to move fast."

He studied her. "And that means?"

"It means I may need your help. No, I *will* need your help." She rushed on, "And you won't like it, but it's going to happen. It has to happen."

He didn't speak for a moment, and then said quietly, "Then why the hell don't you stop standing there like a drama queen and tell me what you're talking about."

FIFTEEN

Jane opened the car door as Joe drew up before the brick building. "Why don't you park and I'll go inside?"

"No way."

"I told you I wanted to do this alone, Joe."

"You can do it alone. After I check out the office and make sure it's safe." He smiled crookedly. "That's the job you gave me and that's the job I'm doing." He parked in a spot near the building. "Now you can jump out and be as independent as you please as long as I'm right behind you."

Jane ruefully shook her head. "Joe, do you know how weird that sounds?"

"It works for me." He got out of the car. "Get moving."

She started quickly toward the double glass doors of the entrance. "As long as you stay behind me. I don't want to scare him off. You can be intimidating."

"I wish I could intimidate you." He opened the door for her. "And you're beginning to be a little intimidating yourself."

She shook her head. "Not me." She moved toward the girl dressed in jeans and a tunic sweater who was sitting at a desk in the foyer while Joe leaned against the wall, his gaze focused on the row of desks and cubicles to the left of the foyer. "Hi, I'm Jane MacGuire. I called this morning and made an appointment with Samuel Drake."

A smile lit the girl's freckled face. "Hi, I'm Cindy. Sam said to send you right in." She lifted the phone and pushed a button. "She's here, Sam." She hung up and nodded. "Go for it."

Both the receptionist and the office itself breathed casualness and informality. The attitude was encouraging and exactly what Jane had hoped it would be. "Thanks." She walked toward the door that bore only the brass letters S. Drake and opened the door.

"I appreciate you seeing me, Mr. Drake. I promise I won't take long."

"Sam." Drake rose to his feet. He was tall and lanky, dressed in khakis and blue T-shirt, and looked not a day over thirty. "Take as long as you like." He grinned. "It probably won't do you any good, but I'll enjoy the show. Your phone call interested me and I'm a simple soul who doesn't need much to intrigue him."

She didn't believe that for a minute. He might be easygoing but there was keen intelligence in those blue eyes. She braced herself for the fight to come. Study him, search out any weakness, and use it. Ambition? Perhaps. Security? She doubted it. It could be he just wanted to be liked and respected. That would be easiest to handle. Sit down and chat for a few minutes and see if he revealed anything. "Then maybe I can entertain you for the next quarter hour or so." She smiled and moved toward the visitor's chair beside his desk. "Or maybe we can entertain each other. You're very young to hold down such an important position. It makes me feel much more comfortable about approaching you. I have to admit I was a little nervous. . . ."

* * *

She phoned Trevor that night when she got back to the lake cottage. "We've got *Archaeology Journal.*"

"What?"

"You heard me. Drake is going to run a short article in this week's issue about Sontag's find. It won't be a total confirmation but close enough. He wants you to e-mail him a photo of the bust of Cira. He promised he'd blur it so that Aldo wouldn't recognize it as the one he sold to that collector. He'll need it right away if he's going to insert the story in—"

"Slow down," Trevor said curtly. "How the devil did you do it?"

"You said you didn't have time and we needed them. So I went to Drake's office and did it myself."

He swore long and obscenely. "You left the cottage and went to Newark?"

"Not alone. Joe went with me. He made sure no one knew I'd left here, and was there to protect me."

"The idiot."

"No, he's smart and tough and did what I asked him to do."

"Where was Bartlett? I'm going to strangle him."

"I told you, Joe's smart. It's not Bartlett's fault. He wasn't expecting to have to watch for us to slip away from the cottage." She paused. "And I did what was needed. I was tired of listening to you tell me about how everything was moving so splendidly when the only thing I wanted was to *do* something. So stop cursing and send Drake that photo."

He was silent a moment. "How did you convince him?"

"It wasn't easy," she said wearily. "I almost blew it. I couldn't read him. Then I saw something in his expression and I had the key. . . ."

"The key?"

"He's aching to be an adventurer. He's tied to a desk reporting on dry-as-dust discoveries when he wants to shake the world."

"And how did you come to that conclusion?"

"I was talking casually, feeling him out, and I hit it lucky. I was joking and mentioned Indiana Jones. He lit up like the Fourth of July."

"He wants to be Indiana Jones?"

"There's nothing wrong with wanting to be a hero. So I gave him his chance. I told him the whole story about Aldo and the connection with Cira and how we needed him to spring the trap. I pulled Joe in to show him how upright and law-abiding we were. And I also promised him an exclusive after we catch Aldo. And, unlike you, I'll keep my promise. Now what's the next step?"

"You stay there and don't move a muscle."

"I'll do what I please. Tell me how we get Eve invited to Herculaneum after Aldo reads the confirmation in the magazine."

"We do two days of prep work in the newspapers having Sontag talk about forensic sculptors and the need to get the foremost professional in the business to do it. Then we wait another couple days and have Sontag announce his choice."

"That's almost another week of waiting."

"Then that's what we'll do."

"I should think you'd be able to hurry it." She yawned. "I'm too tired to argue right now. I was up all last night researching the magazine and convincing Joe that helping me was the right thing to do. I'm going to bed. Remember to fax that—"

"My God, you're formidable."

She felt a pang of hurt. "I don't know what you're talking about. There was a job to do and I did it."

"And the most formidable thing about you is that you don't realize it. You probably made Drake so dizzy that he didn't know whether he was coming or going."

"I only gave him what he wanted."

"Heaven protect us poor males if you ever pull out the big guns."

"If you have to rely on heaven, then you're pretty sorry and don't deserve to be protected. And I'd think you'd be grateful instead of whining."

"I am grateful. And mad. And scared."

She couldn't deal with this any longer. "The hell you are. Get over it. Send the photo." She hung up the phone.

"He didn't like you leaving here?" Eve asked from behind her.

"No." She turned to face Eve. "Why should he be any different? You and Joe hated it too. But you finally agreed that I could do it."

"Oh, I didn't have any doubt you could

do it. I just wish I could have been there to watch you in action."

Jane frowned. "But you were angry when you thought I was manipulating Joe."

"That was Joe. Aldo's made this a war zone. As long as you don't hurt innocent bystanders, use any weapon you can." She smiled. "But next time I don't want to be the one to stay here and keep the home fires burning."

"You'll be in the middle of it once we get to Herculaneum. If we ever get there. Trevor is taking baby steps during this stage of his precious con."

"Which is probably smart," Eve said. "I approve of delicacy in the final stages. I've learned I can ruin everything in my reconstructions if I get in too much of a hurry. Though I agree it's hard to wait. Get to bed soon. You look like you're ready to drop."

"I am." She motioned to Toby and moved down the hall. "I'm going to sleep like a rock tonight."

"With no dreams?" Eve asked quietly.

"You mean of Cira?"

Rocks falling, striking. Pain. Blood.

She shook her head. "I haven't dreamed

of Cira for a long time. Maybe it's over. Maybe I'll never dream of her again."

"Don't be too sure. Considering that everything we're doing is about Cira, I'd be surprised if she weren't front and center in your mind."

"So would I. But then she's always there. Did I tell you that she was probably the Herculaneum version of a musical comedy star?"

"No. Really?"

"Isn't that strange? She had such a tough life. It must have been hard for her to act the clown. I can't see her cavorting around singing and dancing." She shrugged. "But I guess she could do anything she wanted to do. Good night, Eve."

"Sleep well."

She'd sleep well, Jane thought as she closed her door behind her. If she dreamed, it would be of Sontag and Aldo and the ruins of Herculaneum with Trevor spinning his web around all of them.

She should be glad that she no longer dreamed of Cira. Maybe the circle was now complete, her story told. Maybe Cira had died when those rocks had crashed down on her.

Sadness. Loneliness.

Instant rejection surged through her. No, she wouldn't *have* it.

She was crazy. How could she prevent something that had happened two thousand years ago? Whatever had occurred in that tunnel, she had to accept it.

She started to undress. "But it's not fair, is it, Toby?" she whispered as she slipped into bed. "She fought so hard. She deserved to live. . . ."

Dahlonega, Georgia

The photograph of the sculpture in *Archaeology Journal* was slightly blurred but unmistakable.

Cira.

Aldo's gaze devoured the woman's features before scanning the accompanying article. Confirmation. The magazine was being very discreet but it was clear they were confirming Sontag's find and had even been given a prized photo of the statue found in the anteroom.

He went to the Florence *La Nazione* site.

Another news conference and Sontag talking about his remarkable discovery and obtaining a forensic sculptor to verify that the bust and skeleton were the same woman. It was the second mention in as many days.

Forensic sculptor.

Cira.

Jane MacGuire.

The circle was closing, tightening like a noose.

Very well, the worst had happened, but he could make it work for him. Maybe this was a challenge so that he could prove how superior he was to that bitch.

Last night he'd dreamed of Cira and woke in an ecstasy of sexual release. Broken bones and blood and her tears of humiliation. But he couldn't have the blood without Jane MacGuire. She was the present manifestation of that bitch. He had to have both to be complete.

He *would* have them. He deserved it.

But fate sometimes stumbled and needed a little help. He had to take control. Look at what happened at that glade when he'd almost had Jane MacGuire in his grasp.

He couldn't permit any slips this time.

* * *

"I need to see you," Sontag said curtly when Trevor answered his phone. "Right away. I never bargained for this."

"You didn't bargain for anything. You were blackmailed." Trevor sat up in bed. "What's wrong? Reporters bugging you?"

"Just get here." He hung up the phone.

Trevor glanced at the clock on the nightstand as he started to dress. Two forty-five A.M. Sontag wasn't one who tossed and turned, worrying in the dead of night, and he'd definitely sounded spooked. Trevor had better move fast before he unraveled and blew everything.

He arrived at Sontag's house on the outskirts of Herculaneum fifteen minutes later.

"You said it was cut-and-dried," Sontag sputtered as he threw open the door. "Just a few news conferences and then I could go to Cannes. You said he was out of it."

"Calm down," Trevor said. "You have only a week or so more and then you can leave Herculaneum."

"I'm leaving tomorrow."

"The hell you are." He strode into the room. "You still have work to do."

"No, I don't." He picked up a large envelope on the coffee table and threw it to Trevor. "I'm done." He was untying his velvet robe as he moved toward his bedroom. "I wash my hands of it. He's trying to take over. He'll expose me. I'm going to pack."

It wasn't going to happen. He wasn't going to let Sontag off the hook. He was tempted to go after him at once and apply pressure but he decided to let him cool down for a few minutes. He opened the envelope and drew out the sheaf of papers inside.

He gave a low whistle as he saw the top page. "Christ!"

"We've got him," Trevor said when Jane answered her phone two hours later. "We've not only got him. I'd bet he's here in Herculaneum."

She stiffened. "What?"

"Sontag phoned me in a panic and tossed an envelope at me as soon as I walked into the room. It contained a complete dossier on Eve Duncan. It was obviously pulled off the Internet, and the story about her reconstruction of the Egyptian mummy was on the top."

"No note?"

"No, but he found it on his doorstep when someone knocked on his door in the middle of the night. It freaked him out. He thought it was Carpenter trying to muscle in on the great unveiling. He loves all the attention focused on him and wants to stay in the limelight."

"You think it was Aldo?"

"He could have hired someone else to do it but I've got a hunch Aldo's tired of waiting and wanted to make contact. Jesus, I didn't think we'd get this lucky. I thought we'd have to have Sontag make the announcement and then sit on pins and needles until we got a response from Aldo."

"Why would he do it?"

"He's been reading about Sontag's mulling over the forensic sculptor selection for a week and decided he wanted to take command. Arrogant son of a bitch. It's all gone his way since he started his killing spree and he can't imagine not being able to call the shots."

"But why drop her dossier off in the middle of the night?"

"Why not? He wants to be feared and he's not been given much of that satisfaction lately. If he's going after the skeleton, perhaps he wanted Sontag to realize how vulnerable he was. He didn't realize Sontag would be more worried about his fifteen minutes of fame than his life."

"But it could have worked the other way. Sontag could have chosen someone else because he didn't want to be dictated to."

"True. My guess is that Aldo may not even be entirely sure that this isn't a trap, but he's willing to take the chance because he's certain he can overcome all obstacles that get in his way."

"To get to Cira." She added slowly, "And he still wants me, too."

"You act surprised. That was the plan, wasn't it? He wouldn't want Eve to do the reconstruction if he didn't think it would draw you."

"I'm not surprised." But she was chilled and a little taken aback at the speed at which Aldo had grabbed the bait. "This has caught me off-balance. I'm just trying to think my way through it. You don't believe he might think it more logical for them to leave me behind under guard?"

"His destiny," he reminded her. "And if they did leave you behind, he'd do something to bring you here."

"So when do we leave for Herculaneum?"

"You've bounced back. You're beginning to sound eager as hell."

"It's a relief to know that we're moving at last."

"It's not a relief to me. I've been having visions of faceless corpses dancing in front of me the closer we've been getting to pushing this final button."

"Then make sure you don't do anything stupid that will make me one." She asked again, "When do we leave for Herculaneum?"

"I'll have Sontag make the announcement that he's hired Eve tomorrow at a news conference. We should probably give it two days before you arrive at Herculaneum. Tell Eve that there will be media at Naples airport when you get in."

"She'll hate that."

"She can put up with it. Everyone knows she's media shy but if I'm wrong about Aldo being here I want to make sure he knows she's arrived. And that barrage of publicity will be salt in Aldo's wounds. I'll make sure they run another picture of the bust of Cira in the local paper. I'll try to make sure Eve's exposed as little as possible after that but media exposure is key here. I'm going to meet you in Rome and fly in here with you."

"Why?"

"I want to be seen arriving at the same time. I'm going undercover until then. If Aldo is already here, I don't want him to see me hovering over Sontag and pulling the strings."

"Can you still control Sontag? I thought you said he was freaked."

"He is, but he has a keen sense of self-preservation and all I had to do was convince him that I could keep him in the limelight. Tell Quinn that I've found a villa on the outskirts of Herculaneum that has some interesting features but I'll leave it to him to hire a security force for protection. He can contact the local police and get recommendations. The backgrounds of the kind of team I'd hire wouldn't meet with his approval."

"I can imagine."

"No, you can't. You're seventeen."

"Will you stop harping on that?"

"No, I have to keep reminding myself. I've called Bartlett and told him to arrange to fly your Toby to California for your friend, Sarah, to puppy-sit. I know you wouldn't rest if you weren't sure he was well taken care of. Is that okay?"

"As long as he's safe."

"He'll be safe. I'll tell Bartlett to hire a private jet for the pooch if he has to do it. I'll call you after the press conference tomorrow night." He hung up.

She pressed the disconnect and sat there for a moment. She felt stunned . . . and scared. She hadn't expected to feel either emotion. She'd thought she'd be prepared.

She was prepared, dammit. All she had to do was shrug off this weird sense of foreboding at the thought of going to Herculaneum. Events were moving as they'd planned, better than they'd planned. She should be happy.

No, not happy, but she was beginning to feel a tingle of excitement and anticipation. She stood up from the swing and headed for the front door. "Eve, Trevor called. Pack your bags. We're going to Herculaneum."

* * *

The two-story stucco villa on the Via Spagnola that Trevor had rented was spacious and charming. It was enclosed by an ornate wrought-iron fence and there were bright geraniums overflowing from the window boxes on the second floor.

Trevor unlocked the front door and stepped aside. "I'll stay here with Eve and Jane, Quinn. Suppose you go in and check it out. I'd do it, but I don't think you'd trust anyone but yourself."

"Right." Joe moved quickly past them and into the foyer. "Though it should be okay. I've had two security men watching the house since you gave me the address yesterday. Stay here."

"I should have known," Trevor murmured.

"Yes, you should," Eve said as she glanced around the marble foyer. "Nice. How many bedrooms?"

"Four. Two bathrooms. Parlor, study, and library. The kitchen is pretty modern and that's a plus for houses this old."

"How old is it?" Jane asked.

"It was built around 1850. Sontag owns it

and I got him to lend it to me when I found out that it's exactly what I needed."

"You twisted his arm?"

"I didn't have to. He'd caved by that time and was doing everything I told him to do. Until the other night when he got his midnight visitor."

"It's okay," Joe said as he came down the stairs. "Eve and I will take the bedroom at the end of the hall. You take the middle bedroom, Jane. Trevor can be on the other side and we'll sandwich you."

"A sandwich," Trevor said. "Interesting idea, Jane. But considering how prickly you are, not very appetizing."

"Shut up," Joe said coldly. "That's not acceptable, Trevor."

"I know. It just slipped out." He started down the hall. "To make amends I'll brew a pot of coffee and fix something to eat while you all get unpacked and cleaned up."

"Sontag appears to be very cooperative," Jane said as Eve and Joe headed for their bedroom. "He's not upset any longer?"

"He's upset. He'd like nothing better than to take off with his tail between his legs. It's all a question of control. Try to get a little rest. You had a long flight." He disappeared through the arched door at the end of the corridor.

She didn't want to go to her room and rest. She wasn't tired. She was excited and on edge and the different sights and sounds and smells of Italy had almost overwhelmed her. She hesitated and then reluctantly headed for her bedroom.

"Want to come with me?" Trevor had come back and was standing in the doorway. He smiled. "I thought you wouldn't be able to tamely shuffle off to rest. Come on. Help me."

She turned toward him eagerly and then caught herself. "Don't be patronizing. It doesn't take two to make a pot of coffee."

"Patronizing, hell. I'm lonely." He took a step toward her, his hand outstretched. He coaxed, "Come with me."

"Come with me. Trust me."

No, she wouldn't let her mind play tricks on her just because they were in Herculaneum. The relationship between them was nothing like the one shared by Cira and Antonio. Hell, they had no relationship, only a common goal.

But it would do no harm to go with him

right now. She was feeling unsettled and, yes, a little lonely, too. She took a step forward, then another, and took his hand.

Her eyes widened. Tingling. Disturbing. Sensual. She started to pull away.

His grasp instantly closed around hers, warm, strong, safe, and suddenly that sensual disturbance vanished. "See? It didn't hurt a bit. Do you want to make the coffee or do the sandwiches?" He chuckled as he led her toward the kitchen. "Sorry. Those 'sandwiches' keep appearing out of nowhere, don't they?"

Three guards at the rear of the house. Two at the front. It would be difficult to get to Jane MacGuire while she was inside the villa.

Aldo watched the lights go on at the house on Via Spagnola. So cozy. They were probably gathered around the dinner table, drinking wine and chatting about Cira and the reconstruction.

Did Eve Duncan and Joe Quinn know the serpent they were hugging to their bosoms? That Jane MacGuire and Cira were one? Probably not. No doubt she had worked her magic and made them believe what she wanted them to believe. She wanted to live forever and this reconstruction could ensure that at least her face would be immortal.

It wasn't going to happen. He couldn't tolerate it. And the longer he stayed here in this city, the more convinced he was that he'd been brought here for a reason. His fear and uncertainty were gradually fading. He'd be shown the way through that army of guards surrounding her.

Or she'd be led to him like a lamb to the slaughter.

"It's beautiful," Eve said, gazing out the kitchen window at the winding streets of the city. "No, that's not right. It's arresting. You can't help but remember what happened here."

"The citizens of the town make sure you don't forget," Joe said dryly. "It's how a good many make their living. And I can't wait to get this job done and get out of here." He turned to Trevor. "I didn't like that circus at the airport. I'm not having Eve go through that again."

"It's not going to be necessary," Trevor said. "There will be at least one more press conference but after tomorrow it's best that she stay out of the limelight as much as possible."

Joe met his gaze. "I agree."

"When am I supposed to be starting to work on this reconstruction?" Eve asked. "It would be nice to have a little more information. I had to tap dance through all those reporters' questions this afternoon."

"But you did it so well." Trevor smiled. "I was impressed."

"I don't need you to be impressed," Eve said. "I need you to be smart, efficient, and to get us the hell done with this horror as soon as possible." She glanced at Jane. "And not to do anything that will give Aldo his chance at her. We agreed to come here because it was a way of ending this nightmare quickly. I'm not planning on spinning my wheels now that we've arrived. Your job was to set up a place where we could trap Aldo. You say you've done it. Is this the place?"

Trevor nodded.

"What makes it so special?"

"The tunnel."

"What?"

"There's a robbers' tunnel running beneath the villa that intersects the network of archaeological tunnels that crisscross the theater excavation. No one really knows how many robbers' tunnels were drilled over the centuries. Sontag discovered this one several years ago and decided to keep its location secret so that he could go down and do a little private excavating for fun and profit."

"Do you honestly think Aldo will try to gain entrance to the villa through that tunnel?" Joe asked. "He'll know we're waiting for him. He may be nuts but he's canny as a fox."

"You're right," Trevor said. "There's no way he'd try to gain entrance to the villa. So we have to draw him down to the tunnel and then go after him. The Via Spagnola tunnels have as many off-shoots and twists and turns as Precebio's tunnel."

"You said that Aldo knew the tunnels like the back of his hand when he was a boy," Jane said.

Trevor nodded. "The one advantage we have is that Sontag is the only one who ever mapped this particular network of tunnels. Aldo wouldn't be familiar with them."

"We hope," Joe said. "And if the tunnel is that complicated we may be as lost down there as he is."

"I've got Sontag's maps and I've been checking out the tunnel every night since I found out about the villa. Besides, with any luck we won't have to know much about the tunnel. We'll set up the trap and let Aldo come to us."

"And I suppose you've already done that," Eve said dryly.

"Pending your approval." He took a notebook from his back pocket and flipped it open. "There's only one place that's really possible for an ambush." He put the notebook on the table. "I know it looks like hen scratching but this is the tunnel that leads to the archaeological tunnels. You take the branch that leads off it here." He drew a line intersecting. "This branch leads to the vomitorium but about halfway you run into an offshoot passage that twists around and then comes back from a different angle. There's a ledge about thirty feet up that will give you a clear shot, Quinn."

"Cover?"

Trevor nodded. “You won’t have a problem. The face of the wall looks like a solid sheet with only a small opening off the ledge.”

“Vomitorium,” Eve repeated. “Is that what it sounds like?”

“Yes and no,” Trevor said. “The exits from public places were generally called that. For years the guards told gullible tourists that the Romans gorged themselves and then made themselves throw up to eat more.”

“Charming. And this vomitorium was an exit from the theater?”

“It could have been. The Via Spagnola tunnel winds around so much that this could have been an exit for another public building or residence. At any rate, it’s damn convenient for us.” He glanced at Joe. “And there are three tunnels leading off that vomitorium. Aldo will probably be hiding in one of them if we can set him up.”

“And the vomitorium is the target area?” Joe asked. “Exactly where is it?”

“A short distance farther along the tunnel. After you pass the offshoot passage that you’ll be taking, you come to a wider area that was evidently the treasure trove the thieves were after when they dug the tunnel. The vomitorium evidently contained several large statues that were stolen. Only the bases are left."

"How's the light?"

"Better have an infrared scope. I'll have four torches scattered on the walls around the area. That's all I can promise you. It's just as important that he doesn't see you as it is that you see him."

"And what's going to bring him to the room?"

"Jane." His glance shifted to her. "And Cira."

Joe shook his head. "Are you going to send him an engraved invitation for the event?"

"I hope we don't have to. If he calls Jane as he did before she left Georgia, she can set him up. There's a good chance that will happen."

"And if it doesn't?"

"We have a backup." He continued, "We're announcing that the coffin containing the remains is being transported day after tomorrow from the tunnel where she was discovered to the lab here at the villa for forensic examination and reconstruction. I've chosen two well-known forensic experts who have the reputation of not being assholes like Sontag and I'll hand out their names to the media to verify."

"How?"

"That's up to you, Quinn. I don't care if you persuade or threaten them. Just get them to lie through their teeth and go underground for the few days they're supposed to be at the villa."

"We're just going to let Aldo follow us to the villa?"

"Right, he's going to follow us through the theater tunnel to the robbers' tunnel leading to the villa."

"What?"

"It's the kind of flamboyant showmanship Sontag would pull. Dramatically revealing the place where the skeleton was found to the media and then leading them through the darkness to the place where Cira's identity was going to be discovered. Or rather to the point where we have the local police barricade the tunnel to keep the media from going any farther and knowing where we exit."

"Aldo would be insane to be in the middle of that mob of reporters."

"He won't be in the middle. But he'll be there somewhere in that network of tunnels keeping an eye on what's going on," Trevor said. "And he'll go back and explore later. We won't make it too hard for him to find the Via Spagnola tunnel." He added to Joe, "Have you made sure the tunnel where the skeleton was found was put off-limits by the local police and guarded twenty-four hours a day?"

"Of course, it made sense. I just suggested it would be wise to protect the area from thieves who might contaminate the excavation site. They were eager to please. There's a good deal of American money being poured into that hole in the ground. So what's going to draw him to the vomitorium if the reconstruction is going to be done at the villa?"

Trevor smiled. "Because we're going to let Aldo believe that Sontag is going to have a news conference down there for the great unveiling of the reconstruction."

"My God," Jane whispered.

"Again, it's the kind of flamboyant thing Sontag would pull. Leading the reporters through the darkness to a mystery destination, the vomitorium."

"And we draw Aldo down there instead. He'd want to destroy the reconstruction before the media got to it," Jane said slowly. "How do we do it?"

"You challenge him, taunt him, make him think you're taking him on one on one. He's a supreme egotist besides being nuts. You find a way to exploit his weakness."

She frowned. "It could work."

"It better." Trevor turned to Eve. "Everything okay?"

She thought about it. "No. How is Aldo going to know about the vomitorium?"

"Once he discovers the Via Spagnola tunnel, he'll reconnoiter and the vomitorium is fairly easy to find for someone used to negotiating tunnels. Once he finds it, he's not going to go any farther."

"Why not?"

"He'll know it's the place. I've set it up. I've got lamps, batteries, and photo equipment all over the place down there. He won't be able to miss what's going to happen."

"How can you be so sure he'll even find it? It's a hell of a lot to assume."

"You're right. That's why I set up a video camera on the ledge where Joe's going to be waiting. It's pointed directly down at the vomitorium. If Aldo's exploring down there, we'll know it. Trust me."

"I don't trust anyone where Jane's safety's concerned. And I *hate* the idea of using her as bait."

"Eve, you knew that this was the only way we could do it," Jane said quietly. "And Joe is going to be there to protect me."

"And I'll be there, too," Trevor said. "I'm taking her down to the vomitorium that night. You go down ahead of us, Quinn. I'll scout out the tunnel before we take her down and be with her as far as the offshoot passage before I join you at the ledge. I'll guarantee she'll be safe until she gets to the vomitorium. After that it's up to all of us to make sure she stays safe."

"Why can't we bring more security down there?"

"The minute he'd see them, he'd flit. As long as we don't let him get near Jane, she'll be safe. He never uses a gun. He wants ritual. It's important to him. We don't give a damn about ritual; a rifle bullet will suit us just fine."

"This had better work, Trevor," Eve said grimly.

"Lord, what's a man got to do? I'm open to suggestions."

"You'll get them if we see any signs that this damn plan is disintegrating." She turned and headed toward the doorway leading to the hall. "And in the meantime I'm going to bed. I'm beat. Joe?"

"I'll be there in a minute." Joe finished his coffee. "I'm going to check with the security boys and see if they've noticed anything."

"It's too early," Trevor said. "Aldo's not going to make a move yet."

"It must be wonderful to be able to see into a crystal ball," Joe said sarcastically as he opened the kitchen door. "Personally, I've always found that it's better to expect the unexpected."

"So have I," Trevor murmured as the door closed behind Joe. "Usually. But Aldo is different. . . . I feel like I know what he's thinking—it's different." He picked up the cups and plates and took them to the sink. "And maybe I'm wrong and Quinn is right on target. Having two varying viewpoints only makes it safer for you." He turned to face her. "You were very quiet while I was sketching in my ‘master plan.’ Don’t you think it will work?”

“I’ve no idea. It’s difficult to imagine. . . .” She moistened her lips. “You said that the tunnel was directly below this house?”

“Yes.” His gaze narrowed on her face. “Does that make you nervous?”

She shook her head. “Not nervous.” Her glance shifted to the window. “It’s getting dark. It will be even darker in the tunnel, won’t it?”

“Yes. What are you thinking?”

She looked back at him. “I want you to take me through the tunnel. I want to see this vomitorium and I want to see for myself where Sontag barricaded the tunnel anteroom where Cira is supposed to be.”

“We couldn’t get close. Quinn has the tunnel guarded. Besides, you’ll see it tomorrow night.”

She shook her head impatiently. “Not with a gaggle of reporters on our heels. Tonight.”

“Because you want to make sure I’m not off base?”

“I want to *see* those tunnels. I don’t care how close or far away I have to be. You said you didn't think that Aldo was in striking distance."

"I also said I could be wrong."

"But he doesn't know about the Via Spagnola tunnel. We'd be safe there. What about the tunnels close to the theater?"

"If he didn't have a reason, he probably wouldn't be down there. It's pretty nasty and those tunnels are lit by electric light and guarded by the locals."

"Would they bother us if we ran across them?"

"I believe I could talk our way out of it."

"Another con?"

"Isn't that what life's all about?" He studied her. "Why is it so important to you?"

She didn't answer.

"You said you'd been dreaming of tunnels. You think you'll recognize them?"

"Of course not. That would be weird."

He was silent a moment. "Quinn will probably kill me."

He was going to do it! "When?"

"In an hour. I have to call Sontag and prime him for tomorrow's news conference." He paused. "Are you going to tell Eve?"

She thought about it. "No, they'd feel

they had to come with us and I don't want to drag them through those tunnels. You said they were pretty unpleasant."

"Slimy." He added, "But they'd still want to go."

"I'll leave a note for Eve in case she wakes up when we're gone. I don't want her worried."

"But you don't want them to go. Why?"

"They'd watch me," she said baldly. "They'd analyze why and what I was doing and wonder if they should have let me go. People who love you do that. But you don't care. If you watch me, it'll be because you're curious. I'll be safe if you go with me because you don't want to lose Aldo, but you're not going to be biting your nails and fretting."

"No, I'm not inclined to fret." He smiled crookedly. "And, yes, I'm curious about everything about you." He turned away. "I'll see you in an hour. Bring a sweater."

"Wait." When he looked back at her, she asked, "How do you get to this tunnel? Where's the entrance?"

"You're sitting on it." He nodded at the rug covering the stone floor beneath her chair. "It's a seven-foot trapdoor that evidently accommodated Sontag's thievery of the larger items he found. And there's a steel ladder leading fifty feet down. Don't get eager and leave me behind. Okay?"

There was no danger of that. The knowledge that she was sitting over that dark emptiness was disturbing. She wanted to get up and move but forced herself not to do it. She kept her tone casual. "I'll wait for you."

SIXTEEN

Darkness. Only the beam of Trevor's flashlight illuminated the blackness of the tunnel.

The chill and damp seemed to ooze into her every pore and Jane found she was having trouble getting her breath.

Night without air.

Imagination. If she couldn't breathe, it was because she was hurrying after Trevor. "Are we going to the vomitorium first?"

"No, I thought we'd do that on our way back. I have a hunch that wasn't your first priority. You wanted to see the theater."

She didn't argue with him. She was filled with eagerness. "Are there rats down here?"

"Probably. When there isn't any human habitation, nature tends to take back its own." His voice drifted back to her. "Stay close. I don't want to lose you."

"But you wouldn't mind giving me a scare."

He laughed. "I admit I'd like to shake you up a little to see if I could do it."

"Well, you won't do it with the threat of rats. I got used to them in some of the foster homes where I lived when I was a kid. I was just curious."

"There were rats at the orphanage where I grew up, too."

"In Johannesburg?"

"That's right, Quinn dug deep into my murky past."

"It wasn't that murky. At least, what he could uncover."

"It wasn't pristine clean. Watch your step. There's a puddle ahead."

"Why is it so damp down here?"

"Cracks, fissures." He paused. "You said you dreamed about tunnels. Was it like this?"

She didn't answer for a moment. She'd told herself that there was no way she'd confide in him about those dreams but the isolation and darkness made her feel strangely close to him. And what real difference did it make what he thought of her? "No, it wasn't like this. It wasn't damp. And it was hot and smoky. I— She couldn't breathe."

"The eruption?"

"How do I know? It was a dream. She was running. She was afraid." She waited for a moment, and then said, "You said you dreamed of Cira."

"Oh, yes. From the time we found the scrolls. At first, it was every night. Now it's not so often."

"What do you dream about her? Tunnels? Eruptions?"

"No."

"What?"

He laughed. "Jane, I'm a man. What do you think I dream about?"

"Oh, for God's sake."

"You asked me. I'd like to tell you some mystic, romantic story but I know you'd prefer the truth."

"She doesn't deserve that."

"What can I say? It's sex. I don't really think she'd mind me having a few fantasies about her. Cira understood sex. She used it to survive. And she probably would have enjoyed the thought that she had that much power over me two thousand years after she died."

"I don't believe you're— Maybe you're right, but she was more than a sex object." She had a sudden thought. "And I don't think that's all she was to you. You spent a fortune for that bust of her you bought from that collector. Why would you do that?"

"It's a wonderful piece of art." He was silent a moment. "And maybe I'm a little obsessed with her personality as well as her body. She was larger than life."

"Then why the devil didn't you say that in the beginning?"

"I wouldn't want you to think I'm sensitive. It would ruin my image."

She made a rude sound. "I don't think you need to worry about your—"

"This is where the Via Spagnola tunnel ends and joins with the network around the theater," he interrupted. "It should be a little brighter because of the electric lights though it's still pretty dim. I'll keep the flashlight on. These tunnels meander around but it's the only way to view the theater since it's still buried."

"Why haven't they worked harder at excavating it?"

"Money. Difficulty. Interest. They've been doing better lately. Though it's an uphill battle since parts of it are buried beneath more than ninety feet of volcanic rock. It's a shame because this theater is a jewel. It sat between two thousand five hundred and three thousand people and it had all the bells and whistles. Bronze drums for making thunder, cranes for flying the gods across the stage, seat cushions, trays of sweets and nuts, saffron water to spray the patrons. Amazing."

"And exciting. It must have seemed magical to them."

"Good theater still seems magical to us."

"And you found out all of this from that newspaper reporter?"

"No, I did a little research. You said you wanted information. I didn't dare disobey."

"Bull. You were interested yourself."

"Busted."

"It's surprising that the theater wasn't destroyed by the lava flow."

"It's one of the freaky things that happened that day. The flow picked up enough mud to encase and protect it. It might have been excavated intact except for the greed of the people who came after it. At one point King Ferdinand was melting down priceless bronze fragments to make candlesticks."

"I thought you had no respect for the preservation of antiquities."

"I respect the artifacts themselves. And I don't like stupidity or destruction."

"Could Cira have been here at the theater when the volcano blew?"

"Yes, it's believed the cast was rehearsing for an afternoon performance."

"What play?"

"No one knows. Maybe as the excavations progress, we'll find out."

"And they might find Cira buried here."

"You mean, fact following fiction? It's possible. Who knows? The archaeologists are discovering new things all the time."

"New things from a dead world. But somehow it doesn't seem dead, does it? I was thinking while we were driving here from the Naples airport that if you closed your eyes, you might be able to imagine what life was like before the eruption. I wonder what it was like for them that day. . . ."

"I was wondering, too. Shall I tell you?"

"Your research again?"

"It started out that way but it's hard to keep a clinical attitude when you're this close to the source." His soft voice came out of the darkness. "It was a normal day, the sun was shining. There had been earth tremors but nothing to worry about. Vesuvius was always rumbling. The wells in the country had dried up but it was August. Again, not unexpected.

"It was a hot day but it was cooler here in Herculaneum because the city was on a promontory over the sea. It was the birthday of an emperor, a holiday, and people were in town to see the sights and celebrate. The forum was crowded with hawkers, acrobats, jugglers. Ladies were carried on litters by slaves. The public baths were open and men were undressing and preparing to be bathed by attendants. There were athletic events at the palaestra and the victors were about to receive their olive wreath crowns. They were only boys, naked and suntanned and proud of their feats. Mosaicists were cutting their polished stones and glass, bakers were making their breads and tarts, and Cira's friends and fellow actors, maybe Cira herself, were rehearsing their play at the finest theater in the Roman world." He paused. "I can tell you more. Do you want to hear it?"

"No." Her throat felt tight and she could almost see and taste the bittersweetness of that morning. "Not now."

"You said you wanted the flavor of her time."

"You certainly gave it to me," she said unevenly. "It seems impossible that it all disappeared in the blink of an eye."

"No, not impossible. We manage to destroy pretty efficiently without the help of nature. Look at Hiroshima. And it was more like a bellow than the blink of an eye. Reports said that great bull-like bellows seemed to come from the earth itself. Acrid sulphuric smoke was everywhere and a mushroom cloud shot up from the mountain."

"And everyone dropped everything that made their lives worth living and ran."

"Those who could do it. There wasn't much time."

No air.

No time.

She was suddenly having trouble breathing. "I want out of here. How close are we to the tunnel where this anteroom is supposed to be located?"

"Just ahead." He shone the flashlight on her face. "You don't look too well. Do you want to go back?"

"No, let's go. Show me. That's why we're here."

"No, it's not. We're here because you had to see this theater. It's been bugging you."

"It's natural that I'd want to see this place when the woman who looks like me—"

"You don't have to make excuses to me. You wanted to be here. I brought you. Now you want to go home. I'll take you home. But you haven't really seen the main excavation. I can get you closer to the stage by accessing the next tunnel."

She shook her head. "I'm ready to go back after I see where you and Sontag have put the coffin."

He shook his head. "Stubborn." He shone the beam on the ground and took her hand. "Come on. We'll take a quick peek and get you out of here. There's nothing much to see. We've walled off the entrance to the robbers' tunnel so that no one stumbles into it before we're ready." He led her forward. "I'm not sure your hot, smoky dream tunnel isn't preferable to this one. It's oozing slime and filth."

"But you know where you're going. You're not lost and continually going down blind alleys."

"No, I know where I'm going. You're safe with me."

She felt safe, she realized suddenly. His voice was as sure as his grasp around her hand, and the darkness was no longer suffocating but . . . intimate. She felt strange. She wanted to pull away. No, she wanted to move closer. She did neither. She let him lead her into the darkness.

Do what she'd set out to do. See the tunnel where Trevor had set up his big con, check out the vomitorium, and then get back to the villa on Via Spagnola.

"Are you sure you still want to visit the vomitorium?" Trevor asked as he moved ahead of her through the tunnel toward the villa. "I think you've had enough for one night."

"Stop treating me like I'm some kind of invalid. Of course I want to go. It's not as if being down here has been particularly traumatic. You were right, we couldn't get that close to the anteroom tunnel."

"And there's nothing major to see in the vomitorium. So let's skip it for now."

"No, I have to know what's waiting for me." Lord, she was tired of this overpowering darkness. What a horror it must have been for the thieves who had dug their way into the bowels of the earth, not knowing what they were going to find around the next bend. "You said some of these tunnels collapsed over the years. Did it happen here?"

"I ran into a couple dead ends while I was exploring. Don't worry, the walls seem pretty sturdy around the vomitorium. I wouldn't let you down here if they weren't safe." He stopped. "We turn here. If you're sure you want to go."

She didn't want to go. She wanted to run straight back to the villa and go to bed. She wanted out into the light, dammit. She felt as if she'd been buried alive.

As Cira had been buried alive by those falling rocks?

"Jane?"

"I'm going." She moved past him down

the turnoff for the tunnel. "You said it's not that far off the main tunnel. It shouldn't take long. Right?"

He moved ahead of her. "It depends on what you consider long. I have an idea time's moving a little slow for you right now."

She tried to think of something else besides this blasted darkness. "Cira probably knew about that vomitorium. This was her town, her place. I can see her walking around, talking, laughing, playing her games with the men of the town."

"So can I. That's not hard to imagine."

"Not for someone like you who definitely thinks about Cira in a physical sense. She did what she had to do to survive."

"She was no martyr. She enjoyed life. According to Julius's scrolls she had an unseemly sense of humor, but he forgave her because in bed she was a true goddess."

"How patronizing. She probably had to have a sense of humor if she was forced to go to bed with him."

"No force. Choice. She made the choice, Jane."

"Her birth and circumstances made the

choice. What else did the scrolls say about her?"

"That she was kind to her friends, ruthless to her enemies, and it wasn't wise to cross her."

"Who were her friends?"

"The actors in the theater. She didn't trust anyone else."

"No family?"

"No. She took a street boy into her home and was said to have been very kind to him."

"No mention of anyone else?"

"Not as far as I remember. Most of Julius's scrolls concerned her beauty and sexual prowess, not her maternal attributes."

"Chauvinist pig."

He chuckled. "Me or Julius?"

"Both of you."

"Chauvinist or not, he was ready to kill for her. In one scroll he was contemplating murdering his rival who was stealing her away from him."

"Who was it?"

"He didn't name him. He referred to him as a young actor who had recently come to Herculaneum and taken the town by storm.

Evidently he had also taken Cira by storm and it threw Julius into a rage."

"Did he kill him?"

"I don't know."

"He's far more likely to have tried to kill Cira if he couldn't change her mind about leaving him."

"You think so? Interesting."

Not interesting. Horrible. And only a small example of the life Cira had lived.

Trevor suddenly stopped. "Here's the passage Joe will take to get to the ledge overlooking the vomitorium." He shone the light on the rocky wall to the left and she saw a shallow dark cavity close to the tunnel floor. "It's barely crawl space and he'll have to wriggle through the opening, but two yards into the passage he can stand and walk upright until he gets to the ledge."

"I would never have noticed it if you hadn't pointed it out."

"And neither will Aldo." He started down the tunnel again. "There are too many offshoot branches in this tunnel for him to notice a small hole in the wall. He's going to have a plethora of choices."

"Aren't we close to the vomitorium yet?"

"Yes, a few minutes' walk from here."

"Then let's hurry. I want out of here."

It seemed longer than the few minutes Trevor had stipulated when he stepped aside and shone his flashlight into the blackness ahead. "Here we are. Not exactly the most elegant example of Cira's time. Though those six marble bases that are scattered around the area probably held statues of gods and goddesses and maybe the current emperor on the throne."

But the bases were now jagged, broken remnants that guarded the darkness of the three tunnels leading off the vomitorium like sentinels with bared teeth. There were three photography can lights and a battery generator next to the bases but she paid no attention to them. She took a step forward, her gaze on the center of the room. A long red velvet cloth lay on the rocky ground.

"What's that?"

"Part of my prep work. I wanted to make sure Aldo knew he'd reached pay dirt."

"I'd think that the lights would tip him off."

"Okay, it's a little dramatic touch. So I'm a ham."

The velvet looked like a splotch of blood in the oozing darkness and she couldn't take her gaze off it. "That's where you're going to put the coffin?"

"Eventually. But we want Aldo to know what's coming. We can lead him so far and then we turn him loose to search for himself. After he spots this place, he'll start setting up his plans." He pointed to the walls. "I've already placed the torches." He indicated a wall to the left facing the vomitorium. "Do you see that small opening in the face of the rock about thirty feet up? That opens to the passage I showed you. Joe will be lying on his ledge and able to point his rifle directly down into this area. And, as a matter of fact, the video camera I mentioned is filming us right now." He pointed to a large flat rock close to the ground. "I'll be right there and able to roll that rock aside to get out and help you if something goes wrong."

Her gaze shifted to the right. "Two tunnels lead off this area?"

"Three including the one you'll be using."

"And Aldo will be in one of them?" She couldn't seem to tear her gaze from the yawning darkness. She could imagine him there now, watching them. "Isn't there any way we could go after him and try to hunt him down once we're sure he's there? You said he won't be familiar with these tunnels."

"Joe and I talked about the possibility." He shook his head. "It could be a nightmare to try to track someone. These tunnels are like a maze and there are at least two exits besides the one at Via Spagnola. He could stumble on one of them and then we'd lose him." He paused. "But if you're having second thoughts about drawing him into the open, tell me. It's your choice, Jane."

"I was only asking. I'm not having second thoughts."

His lips twisted. "I believe I was hoping you were."

"How strange." She took another step toward the velvet cloth. "It looks . . ."

Blood. Pain. Aldo standing looking down at the velvet in triumph.

Imagination.

Crush the fear. She swallowed. "It looks very theatrical." She turned away and started back toward the tunnel. "I'm sure Cira would have approved."

"Only if it was a comedy. Tragedy wasn't her forte."

"Not mine either."

His hand was on her elbow, supporting, comforting. "And I intend to keep it that way. Let's get out of here."

"I'll go ahead." Trevor climbed the ladder and opened the trapdoor to the kitchen. "If Quinn is awake and stirring, then I'll be the one to face his wrath first." He glanced around the room, and whispered, "All clear."

She hadn't realized how relieved she'd be to know she wouldn't have to confront Joe and Eve. She was shaken enough without having to deal with any other emotion.

"Get to bed," Trevor said as he pulled her up into the kitchen and shut the trapdoor. "Tomorrow's a big day."

"For Eve," Jane said. "Not me. As far as the media is concerned, I'm only here because I'm Eve's kid and she wanted to expose me to European culture."

"But since she's not too accessible, they may try to get at her through you. And anyone who read the *Archaeology Journal* article might see the resemblance with the statue."

"It was too blurred. Sam did a good job."

He stiffened. "Sam? You're on first-name terms?"

"He's that kind of man. And we hit it off."

"I'm sure you did. I'd bet you had him wound around your finger before you'd been in his office fifteen minutes."

She frowned. "It wasn't like that."

"Really? What was it like?"

"I told you how difficult it—" She broke off. "I don't have to make explanations. What's wrong with you?"

"Not a damn thing. I was just wondering what you did to get—" He stopped and turned away. "You're right, I'm out of line. Sorry."

"Apology *not* accepted. If you mean what I think you mean."

"It was a mistake, okay?"

"No, it's not okay. Are you some kind of sex maniac? First, that stupidity about Cira and now this. I don't sleep with people to get my way. I have a mind and I use it."

"I said I was sorry."

Anger was searing through her. "It's no wonder you have those disgusting dreams about Cira. You believe all women are prostitutes." A sudden thought occurred to her.

"It's my face. Because I look like her, you think I'd behave the same way."

"I know you wouldn't."

"No? In some part of that pea-sized, chauvinistic brain the thought must have been there or you wouldn't have acted like such an asshole."

"I don't think you're like Cira."

"No, I'm not. But I'd be proud to have her strength and her determination, and I resent you intimating that she was less than she was."

"May I point out I've never admitted comparing the two of you? You're the one who's so sure that I—"

She turned to leave the room.

"No." His hand was on her shoulder, spinning her around. "Don't turn your back on me. I've stood here and listened to you condemning me for a sex crazy son of a bitch, but I won't let you run away until I have my say."

"Let me go."

"When I've finished." His eyes were glittering in his taut face. "First, you may be right. I've lived with the image of Cira for so long that I could be unconsciously comparing you. Not consciously. I realize the differences. One of which sticks in my throat and nearly chokes me every time I look at you. Second, just because I've got my share of healthy lust doesn't mean I think less of her . . . or you. I told you that I thought she was bigger than life. Sex is part of the package, but only a part. Third, if you were older and had a little more experience I wouldn't have to tell you all this. I could show you."

She stared up at him, anger ebbing away, replaced by that odd breathlessness she'd experienced once before.

"Don't look at me like that," he said thickly. His hand left her shoulder and moved up to cup her cheek. "God, you're beautiful. You have so many expressions. . . ."

Her skin was tingling beneath his touch yet she couldn't seem to move away. "Everyone has expressions."

"Not like you. You light up, you cloud, you sparkle. . . . I could watch you for the next millennium and not get tired of—" He drew a deep breath and his hand slowly dropped away from her. "Go to bed. I'm not behaving well and it could get worse."

She didn't move.

"Go to bed."

She took a step closer and tentatively touched his chest.

"Oh, shit." He closed his eyes. "Now you've done it."

His heart was beating so hard beneath her palm. . . .

His eyes opened and he stared down at her. "No."

"Why not?" She took another step. "I think I want—"

"I know you do." He drew a deep shaky breath and took a step back. "And it's killing me." He turned and headed for the door. "Sex maniacs are like that."

She barely remembered calling him that. "Where are you going?"

"To get some air. I need it."

"You're running away from me."

"You're damn right."

"Why?"

He stopped at the door to look back at her. "Because I don't screw schoolgirls, Jane."

She could feel the heat flush her cheeks. "I didn't say I wanted to screw you. And that's not a very pleasant way of—"

"I didn't want to make it pretty. I'm trying to discourage you."

"You act as if I attacked you. I only touched you."

"That was enough. When it's you."

She lifted her chin. "Why? After all, I'm only a schoolgirl. Not important enough to be of any account."

"No more than the black plague was during the Dark Ages."

"Now you're comparing me to a plague?"

"Only the devastation factor." He studied her expression. "Have I hurt you? Christ, I keep forgetting you're more fragile than you pretend."

"You couldn't hurt me." She stared at him defiantly. "I wouldn't let you. Even though you tried your best. Let's see, you called me a plague, a schoolgirl, Cira."

"I did hurt you." He didn't speak for a moment and when he did the harshness was gone from his voice. "Look, I never want to hurt you. I want to be your friend." He shook his head. "No, that's not true. We may be friends someday but there's too much in the way right now."

"I can't imagine being friends with you."

"Ditto. That's the problem. Oh, what the hell. I'm just digging myself deeper." He slammed the door behind him as he left the house.

"I never want to hurt you."

But he had hurt her. She felt rejected and uncertain and lonely. She had acted instinctively, compulsively, and he'd refused her.

It was only her pride, she told herself. She was far from ignorant, but she didn't know anything about sex on a personal level. He obviously wanted to have nothing to do with a novice.

Well, she wasn't to blame. He was attractive and she'd responded to him. And it wasn't as if she'd been alone in that attraction. He'd touched her and made her feel—

And then the bastard had treated her as if she were a teenage Lolita.

Screw him.

She turned on her heel and went down the hall to her bedroom. Wash up and go to sleep and forget about Trevor. Look upon tonight as a learning experience. Didn't most teenage girls have a fixation on older men at one time or another?

She wasn't most girls. She didn't feel any

younger than Trevor and he hadn't been fair. She had a right to make a choice, not be sent away with a pat on the head. It wasn't as if she didn't have friends her own age who already had sexual experience. One of her classmates had even gotten married last quarter and was going to have a baby in August.

And the only reason she didn't have experience was that she hadn't been tempted. The boys at school were . . . boys. She'd felt like their older sister. She had more in common with Joe and the guys at the precinct than she had with her peers.

But not with Mark Trevor. She had nothing in common with Trevor and there was no reason she should feel this closeness to him.

She opened the bedroom door and started to get undressed as quietly as possible. Her face and hands were smudged from the tunnel but she wasn't about to go down to the bathroom to clean up. She'd been lucky Eve and Joe had slept through their excursion in the tunnels and wasn't going to risk waking them. She'd get up early and shower before they got out of bed.

She moved over to the window to look out at the winding street. Was Aldo standing somewhere in the shadow of one of those shops? Down in the theater tunnel she'd been overwhelmed by death but not the death that Aldo represented. Trevor had made her see that ancient Herculaneum far too clearly. Young suntanned athletes, languid women on litters, actors rehearsing their lines. All cut off in the prime of their lives. She'd been deluged, chilled, and crushed by the realization of the scope of those deaths.

Yet she'd never felt more alive than that moment when Trevor had touched her cheek. Perhaps that was why she'd been so affected and caught off-balance.

But now she was back to the real world.

Aldo's world.

It was truly like a funeral procession, Aldo thought. The metal coffin was being carried by four of Sontag's students and the mourners were Joe Quinn, Eve Duncan, and the reporters and soldiers following the procession.

The coffin.

He stared with feverish intensity at the box that contained Cira's remains. He'd seen specially constructed coffins like that as a boy when he'd played around his father's archaeology sites. Sontag had obviously done everything possible to preserve that skeleton from disintegration.

It would do him no good. He would smash those bones, grind them to dust. He would defile and—

Jane MacGuire and Mark Trevor had come around the corner, trailing behind the crowd around the coffin. She looked pale and composed beneath the dim electric lights illuminating the sepulchral darkness. Her gaze was fixed straight ahead, not on the coffin. What are you feeling? Anticipation? Triumph? Or is it too painful, bitch? You don't know pain yet.

Do you feel me looking at you? Does it frighten you? But then you like to have men stare at you, don't you? Trevor is watching you now, devouring you with his eyes. How long did it take you to lure him into your bed, whore?

He could feel the fury explode inside him. It shouldn't have happened. Trevor had no business coming between them. It should have been him. It *would* be him. Before he took her face, he'd take her body. He'd spend himself, cleanse away the evil that was Cira.

But it might not be enough. What if he had only a few moments to enjoy that final victory? He needed more. He needed contact again, her voice, her words.

The procession had passed out of sight down the tunnel and he had to catch up before he lost them. He moved quickly down the robbers' tunnel that ran parallel with the theater tunnel. He wasn't really worried. He'd be able to follow them. He knew these tunnels well and the darkness was his friend. The blood was singing through his veins with a rhythmic refrain that repeated over and over.

It was his time.

SEVENTEEN

"You went to pretty elaborate lengths to make this look authentic," Eve murmured to Trevor as she watched the students carefully placing the coffin on the table in the large, high-ceilinged library. "It wasn't easy for them to get that coffin up that ladder."

"Not as hard as it would have been if Sontag hadn't made sure that the opening would accommodate large art items."

"As far as I can see, you only did one thing wrong," Eve said. "If those tunnels underneath this villa location are supposed to be such a big secret, won't those students talk?"

"Not if they want to keep their internship with Sontag. He'll give them their walking papers if they exchange even a passing remark with anyone. I told you he wasn't a very nice guy. But in this case, it serves us well." He turned to Jane. "It's starting. Last chance to back out."

"Don't be ridiculous." She moistened her lips. Why couldn't she take her gaze from that coffin? It was a fake, a con. There was no reason to be disturbed. "What's in the coffin?"

"A skeleton."

Her gaze flew to his face. "You're joking."

He shook his head. "I don't know how close we're going to be observed by Aldo and I didn't want to take any chances."

"Where did you get it?"

"I visited a small museum outside Naples and borrowed it from them. It took some pretty fast talking and I made a hell of a lot of promises in Eve's name to get it." He turned to Eve. "The woman's skeleton was one of the bodies found in the marina."

"You want me to do an actual reconstruction?"

He nodded. "Everything should give the appearance of being absolutely authentic. You told me once that you had to be careful not to see any photographs because you were afraid your hands and mind would betray you. This time I want that to happen. Think Cira. Or Jane. I've set up a pedestal and bought supplies for you. How about it?"

"It depends on what promises you made in my name."

"I promised after we finished with the skeleton that you'd erase the Cira face and do a true reconstruction. The museum's poor as dirt and your name would be a great drawing card. It didn't seem too unreasonable. Will you do it?"

Eve nodded slowly, her gaze on the coffin. "What do you know about her?"

"She was young, somewhere in her teens. She had a broken shinbone. The museum thought from the lack of nutrition evidenced by her bones that she was working-class. They call her Giulia." He smiled. "And that's all I know. It's all they know." His glance went to Joe and Sontag, who were ushering the students from the room. "I'd better go and be sure Sontag doesn't make any major foul-ups. He takes a firm hand."

"Then I'm sure he'll get it." Eve was moving toward the coffin. "Where is this studio you set up for me?"

Eve's tone was absent and Jane could tell she was already absorbed in the project to come. "Can you wait until you unpack and have dinner?"

"The study," Trevor said. "And I'll bring the skull and set it up for you after I talk to Sontag."

"I want to look at her now."

"Go ahead. There's no lock on the coffin." Trevor strode toward Joe and Sontag.

Jane followed Eve across the room. "Why are you in such a hurry? She's not one of your lost ones, Eve."

"If I do her reconstruction, she will be. Not only that, I'm going to take liberties giving her your face and I want to get to know her." She lifted the lid of the coffin. "What did the people at the museum call her?"

"Giulia."

She gently touched the skull. "Hello, Giulia," she said softly. "We're going to get to know each other very well. I have nothing but respect and admiration for you and I'm eager to see who you are." She stood for a moment looking down at the skeleton and then closed the lid. "That's enough for now." She turned away. "I couldn't work on her without introducing myself."

Jane nodded. "I know you couldn't. I've seen you do it with the lost ones. Do you think they hear you?"

"I've no idea. But it makes me feel better about the intrusion." She headed for the staircase. "At least working on Giulia will keep me busy. I've been twiddling my thumbs since the day you sprang this plan on us. It's going to be a relief to get back to work. You know, she has very small, interesting facial bones. . . ." She looked back at Jane standing at the foot of the stairs. "Aren't you coming up?"

"Not now. I think I'll go out in the garden. I'm restless." She smiled. "I don't have a Giulia to think about. I'll see you at dinner."

"Stay close," Eve said as she started up the stairs again. "Joe has so many guards around that I suppose the gardens are just as safe as the house, but I like the idea of four walls around you."

"I went for walks at the lake."

"This place is different. It seems alien."

It didn't seem alien to her, Jane thought as she crossed the foyer and opened the French doors leading to the rose garden.

Ever since she'd arrived in Herculaneum she'd felt a strong sense of familiarity. Even now the sun warming her cheeks, the scent of roses, the tinkle of the fountain as it fell on the tiles were all strangely comforting.

"You look very content. I almost hate to disturb you."

She stiffened and turned to see Trevor coming out of the house. "Then don't do it. Unless you have a good reason."

"I do. I wanted to lay down the house rules now that the game's in play." His glance traveled around the garden. "This is a pretty place. It's like a garden caught in a time warp. You can almost see ladies in white gowns with bustles drifting down those paths."

"At least you didn't say ladies in togas. I'm getting an overload on ancient history."

He studied her expression. "You don't look stressed."

"I'm handling it." She looked away from him. "Did you really need to spring that skeleton on Eve? What are the chances of Aldo getting close enough to see her working on it or seeing the reconstruction itself?"

"High enough. There's no telling if he'll

get a glimpse of the reconstruction in the coffin. It was safer. Beside, Eve will be happier working."

"And that's why you did it?"

He didn't answer directly. "I like Eve. It's hard for a woman of her mind-set to sit around doing nothing."

"Yes, it is." And he was very perceptive to realize the need and fill it. "Okay, what are the house rules? Am I supposed to stay away from the garden?"

"No, just don't wander toward the gate. And you don't leave the villa without Quinn or me."

"I didn't intend to leave here. There's no reason." She paused, her gaze going to the wrought-iron gate. "He's coming to me."

"He probably will." Trevor's gaze followed hers. "But don't play into his hands."

"You didn't have to tell me that. I may be a schoolgirl but I'm not stupid."

He grimaced. "That really stung, didn't it?"

"You called it the way you saw it." She gave him a cool glance. "I *am* a schoolgirl and I'm not ashamed of it. But being my age and in school doesn't mean I'm ignorant. From the time I was five years old I ran the streets and knew every prostitute and drug runner in south Atlanta. By the time I was ten I'd bet I knew more than you did when you left that orphanage. Yes, it stung, but I thought about it and decided that you didn't know beans about me and that was your loss."

"It certainly is." He smiled. "And I'm feeling it more every minute. Do you forgive me?"

"No." Her gaze shifted to the fountain. "You didn't look at me as an individual. That's what I can't forgive. You lumped me in with the rest of my age group and walked away from me. That's okay with me. I don't need you. But, in a way, you're as bad as Aldo. He looked at my face and didn't see past it."

"Tampering with a girl of your age is a big responsibility," he said quietly. "I didn't want to hurt you."

"No one hurts me but me. And you didn't want the responsibility. Fine. I don't even know why we're talking about this. It's over." She stood up. "And it's not as if anything really happened."

"Something happened."

She knew what he meant and she

wasn't going to deny it. "Nothing that I can't forget."

He grimaced. "I wish I could say the same."

"You shouldn't forget. You fouled up." She had to get away. She was forgetting anger and remembering the hurt. She turned and started down the path. "Maybe you'll learn something from it."

"I already have." His voice followed her as she reached the arbor. "Don't go too far, Jane."

She didn't answer. She desperately hoped he'd leave. The peacefulness of that moment before he came into the garden was gone. She'd thought she'd armored herself against him but, good Lord, she was actually trembling. Was that what sex did to you? Then she could do without it. She wanted full control of her body and didn't like the way it was betraying her. She didn't want to remember how he'd looked with the mellow sunlight turning his tanned skin to gold. She didn't want to remember how it had felt to touch him.

She wouldn't remember. She'd behaved with strength and intelligence and this aftershock would disappear soon. She glanced back over her shoulder. Relief flooded her as she saw that Trevor had gone back into the house. She'd stay here a little longer to regain her composure and then leave the garden and go up to her room. She needed a shower and she needed to see Eve. Not to talk. She wasn't good at confidences, but being with Eve always calmed her. Whenever she was filled with hurt or—

Her phone rang.

Probably Eve concerned that she'd been out here too long.

"I'll be in soon, Eve. You should smell the roses. It almost makes you drunk with—"

"Are you in the garden?"

Aldo.

Shock turned her rigid and she couldn't speak.

"You're not answering."

"Yes, I'm in the garden." Her voice was uneven and she had to steady it. "Where are you?"

"Close. I watched you down in that tunnel today. I was almost near enough to touch you. I will touch you soon. Shall I tell how?"

"I'm not interested. You're being ridiculous. You can't—" She stopped. As much as she wanted to argue with him, it would ruin everything if she actually convinced him she wasn't Cira. Play along with him. Stop protesting and try to set him up. "Suppose you're right and I am Cira. You can't stop me. I'm too close. Eve is doing the reconstruction now and when it's finished, I'll be famous. Even after I'm dead I'll still live forever. My face will be posted on the sides of buses. They'll do documentaries about me. They'll name perfumes Cira. You can make your telephone calls, spit all the poison you like, but it's not going to do you any good. You'll lose."

"Bitch." He was clearly having to smother his rage. "You think you're so safe sitting surrounded by Duncan and Quinn and that bastard, Trevor. None of them can protect you. I'll kill you and then I'll kill them."

Her heart jerked and her hand tightened on the phone. "Why kill them? I'm the one you want."

"You infected them. They'd never give up hunting for me." He was silent a moment. "That bothers you."

"No, it just seems stupid."

"You're trying to deceive me. It does bother you. Perhaps when you draw them to you, it causes you to form an attachment yourself."

"If I'm as cold as you think, then you couldn't be more wrong."

"But you aren't always cold. Julius Precebio wrote with disgusting detail about your passion. You can be touched. Trevor has touched you, hasn't he?"

"No."

"You lie. I saw him look at you." His voice turned soft. "And I saw you with Eve Duncan on the porch one night. You were very emotional."

She felt a cold chill. "I was pretending."

"Maybe. But maybe not. I hear something in your tone. . . ." His own tone was suddenly laden with malice. "At any rate, it's too promising not to explore. Shall I tell you what I'm going to do to Eve Duncan?"

"No."

"She works very hard giving victims back their faces, doesn't she? I'm going to take her face away. I've gotten very proficient at slicing away that evil face of yours. Sometimes those women stayed conscious until the end. I'll go slowly with Duncan and make sure she suffers the full torment she deserves."

She tried to keep her voice from shaking. "You truly are a monster."

"Oh, no, I'm the sword of justice. You're the monster. It's you who twisted my father's mind until he could give me nothing but scorn, it's you who lured Duncan and the others here when Sontag found that skeleton. You knew I'd kill them if they got in my way."

"You're not talking about killing them if they get in your way. You're saying that you'll kill them anyway."

"Once you started using them, they automatically had to be removed." He chuckled. "And now that I know it's going to upset you, I may have to plan a way to do it while you're still alive. It will be an added pleasure."

"Aren't you getting distracted? I'm your target."

"I couldn't be more focused. It's been a pleasure chatting with you. We'll do it again soon. Good-bye, Cira." He hung up.

Dear God, she was shaking.

She reached out and grabbed the

wrought-iron post of the arbor to steady herself. Ugliness. Madness. Death.

Terror.

Her heart was beating hard, painfully hard.

Eve. Joe. Trevor.

God help her, Eve . . .

"Jane?"

She looked over her shoulder to see Trevor coming down the path from the house.

"What's wrong?"

She shook her head.

"What's wrong, dammit?" He reached out and grabbed her shoulders. "I was keeping an eye on you from the house and I saw you reach out and grab that fence as if it were a lifeline."

"Phone call," she said numbly. "Jesus, Eve."

"The call was from Eve?"

"Aldo."

He stiffened. "What?"

"He said he'd call me. We were expecting it. I just didn't—" She tried to pull away. "Let me go."

"When you finish telling me what the hell's happening."

"Aldo."

"What did he say?"

"Too much." She moistened her lips. "He's really nuts. And I'm worse. I fouled up. I was going to try to set him up but then I lost him. I let him see . . . I blew it. I got so scared and he could tell." Her hands clenched into fists but she couldn't stop the trembling. "He could tell and now he'll do it. But I can't let him. It's my fault. I won't let him near her, not a—"

"Jane, shut up. Do you want me to slap you?"

She looked up at him in shock. "You do and I'll kick you so hard in the nuts, you'll be a soprano."

"Okay, you're back to normal." His hands loosened on her shoulders. "Come on and sit down on the bench and get your breath."

She'd already gotten her breath back but she still couldn't control the shaking. She sat down and crossed her arms over her chest. "I'm not back to normal. I'm scared and sick and I want to be alone. Go away."

"The hell I will. When you're ready to talk to me, I'm going to be here."

Oh, let him stay. It didn't matter. Give him

what he wanted. She took a deep breath. "He's going to kill her. It doesn't matter if he kills me first. He's going to kill her anyway."

"Eve?"

"Eve and Joe and you. But he got a good deal of pleasure out of telling me how he was going to kill Eve." Her nails dug into her palms. "I won't let him do it. I'll keep her safe."

"Jane, Eve knew there was a certain amount of danger when she decided to come here. You knew it too."

"But I didn't know that he'd make her a target. I thought he'd focus on me. All his other victims were women with my face. How was I to know he'd decide everyone I was close to had to die? He even wants to kill you."

"I'm flattered he thinks you'd care, but he had his reasons to kill me before you came on the scene."

"He had no reason to kill Eve or Joe."

"Aldo's phone call actually changed nothing, Jane. He made a few threats and tried to panic you."

"He did panic me." But the terror was beginning to ebb and she could think again. "And he enjoyed it. He caught me off guard and I let him see how much he could hurt me."

"Okay, but you didn't blow it completely. Right? You didn't set him up, but he's going to call again?"

"He said he was." She added bitterly, "He enjoyed it so much that he probably won't want to wait to do it again."

"Then you can see that this call basically changed nothing."

"You're wrong. I didn't realize to what extent I was risking Eve and Joe. I do now. And I made it worse for them by letting Aldo know how much they meant to me." Her lips tightened. "And that makes everything different. We've got to keep Eve and Joe safe."

"We'll do our best."

"That's not good enough." She stood up. "You were right to treat me like an idiot schoolgirl. I should have been able to fool him, turn him in another direction. But I didn't. I was so scared that I couldn't think fast enough. I'm not waiting around for him to come after Eve."

"Eve won't be down in the tunnel with us and she'll have protection here at the villa."

She whirled on him. "And what if he kills me? Do you guarantee that he won't get past her security and slice her to ribbons? He's not going to hurt Eve. He's not even going to get close to her," she said fiercely. "Do you have any idea how much I care about her?"

"I think I do," he said gently.

"Then you should know that I'll never let that piece of filth within a mile of her. So if you want Aldo, you'd better make me a promise. No matter what happens, you're going to keep Eve and Joe from being hurt. I don't care if Aldo gets away. I don't care if you think I'm in danger. Nothing happens to them."

"That's a difficult promise to make but I'll do my best."

"*Promise* me."

"I promise." His smile was twisted. "And I guess I should feel fortunate you don't care enough about me to demand the same promise about my safety."

"You can take care of yourself. You weren't pulled into this like Eve and Joe. Besides, it's all about Aldo with you."

"Of course. What else? It's all about Aldo."

* * *

"What's wrong with her?" Bartlett asked as he met Trevor at the French doors. "She looked like she'd run into Godzilla."

"Close. She got a phone call from Aldo."

Bartlett's eyes widened. "Indeed."

Trevor nodded jerkily. "And he scared the hell out of her."

"That doesn't really compute," Bartlett said. "Jane doesn't scare easily."

"She does when it concerns Eve and Joe Quinn. Evidently Aldo's threats were specific and very ugly."

"I see." Bartlett nodded gravely. "Yes, that would tip her over the edge. She's very wary of most people but Eve and Joe are her entire world."

"She made me promise to keep them safe. How the hell am I going to do that in a situation like this?"

"I'm sure you'll find a way. Ever since we met, you've been juggling ideas and possibilities and twisting events to suit yourself. It's automatic with you." He smiled. "I find it quite exhausting to watch since my mind doesn't have that capability. But whatever you decide I'm going to have a part in it. I notice that I've been left out in the cold in all this planning that's going on. It hurts my feelings." He added quietly, "I won't get in your way but I'm tired of hovering on the edge. I have to help."

"I told you that you were to stay here and protect Eve."

"Quinn's arranged security for her that's much more qualified than I am."

"According to Jane, she can't have too much."

"I'm going with you."

"Bartlett, I don't need you to—" He stopped and shrugged. "Come ahead. Why shouldn't I risk your neck, too? I'm putting everyone else on the chopping block."

"Dear me, you are having guilty twinges, aren't you? May I point out that I'm a grown man with free choice? And you told me that it was Jane who concocted the plan to use herself as bait."

"But I gave her the rope to stake herself out for him." He turned on his heel. "Oh, what the hell. Why should a bastard like me give a damn? Do what you like."

The red velvet cloth lay on the rocky floor waiting in the darkness.

Waiting for her.

The beam of Aldo's flashlight played over the gleaming marble bases, the photography lights and battery, and then beyond them to the tunnels leading off the vomitorium. He was tempted to go and explore but there was no telling what traps the bitch had laid for him. It was bad enough she'd managed to find this tunnel of which he had no prior knowledge. It had come as a complete surprise to him when he'd seen them carry the coffin down an unexpected turn. He'd followed them to the ladder leading to the Via Spagnola before he'd doubled back. It was only after he'd phoned Jane MacGuire later that day that he'd come back down and started to reconnoiter in depth.

And then he'd found this cloth, red as blood, living blood.

Waiting for the coffin. Waiting for her.

I've *got* you, bitch.

Did you think that you could find a place in this city where you'd be safe from me? There were ways to find out what he needed without risking being caught in her trap.

He bent down and touched the velvet

with his fingertips and a thrill went through him.

Soft. Smooth. Cold.

Like the flesh of a dead woman.

“You’re almost finished.”

Eve glanced at the doorway of the study where Joe stood watching her. She nodded. “Close. I started the final molding.”

“And you’re eager as hell. You’ve been working full steam ahead.” He walked over to the pedestal to stand beside her. “Why? We’re setting the pace. Aldo’s not going to be moving until we do.”

“I want to be done with it. It feels strange making this skull with Jane’s features. It’s almost like a betrayal.” She smoothed the clay at the temple. “I’m glad I’ll be able to make it up to Giulia later.”

“Maybe if she knew she’d be glad that she was helping to save Jane.” Joe smiled. “I should have known you’d become involved with her.”

“She’s interesting. The museum said she was working-class, possibly a laborer. I wonder what her life was like.” She tilted her head. "And I wonder what she really looks like. . . ."

"You'll know soon."

She nodded. "You bet I will. As soon as this is over. This is so weird. . . ." She brushed the hair back from her forehead. "First, that reconstruction of Caroline Halliburton and now this one. Both Jane. Do you know, Jane was talking about how things seem to go in circles."

"You've got clay on your face." He took his handkerchief and carefully wiped her forehead. "How many times have I done this over the years?"

"I'm sure enough to qualify for the Guinness Book of Records. Since my profession isn't the most popular one in the world." She smiled. "And you're very good at it."

"My pleasure." His finger gently touched her upper lip. "Always. Taking care of you fills me with— It warms me."

"I know." Her smile faded. "And that's why you're trying to keep me away from that tunnel."

"I am keeping you away." His lips brushed her nose. "You've done your part. Now let me do mine."

"I didn't argue when you were all talking

details because I knew it wouldn't do any good." She slid her arms around his waist and buried her face in his chest. "But if you think I'm going to let you go down there without me, you're crazy."

"Then I'm crazy."

She looked up at him. "No," she said firmly. "I'll do anything you say to keep safe, but I'm going to be there. Get me a gun. You know I can use it. You're the one who taught me."

He shook his head.

"You're going to be down in that hellhole. So is Jane. Do you think you can keep me away? Either take me yourself or watch me go down alone."

He sighed. "I'll take you." His lips tightened. "You'll go into the passage with me. You stay quiet. You don't move a muscle no matter what you see happening. You let me take care of it. Understand?"

She didn't answer.

"If you don't, the first thing I'll do is knock you out to make sure you don't get yourself killed."

"I wouldn't forgive you for that."

"I'd take my chances. It's better than the alternative." He smiled recklessly. "You forgave me for doing something a hell of a lot worse. Well, maybe not entirely, but you let me stay with you. And after all I've done to mend my fences, I'm not losing you to that son of a bitch."

"It's Jane you have to worry about."

"No, it's you. First, and always. Then it's Jane and the rest of the world." He kissed her, hard. "I can't be any other way. You should know that by now."

Yes, she knew, and that knowledge had been her shelter and her armor all these years. Dear God, she loved him. Her arms tightened around him. "Me, too. You first, Joe."

He shook his head. "Not yet. Someday, maybe. I'll take my turn." He rubbed slowly, sensuously, against her. "But in the meantime . . . I've never made love to you in Herculaneum or any other ancient city. Don't you think we should rectify that?" He glanced at the skull on the pedestal. "Since this lady's first reconstruction's not going to furnish any surprises, I definitely think Giulia would approve."

"So do I." She started unbuttoning his shirt. "And, anyway, I need to show you. You first, Joe . . ."

EIGHTEEN

October 20
10:40 A.M.

"He found the vomitorium." Trevor strode across the parlor and popped the tape into the player. "At four-seventeen this morning. I do love cameras with all the bells and whistles."

"You're sure?" Jane asked.

"Oh, yes." He pressed the button. "It's dark as hell but the camera's built for low light. You can make him out."

Yes, she could make him out, Jane thought numbly as she watched Aldo bend and touch the red velvet throw. Dear God, his expression . . .

"Evil," she whispered. "How could anyone be that evil?"

The picture disappeared from the TV

screen. "That's enough," Trevor said curtly. "I just wanted you to know that we weren't doing all this planning for nothing. He found the bait and now we have to get him to go after it."

"No, *I* have to get him to go after it." She swallowed to ease the tightness of her throat. "It shouldn't be that difficult. He wants Cira and me so bad he can taste it. He's . . . hungry. When he reached down to touch that cloth he looked like a cannibal."

"Then it's our job to give him a bellyache." He headed for the door. "I'll show this to Joe and Eve. They'll be glad to know we're on target."

"Is that the only time you caught Aldo on tape?"

"Yes, no more sightings at the vomitorium, but you can bet he was exploring those tunnels after he found it."

She sat there for a moment after he'd left, staring blindly at the blank TV screen. She shouldn't be this shocked by that brief glimpse of Aldo. She knew exactly what he was. She didn't need this reminder.

But, God in heaven, his expression . . .

* * *

Jane was sitting in the parlor when her phone rang at two-thirty the next afternoon.

She tensed.

"Answer it," Trevor said from across the room. "You know what to say."

Yes, she knew. She'd rehearsed it enough mentally since she'd blown that other opportunity. She pressed the talk button. "Aldo?"

"You've been waiting for my call? That's good. That's the way it should be. I've been waiting a long time for you. Years."

"You can wait forever. It won't do you any good. I'm too close. In another two days you can kill all the women with my face on earth and I'll still survive. My face will be everywhere."

There was a silence. "Two days? That's not the truth. You told me only two days ago that Duncan had only started the reconstruction and that you needed—"

"Two days is a long time for Eve when she's motivated. And you can bet that I motivated her. I was hoping you'd believe you had all the time in the world so we could complete our plans. Trevor managed to get the reporters from all the major newspapers to commit to the great unveiling. Eve's doing a wonderful job. The face of the reconstruction looks young and strong and when I look at it I see myself."

"You see the devil."

"No, you see the devil. I see life and power enough to rid myself of enemies like you."

"You'll never rid yourself of me. I'm your nemesis."

"You're a poor, pitiful pervert who has delusions of grandeur."

"You're not going to make me angry again." He was silent a moment. "Where is this photo shoot going to take place?"

She waited a moment before saying, "Here at the library in the villa, of course. At nine o'clock in the evening, day after tomorrow." She tried to make her tone mocking. "You have an invitation. Don't you want to see the huge splash the reconstruction makes?"

"You're lying. It's not going to be at the villa."

"No? Then where is it going to be held?"

"Did you think I wouldn't find all that equipment at the vomitorium?"

"Dear me, you must have been doing a little spying. You're right, of course. We think the photo shoot will be much more effective down in the tunnels. That should be to your advantage if you decide to join us."

"Do you think I don't know you'll all be waiting for me?"

"All? I don't need anyone else to rid myself of vermin like you. But I'll be waiting for you. I need to destroy you before you destroy me."

"I won't be there. I'm not a fool."

"But you're a coward." She paused. "Okay, don't come to the press conference. I'll meet you at the vomitorium tomorrow night at nine o'clock. I'll have Trevor take down the coffin with the reconstruction and then leave. You'll have us both, if you're man enough to kill me and destroy the skeleton."

"Tomorrow night."

"Tempted? No skeleton for the press conference the next night and you rid yourself of me."

"It's a trick."

"If it is, are you clever enough to turn it against me? I don't think you are. You won't be there. You'll be too frightened. You know I've beaten you all your life. I took away your father. I took away your childhood and now I'm going to show you what a sniveling failure you really—"

"Shut up."

"Why should I? You're nothing. You're weak. I don't have to have help to crush you."

"No, you're so proud of yourself." He sneered. "You've been preparing yourself to meet all comers. Do you still have that thirty-two Smith and Wesson Quinn gave you?"

She was silent, surprised.

"See? I know everything about you. I know you can fire a gun and you were issued a hunting license when you were sixteen. The computer is a wonderful source of information and I even know the name of the firing range where Joe Quinn took you to teach you."

"If you're so sure that destiny is on your side, then that shouldn't bother you. Don't you think you're smart enough to find out if there's anyone down there but me?"

"Of course I am."

"Did that sting? Good. You deserve it. Poor bastard, afraid of a seventeen-year-old girl."

"I'm not afraid."

"Admit it. You're out of your league, Aldo. I'll be there tomorrow night. Come or don't come. I don't care. I'll have a chance to kill you another day. But this is your last chance. After that press conference it won't matter if you destroy the reconstruction. I'll live on forever."

"No! It won't happen and I won't be taunted by you."

"Then don't come. Read about it in the newspapers." She hung up, drew a deep breath, and looked at Trevor. "How did I do?"

"You could have fooled me," Trevor said.

She shook her head. "He was very wary." She paused. "I keep thinking about that video of him in the vomitorium. He looked so triumphant, so at home in that tunnel." She shivered. "I felt caught, smothered, down there. And you said they were like a maze."

"But you're not going to have to know anything about the tunnels. And remember, Aldo is in the same boat as you are. He's not familiar with the Via Spagnola tunnels. Even if he's been doing some tentative exploring, it would take months to learn them without a map."

"Do you think he'll come?"

"If he can find an advantage, if he can see any way he can kill you and survive."

"It won't be easy. He's going to be suspicious. He knows you and Joe will be trying to trap him."

"But you threw down the ultimate challenge and he's just nuts enough to try to do it. Isn't that what we've been counting on?"

Madness and that sick hunger to kill. "Yes."

"And he'll be down there checking out the immediate area. He won't find anything but what we want him to find. Our principal advantage is the temptation you offer and his desperation at the thought of Cira becoming a household name. If anything will draw him out of his hole into the open that will be it."

She tried to think, mentally going over the conversation word for word. "I have to look vulnerable. He's not going to show his face if I show up armed to the teeth."

His lips tightened. "There's no way you're going down there without a weapon."

"Do you think I'm crazy? But no jacket or pockets that could hide a weapon." She repeated, "I've got to look vulnerable. You'll have to plant a gun somewhere I can get to it fast."

He thought about it. "Underneath the red velvet throw. Lower right-hand corner as you come out of the tunnel. It will only take you seconds to get to it. And we'll plant another in the coffin itself. Just in case."

Just in case something went wrong. She didn't want to consider that possibility. "Tomorrow night." She tried to keep her voice even. "After all this time it seems impossible it's finally—"

"Stop thinking about it," he said roughly. "If you're going to opt out, do it. I did the best I could but I don't like it. You'll be lucky if we don't get you killed."

"You don't have to like it. All you have to do is protect Joe and Eve." She paused. "You keep trying to talk me out of this. You seem . . . torn. Maybe it wasn't only the money. Perhaps this Pietro did mean something to you."

"How kind of you to grant that I have a few human feelings."

"How am I supposed to know what you're feeling when you don't let anyone see them? Was it the gold or was it Pietro Tatligno?"

"The gold, of course."

"Damn you, talk to me."

"What do you want from me?" His lips twisted. "Do you want me to tell you that Pietro saved my ass in Colombia? That he was the only person I ever knew that I felt I could trust? That he was closer than a brother to me?"

"Was he?" she whispered.

"Hell, no. It's all a bunch of lies. Of course it was the gold." He stood up and headed for the door. "Let's go tell Eve and Quinn we've made the connection."

October 21
7:37 P.M.

It was getting dark.

"It's time," Trevor said quietly from the doorway. "You told me to tell you when Quinn was going down to the tunnel. He's heading for the kitchen now."

Jane turned away from the parlor window and started for the hall. "You checked out the passageway?"

"I've just come back." He smiled. "Can't

you tell? I look like I've been crawling through a sewer. It's safe. First, Bartlett and I carried the coffin down and positioned it and then I checked out the passage. And I've left Bartlett down there to make sure it stays safe until Quinn gets to his ledge."

She stopped. "Bartlett?"

"Don't worry. I gave him a shotgun and orders to fire at anyone but me or Quinn. You don't have to have much martial skill to be intimidating with a shotgun. After we get down there, Bartlett is going to stay near the ladder and guard the entrance to the villa. It's best that someone is outside those tunnels to give warning, if something goes wrong."

If something goes wrong. Yet another qualification that filled her with panic. "I thought Bartlett was going to stay up here with Eve."

"So did I. But he decided that wasn't going to happen. I arranged for there to be four security men to stay with her instead. Lord knows what other security Quinn's set up."

"You promised me."

"And I'll keep it. I won't let Aldo get past me to climb the ladder to the villa." He nudged her toward the kitchen. "If you want to see Quinn before he goes down, you'd better hurry. He was opening the trapdoor when I left him."

"We give Joe fifteen minutes and then we follow him?"

Trevor nodded. "That should give him time to get up on the ledge and position himself. I'll be there to back him up in—"

"Eve!" Jane ran toward the trapdoor. "What are you doing?"

Eve was on the third step descending the ladder. "What does it look like?" She took another step down. "Really, Jane. What did you expect? I wasn't going to let Joe or you go down there without me."

"You were supposed to—" She whirled on Joe. "Tell her— Keep her out of there."

"Do you think I haven't tried? Can't do it. You know her. All we can hope for is damage control."

"Why didn't you tell me?" Her voice was anguished. "Why didn't you—"

"Because I knew you'd be upset." Eve grimaced. "And you are. But now you don't have to stew about it for days. Come on, Joe. Let's get going."

"Don't do this, Eve," Jane pleaded. "Please."

Eve shook her head. "Jane, we're a family. We do things together." She took another two steps down and disappeared from view.

"No!"

Joe started down the ladder. "You can't budge her. I'll take care of her, Jane."

"Take care of yourself, Joe," she whispered. Dear God, she had a terrible sinking feeling. It was only beginning and everything was going wrong.

Joe was out of sight. Lost in the darkness of the tunnel.

"I didn't know," Trevor said. "As God is my witness, I thought Eve was staying here in the villa."

"I know you did," she said shakily. "It almost makes you believe in fate, doesn't it?" She shook her head to clear it. "But not Aldo's version of destiny. We can't let that happen."

"She'll be with Quinn and me. I'll keep my promise."

"You'd better." She wanted to start down that ladder, run after Eve and Joe through the darkness. She couldn't do it, she realized frantically. She had to wait until they got into position on that ledge.

Fifteen minutes.

October 21
8:02 P.M.

"I leave you here," Trevor said in a low voice as he fell to his knees at the entrance of the passage leading to Joe's ledge. "I'm going to work my way around to where Joe and Eve are waiting. The vomitorium is right ahead." He handed her a flashlight. "Remember, a thirty-two Smith and Wesson is under the velvet throw and another gun is in the coffin. Joe said you knew how to use it, but don't do it unless you have to. If Aldo sees you with it, he may decide that a long-range killing isn't that bad. When you get up ahead, the torches are lit. But it's best if you try to stay in the shadows."

She moistened her lips. "Then how will he see me?"

"He'll be able to see you. Just don't make it too easy for him."

She laughed shakily. "Don't worry. I've no intention of doing that. But hiding in the shadows isn't going to do much good. You said he wouldn't shoot me and the whole point is to draw him toward me so that Joe can get his shot."

Trevor muttered a curse and shone the beam of the flashlight on her face. "You're scared. We can call this off. It's not too late."

"No, we can't." She shielded her face from the light. "And of course I'm scared. I'm not an idiot. Get going. I want you there to protect Joe and Eve."

He hesitated a moment and then began to crawl through the opening.

He was gone.

Silence.

Darkness.

Alone.

Or was she alone? Was Aldo somewhere behind her in the darkness?

No, Trevor had positioned Bartlett outside the tunnel to keep an eye out. If Aldo was in this tunnel, he was ahead at the vomitorium. Waiting for her.

Her heart was pounding so hard she felt

as if it were reverberating like thunder through the tunnel.

It was going to be all right. Joe would warn her if Aldo were waiting for her at the vomitorium. He'd either shoot Aldo or he'd fire off a warning shot if that weren't possible.

She drew a deep breath and started forward. Right ahead, Trevor had said. Look straight in front of her, move fast, and it would soon be over.

Christ, how she hated this darkness.

Is that how you felt, Cira?

"Shit. Shit. Shit." Trevor ground out the curse like a mantra as he ran through the tunnel, playing the powerful beam of the flashlight on either side of him. She'd been afraid. Of course she'd been afraid. She was only a kid.

Aldo didn't think of her as a kid. He thought of her as a demon. He thought of her as dead meat. Damn him. Damn him.

Why was he damning Aldo? Trevor was the one who'd let her walk down that tunnel alone.

It should be safe. He'd taken every precaution he could.

No, he could have taken another precaution. He could have found some way other than using Jane as bait. He could have forgotten Pietro and remembered that she deserved to live a—

Red.

He skidded to a stop.

The beam of his flashlight had picked up something red on the ground near a boulder up ahead. It was just a trace, a glimpse, and he'd almost missed it.

Blood?

He lifted the light and warily scanned the darkness ahead.

Nothing.

He moved slowly toward the boulder. As he reached it he saw the red substance was trickling from behind the rock. He bent and touched his fingers to it.

Yes, blood.

He drew his gun from his jacket and inched closer. He was almost on top of the boulder before he saw the huddled body of the man behind it.

Blood everywhere. Blood on his face.

Blood on his shirt. His throat was cut from ear to ear.

Quinn?

Dear God, it looked like a scene from a horror movie, Jane thought.

She stared in morbid fascination at the coffin resting on the red velvet cloth and then up to the opening where Joe was waiting with his rifle.

No, don't look up there. She couldn't be sure that Aldo wasn't watching her. She tore her gaze away and looked back at the coffin.

Why was Aldo letting her stand here? Why didn't he make his move?

Throw the dice. Make it strong. Make it bold. She took a step forward out of the shadows. "Here I am, Aldo." Her tone was challenging. At least, she hoped it was. "Are you there? Did you screw up your courage enough to meet me?"

No answer.

"I can feel your eyes on me. Coward." She took another step forward. "It's just as I thought. You're afraid of me. Your father was afraid, too. But he still loved me. More than anything. Much more than you. You didn't matter at all to him."

No answer.

"Not that I blame him. He needed a son he could be proud of, not a stupid coward like you." She started for the coffin. "Well, if you're not going to show yourself I'll just take a look at the reconstruction and make sure it's okay after the trip down that ladder. Eve did a magnificent—"

"Get away from the coffin. She's mine now. And soon she won't exist."

She whirled toward the tunnel to her right from where the voice had come. She could see nothing but darkness. "Aldo?"

"Get away from the coffin."

"Why should I?" She moistened her lips. "Come out from under your rock and stop me."

He laughed. "Under my rock? That's very apropos. As it happens, I deposited a troublesome bundle under a rock very recently. Well, he was partially under, mostly behind. I had to take what I could get. It's difficult to find large loose boulders in these tunnels. The thieves who dug them were very efficient in clearing them."

She stiffened. "He?"

"It wasn't your Eve. Not yet. She'll have to take her turn. But that turn will come very shortly. Let's see, only a few minutes . . ."

It could be a bluff. "I don't believe you."

"Too bad. It will come as such an unpleasant shock. . . ."

Christ.

Trevor tore through the tunnel toward the ledge.

He'd promised her Eve would be safe.

Blood.

Throat slit from ear to ear.

Run faster.

Next turn.

Faster.

NINETEEN

"One more minute," Aldo said. "I hope you said your good-byes to her."

Fear surged through her. He had to be bluffing, but the threat was terrifying her. She had to force him to come into the light. She stepped toward the coffin.

"Don't move."

She took another step.

"Don't take another step. I don't have to wait. I can make it happen now."

One more minute.

I can make it happen now.

What could Aldo do that—?

And then the realization hit home.

Oh, God.

"Eve! Joe!" she screamed. "Get out of—"

The earth bellowed and shook as the tunnel exploded around her!

She fell to the ground.

Flying rocks.

Blood on her cheek.

Darkness.

The explosion had shaken three of the torches from the wall.

Dear God, and the wall and boulder behind which Joe and Eve were hidden were no longer there. It was a pile of rubble and stone.

Get up.

He'd be coming.

He was already coming. She saw his shadow move in the opening of the offshoot tunnel where he was standing.

The guns.

One underneath the cloth. One in the coffin.

Dear God. Both the coffin and the cloth were buried under rocks and rubble. She'd never be able to get to either gun in time.

She heard his footsteps. "We're alone now, Cira. I set the dynamite too close to the opening for them to survive."

She was on her feet and running back toward the main tunnel.

Pain.

In her cheek. The back of her neck. Her shoulder.

Forget it. Get to the main tunnel. Get to the ladder to the villa.

Joe. Eve.

Don't think of them. It hurt too much.

Trevor. Trevor had been in that tunnel with them. . . .

Death.

Stop crying. Run faster. Get out of here so that you can kill the bastard.

"Not so brave now." Aldo's voice was mocking. "Run, little rabbit."

She should be near the passage where Trevor had crawled into the auxiliary tunnel and left her. The main tunnel leading to the villa was four turns beyond it.

Yes, there was the opening. Go faster. Only a little more distance and she'd be past it and—

Rumbling.

Falling rock.

The ground shook beneath her feet.

Another explosion!

"That should take care of the main entrance," he said mockingly. "Did you think I'd let you get back to your fine villa? I always knew there was a chance you'd try to trap me. But I'm too clever for you."

He was still far behind her. He was showing his contempt by walking slowly, strolling, she realized in a fury.

The passage. She fell to her knees and dove into the tunnel Trevor had taken. Aldo had said he'd set the charge close to the ledge near the vomitorium. Let this passage not be totally collapsed, she prayed. Let her be able to—

She could straighten, stand up. She could run!

"But how are you going to get out of here?" Aldo's voice was mocking as he crawled after her. "The other end has to be blocked by stone . . . and bodies. Are you going to crawl over them?"

"And how are you going to get out?" she called back to him. "That explosion closed your way out too. Trevor said it was like a maze down here. You'll get lost and die."

"There are other ways out. I won't get lost. I know everything about these tunnels I need to know."

"You lie. It would have taken you weeks to learn them."

"Is that what Trevor told you?" He was

closer behind her. Moving faster. "Wrong. You'll see why in—"

She stumbled over something . . . soft.

A body!

Blood. Throat cut.

The intake of her breath was almost a sob.

"Oh, you found him," Aldo said. "Actually, I thought I'd have to point him out to you. I hid him behind that boulder. Someone must have moved him. Perhaps I'd better get on with this a little more quickly."

She forced herself to move beyond that grisly body. "Who is it?"

"Quinn, of course."

She forced herself to think, remember. Relief soared through her. "It's not Joe. Joe is thinner, tougher looking. So is Trevor."

Aldo chuckled. "You're right. Just a little joke."

"Sadistic bastard."

"I'm entitled to my enjoyment of the situation. I've waited a long time for this."

"Who is it?"

"Sontag. I looked up the real estate records in my computer and found the deed to the villa under Sontag's name. If Sontag owned the villa, then he must have known about the tunnels. My father told me he was a crook and there's no question he'd use those tunnels for his own ends. But when I realized you were going to use the vomitorium for that foul photo shoot I knew what a monumental task it would be to familiarize myself with this tunnel. I knew I had to go to the source.

He sounded closer. Find a weapon, any weapon.

He started again. "I paid him a visit and persuaded him to come down here with me and stroll around a bit. He was very cooperative. He even pointed out the secret passage and ledge he'd shown Trevor. After I got copies of the maps from him, I decided that he'd outlived his usefulness."

"So you killed him."

"I couldn't risk him running to Trevor. He had Sontag very intimidated."

Another turn in the tunnel. She must be getting close to the end. She might run into a blockage at any moment. "You would have killed him anyway."

"That's true. I admit it was a release. I've been very frustrated lately. Now that's at an end."

"Even if you kill me, the coffin is buried

under all that rubble. You won't be able to destroy that skeleton."

"I'm in no hurry. It will take time for anyone to get past those rocks blocking the entrance. I'll have my chance. I hear you breathing. Hard. Very hard. You told me you were strong. How strong are you now, Cira?"

"Strong enough." The rock was looser here. Shards were lying on the ground. She must be coming closer to the site of the explosion.

She'd be trapped. Find a weapon.

Get out of his sight.

She put on speed and dashed around the next turn. Her gaze searched wildly.

There!

She picked up an eight-inch shard and thrust it in the waistband of her trousers. Was it sharp enough?

Run.

Hot. Smoky.

Night without air.

"You're almost at the end," Aldo said. "I have my knife in my hand. It's a surgeon's knife. Beautiful. Sharp. Efficient. One last face to remove. Do you know how much it hurts?"

"It won't be the last. You talk as if you have a mission but you're only a murderer. You like it too much."

"It's true, it's my pleasure as well as duty to remove your face from the universe."

"You see? But killing me won't do you any good. The skeleton in that coffin isn't Cira. Her name is Giulia."

Silence. "You lie."

"It was all a con."

"Bitch," he snarled. "You're lying. It's my time. My destiny."

"You're a loser. Trevor got her skeleton from a museum in Naples. You can check it yourself."

The walls were closing in on her.

No air.

Antonio . . .

The rubble was getting heavier, deeper here.

He was right behind her.

Jesus, she could see a wall of rock ahead!

Don't wait until she came to the blockage. Give herself time to maneuver.

"You're a fool. It was so easy to deceive you. You haven't won any—" She cried out as she stumbled and fell to the ground.

She heard his grunt of triumph. "Who's the fool?" His hand grasped her shoulder and jerked her over. "Even if I believed you, I'm still too—"

She drove the rock shard up into his chest with all her strength.

He screamed!

She rolled sideways and struggled to push him away from her. Lord, he was heavy, a deadweight.

But he wasn't dead. He was moving, the knife in his hand gleaming in the dim light of the flashlight she'd dropped on the ground.

She scooted away, searching wildly for another shard, anything she could use as a weapon.

"I won't die," he whispered. "I can't die. It's not . . . meant. You're the one who has to die."

"The hell I will."

That rock—it was lying within reach. She crawled toward it.

Pain.

His knife had entered her calf.

Ignore it.

Her hand closed on the rock and she rolled over.

Hit him. Hit him. Hit him.

But he was close, almost on top of her again. The first blow she aimed at his forehead barely touched him.

His knife was raised.

She struck his arm with the rock. Weak blow. It deflected the thrust but he still held the weapon. Try again.

"You're fading," he muttered. "Where's your power now?" He raised the knife again. "Burn in hell, Cira. I'm the one who has the—"

A shot.

He jerked as the bullet struck him between the eyes. He fell on top of her.

Bullet? she wondered dazedly. She could feel the cold metal of Aldo's knife pressed against her breast. She half expected him to move, attack her again.

Then he was gone, pulled roughly off her body, and thrown aside. "Are you hurt?"

Trevor. It was Trevor, she realized numbly.

"Answer me. Are you hurt?" His shirt was torn half off his body. His face was covered with dirt.

"You're alive."

"I won't be for long, if you're not all right. Quinn will strangle me. What hurts? Answer me."

She tried to think. “Shoulder. The rocks.”

He shone the light on her shoulder. “Bruising. It doesn’t look like anything is broken. Anywhere else?”

“Right leg. Aldo . . .” She shook her head to clear it. “Where did you come from?”

“I burrowed my way through that cave-in up ahead. I was working my way through it when I heard your voice.” He was tearing her khaki trousers. “It nearly drove me nuts. I could hear you, but I couldn’t get to you. I didn’t think I’d be in time.” He examined the wound. “He missed the artery. Not too much bleeding. It will need stitches.” He made a pressure bandage with his shirt. “But maybe I’m safe from Eve’s wrath.”

“Eve?” She forgot to breathe. “Eve’s alive?”

He nodded. “We couldn’t get to her but she said she wasn’t hurt.”

“Joe?”

“Minor cuts, I think. I didn’t take time to check.”

“Why not?”

“The vomitorium entrance was blocked by the explosion. I had to try to go the long way round to get to you. Joe was digging

Eve out of the rubble so I told him I'd go for you."

"Aldo said— You shouldn't be alive. None of you should be alive. Aldo said that he set the explosives close to the ledge by the vomitorium."

"He did, but we weren't there when they went off. I got to Eve and Joe in time to get them out of the immediate area. Dammit, I checked that ledge earlier this evening and so did Joe. He must have stuffed some plastique in a crevice and camouflaged it. It's so dark back there that without instruments we—"

"I don't *care* about the plastique. Then Eve and Joe got out safely?"

"Not exactly." He finished the bandage and sat back on his heels. "We got out of ground zero, but not in time to avoid the blast. Eve was ahead of us and got caught in a rock slide."

"Then she must be hurt. We have to get to her."

"You're not going anywhere. Joe is digging her out."

"We have to go and help."

"She's okay. I'm going to get to the main tunnel and get men and—"

"Aldo blew the Via Spagnola entrance, too."

"Bartlett is probably trying to get a rescue team in operation. If he can't get through the blockage, I'll have to make my way through that maze of tunnels to find the way out."

"That's what Aldo was planning. He said he knew the way. Sontag told him." She shuddered. "Sontag's dead. His throat . . ."

"I know. I saw his body and it scared the hell out of me. I knew if Aldo had gotten to Sontag that he would have told him everything he knew. And since I found Sontag in this passage of the tunnel, Joe and Eve were clear targets. I didn't know what he had in mind, but I knew I had to pull them out quick." He got to his feet. "Stay here and try not to move. You don't want to start that bleeding again." He was heading back down the tunnel. "I'll get help to you as soon as I can."

His voice faded as he went around the turn of the tunnel.

Stay here?

She looked at Aldo's body only a few feet away and felt a shiver of revulsion.

Eve and Joe.

Her flashlight suddenly went out and she was in darkness.

That settled it.

She started to cautiously crawl toward the blockage Trevor had broken through. If he'd been able to wriggle through that cave-in to get to her, then she could get to Eve and Joe.

She heard Joe tossing rocks aside and talking to Eve before she'd gone fifty yards past the blockage.

She called, "Joe, my flashlight's out. Keep talking."

He was silent. "Jane? Thank God."

"Trevor said Eve was trapped but okay. Is she still—"

"Fine." It was Eve's voice. "Are you hurt?"

"Not much." Relief flooded through Jane. Eve sounded as fine as she claimed.

"What the hell is that supposed to mean?"

"Well, I didn't get buried in a cave-in."

"Aldo?"

"Aldo's dead." She could see the light of

Joe's flashlight now. "Trevor's gone for help."

"Why didn't you go with him?"

"I wasn't invited. And if I had been, I'd have refused. How could I leave you down here?" She sat down beside him, picked up a rock, and threw it to one side. "Joe, how much farther do we have to go to get her out?"

"Not far." He smiled at her. "Less than when I was doing it alone."

She nodded as she picked up another rock and hurled it aside. "You bet it is. Being alone sucks. Two is always better."

"How's Jane?" Joe asked as Eve came out of the emergency room.

"Not pleased." She grimaced. "They've sewed up her calf and it's a minor wound but they're going to keep her overnight for observation. She was most indignant they didn't keep me here instead."

"It wouldn't be a bad idea."

"Yes, it would. I'm fine. Just a few bruises."

"Then let's get you back to the villa to

bed." He started down the hallway. "You need a little rest and—"

"No."

"No?" He looked at her. "You're going to stay with Jane?"

She shook her head. "She doesn't need me and there's something I have to do." She punched the button for the elevator. "And there's something you have to do, too."

"This is a lousy idea, Eve." Joe set Giulia's skull on the pedestal. "You should be in bed resting, not working."

"I have to get it done." She turned the light on over the reconstruction. "Did you have any trouble with the local police about taking it out of the coffin?"

"I didn't ask them. I just dug my way through the rubble on top of the coffin and took it. It's mass confusion down there. There are so many rescue workers, archaeologists, and police getting in each other's way that all I had to do was look like I knew what I was doing. There's no way that could happen at home. Jesus, I'll be glad to get back to Atlanta."

"So will I." She shivered as she gazed at the reconstruction. There was something macabre about seeing Jane's face on this ancient skeleton. Snap out of it. Jane was alive and this was Eve's own work. "I'm sick to death of this mess. While I was pinned under those rocks all I could think about were Jane and that murderer. I nearly went crazy." Her lips tightened. "There's no telling what damage dealing with that bastard has done to her. If she was like most girls she'd be looking over her shoulder for the rest of her life."

"She's not like most girls. She'll be fine."

"I hope so. But it went on for too long. It hurt her and I can't stand that. I want her back home living a normal life."

"A few more days won't matter."

"It will matter to me." She took the glass eyes out of the reconstruction. "I want out of here and this is the last thing I have to do to cut our ties. I have to give Giulia her true face and hand her over to Trevor to take back to the museum." She carefully began to erase the features she'd created. The depth was accurate and she mustn't change that as she did the final sculpting.

"So leave me alone and let me get to it. It's going to be a long night."

"I'll hang out and keep you company."

She shook her head. "If you want to help, phone and make our airline reservations out of here for tomorrow night. And then talk to the Italian authorities and make sure that they're not going to put any barriers up to keep us here."

"They already took our statements. And I pulled a few strings to get them to leave it at that for the moment."

"Be sure. I have to have an end to it." She added wearily, "Dear God, and my Jane has to have an end to it."

He nodded. "I'm on my way."

Smooth.

Work fast. Don't think. Let Giulia's face tell the story.

More curve to the upper lip.

Smooth.

More definition beneath the cheekbone.

Smooth.

Her hands were moving quickly, deftly over Giulia's face.

Keep your mind empty.

Should the nose be shorter? It seemed right.

We're almost there. Just a little more over the brow.

No, that was wrong.

"Help me, Giulia. You've been lost for too long."

Smooth.

Her fingertips were hot, though the clay was cool.

Smooth.

Tell me. They said you were a worker but that's not enough. You need a face so we'll be able to *know* you.

Smooth.

That's it, help me.

A little more.

Done!

She drew a deep breath and took a step back. "It's the best I can do, Giulia. I hope I got it— Oh, my God." She closed her eyes, and whispered, "Dear God in heaven."

"I want out of here, Eve." Jane scowled. "The emergency room should have checked me out and let me go last night.

There's nothing wrong with me. You're the one the tunnel fell on."

"But I got by with bruises." Eve filled Jane's water glass and handed it to her. "You had cuts, a strained shoulder, and loss of blood from that leg wound. Incidentally, the doctor said that you'd aggravated that shoulder injury by tossing those rocks around to get me out."

"It didn't hurt." She amended as she saw Eve's skeptical expression, "Much." She took a sip of water and set it down. "When can you get me sprung?"

"This afternoon. And Joe made reservations on the midnight flight tonight. We're going home."

"Good. You're sure you're feeling okay?"

"Jane, I'm fine. Joe is fine. That's the third time you asked that today. Now stop fretting. It's not like you."

"I've never been responsible for nearly getting both of you killed before." She reached for her hand. "I'm sorry. I'd never have forgiven myself if you'd really been hurt."

"It was our choice. We'd do it again." She smiled as she squeezed her hand. "We couldn't get along without you. Like I told you, family is everything."

"Not when I almost got you—" She stopped as Eve's hand covered her lips.

"Hush," she said. "It wasn't easy for you to crawl through that tunnel in the dark to get to me. Why did you do it?"

"You needed me."

"I rest my case." She stood up. "Now I don't want to hear any more about it. Okay?"

She swallowed to ease the tightness of her throat. "Okay. But you can't stop me from thinking." She drew a deep breath. "Where's Trevor? I haven't heard anything from him since he and Bartlett dug us out of the passage."

"I saw him this morning before I came to the hospital. He picked up Giulia to return her to the museum."

"But you didn't finish her."

"Yes, I did. Last night. I worked all night to complete her. It wasn't that difficult. I'd done all the basic measurements. I only had to do a final."

Jane smiled as she shook her head. "Only you would decide to do a reconstruction after you were dug out of a cave-in."

"It was important to me." Her hand tightened around Jane's. "I wanted this nightmare over. I *had* to have it over."

"I understand. Me, too. After I call Sam Drake and give him his scoop, I'll be glad to put an end to all of this. What did she look like? Was she pretty?"

Eve looked away. "Not really pretty. She had a strong, interesting face."

"And Trevor took her back already?" She paused. "He hasn't been by to see me. Not that I really expected him."

"I imagine he's trying to stay out of Joe's way."

"He thinks Joe will arrest him? He saved your life. He probably saved mine, too."

"It would probably be more comfortable for Joe if he just disappeared. Then he wouldn't have to make a decision."

"He won't stay around for long. He's got what he wanted." She added, "But it wouldn't have hurt him to say good-bye."

"Sometimes it does," Bartlett said from the doorway. "Take me. I'm feeling very sad to say good-bye to you, Jane." He came forward and took her hand. "But good friends never say permanent farewells, do they?"

"Are you going back home to London?" Eve asked.

"I'm considering it." He smiled. "Or I may tag along with Trevor for a while. Life is never boring with him."

"Where is he going?" Jane asked.

"I have no idea. You'll have to ask him." He turned to Eve. "Good-bye. Thank you for all your kindness."

Eve gave him a quick hug. "Take care. Call me if you need anything." She brushed a kiss on Jane's forehead. "I'll pick you up at two this afternoon."

"I'll be ready. 'Bye." Jane watched her leave the room before turning back to Bartlett. "I'm not going to have the chance to ask Trevor anything, am I?"

"You might. Although it would be wiser for him to fade into the sunset."

"Where is he?"

"He said he was returning that skeleton to the museum in Naples. Then he's taking the six o'clock flight from Naples to Rome. After that, I've no idea."

"Why are you telling me that, if you believe it's wiser for him not to see me?"

He shrugged. "It's been brought to my attention lately that life is very short and wisdom may not be all that it's cracked up to be. When I was digging through that rubble with Trevor and the rescue crew, trying to get all of you out of that tunnel, I was thinking how sweet life could be and what a shame it was to miss a minute of it." He turned away and headed for the door. "And that's why I'm probably going with Trevor and not back to my accounting job. I'll stay in touch, Jane."

She lay there after he left, staring at the soothing seascape on the wall across the room. Everything in this room was bright and soothing, meant to help heal and make everything right. So different from the oppressive darkness of that tunnel. That nightmare time seemed remote and far away.

Can't breathe.

Hot. Smoky.

Night without air.

Would that dream of Cira fade away too?

It would no doubt be better if it did. She had spent far too much time researching and racking her brains to find some logical reason for a totally illogical experience. She should chalk those dreams of Cira up to one of life's mysteries and move on with reality. Yes, that was sensible.

And Mark Trevor should be dismissed with the same logic and practicality. He had been an interesting experience and she had learned something about herself from meeting him. Yet in six months the chances were that she would be on her way to completely forgetting him. She'd be starting her life and not looking back.

It was finished.

Naples was bathed in twilight, bustling, busy, old, yet trying to come to terms with its age and concentrate on the future.

Different from Herculaneum, Trevor thought as he looked out the plate-glass window at the airport. Herculaneum lived in the past and was content to stay that way. Why not? Cira's city possessed a glorious past that fit her—

"You're very rude."

He stiffened and slowly turned to see Jane standing behind him. "This is a surprise." She was dressed in khakis and a loose white shirt. Her cheek was bruised, she was pale, and her expression was grim.

And, God, she looked beautiful.

"It's a surprise to me, too." She took a step toward him. "Because I'm angry that you could be so rude and stupid. You could have come to the hospital to say good-bye. I shouldn't waste my time on you."

"I agree. You shouldn't be here. How's the wound in your leg?"

"Sore. I'll survive. Bartlett must have told you that I'm going to be fine. Where is he? Did he decide to go with you?"

He nodded. "He's in the coffee shop."

"And where are you going?"

"Switzerland, first."

"But you won't stay there. You'll be going after Precebio's gold."

He smiled. "It's Cira's gold. Perhaps eventually. It's a little too hot around here for me right now."

"I don't believe Joe's going to turn the law loose on you."

"I imagine Scotland Yard will have its own agenda. They don't like tampering with their Web site or interfering with their case-load." He shrugged. "At any rate, I'm always one to avoid trouble."

"Liar."

He chuckled. "Well, unless there's a fifty-

fifty chance I can talk or buy my way out of it."

She nodded. "Bartlett said that you're addicted to walking a tightrope. That's stupid, too. You should grow up."

"I'll work on it."

"No, you'll just continue taking the same chances year after year until you get yourself killed. That's why I'm surprised I even took the time to come here."

"Why did you?"

"You saved my life. You saved Eve and Joe."

"I also helped put all of you at risk." His gaze searched her expression. "No, that's not the reason."

"No, it's not." She took another step closer. "I came because it's not finished. I was lying in that hospital bed telling myself that I was going to forget those dreams of Cira and put you completely out of my mind. I was going to put a period to the whole episode."

"Very smart."

"Only it's not finished and I'm not going to look back and have it gnaw at me for the rest of my life. That's not my nature. There's no one more of a realist than I am and I hate the idea that I can't figure out this connection with Cira. So shall I tell you what I'm going to do?"

"I can hardly wait."

"Don't be sarcastic. You do want to know."

"Sarcasm can be the first line of defense. Hell, yes, I want to know everything about you. I always have." I always will. Don't say those words. Keep your distance. It will only be for a little while longer.

"Good. Then you'll be glad to know I'm going back to school and then on to Harvard. After that I'm going to find out what happened to Cira. I may wait until I graduate from college or I may not. I'll decide later."

"You're coming back here?"

"Wherever I have to go to find the answers. I don't give a damn about your gold, but I have to read those scrolls. I told you, it's not finished. I have to find out if Cira died in that eruption. If she didn't, I have to know what happened to her. And I have to know how I knew about her, why I had those dreams. It's important to me."

"You saw that excavation. It could take years to find an answer."

"I've got years. I'm only seventeen." She looked him directly in the eye. "No matter what you think, that's a plus. I'm going to go home and live every minute of every day. I'm going to grow and learn and experience. I'm going to see if I can find a man who makes you look boring in comparison. It shouldn't be so difficult. And, God knows, I don't want to have to deal with you and your antiquated sense of what's proper and not proper. I can't understand how a man who admits to being a criminal and a scoundrel could be so idiotic. Someday you're going to regret turning away from me."

"I already do."

"Well, it's too late. You had your chance." She turned and started away. Then she whirled back to face him. "But you may get another one if I decide you're worth it and I don't find anyone better. So you'd better work on clearing Cira out of your head. I don't like the competition. She's dead and I'm alive, and by the time I'm through with making myself into the person I want to be there won't be any comparison."

She didn't wait for an answer. Trevor watched her stride across the lobby. Her head was high, her shoulders straight, her carriage indomitable.

"I thought she might come to say good-bye." Bartlett was standing beside him, his gaze on Jane. "Or perhaps *au revoir*. Which was it?"

Au revoir. Until we meet again.

"I'm not sure." She'd almost disappeared from view but he could still see the strength and determination that radiated from her every movement. He suddenly felt a surge of exhilaration. "I think it was *au revoir*." He started to laugh. "And, if it was, God help me."